'In her debut fiction nov[...]ls up the roots of trauma, b[...]ly. It probes what can happen when life confronts you in unmistakeable ways that force you to take back control'
Jenni Fagan

'A truthful, funny, beautifully written and compulsive read. Lynsey May dissects the everyday traps women manage to set for ourselves with forensic wit and a fine eye for detail'
Kirstin Innes

'Compulsively readable, darkly funny . . . May has a keen eye for the manifestation of emotional complexity in all human interaction and a talent for dramatising it'
The Skinny

'There's a huge emotional punch packed into this deceptively light novel . . . May's darkly funny take on vulnerability, responsibility and complicated relationships promises more to come'
Daily Mail

'An agreeably light novel which is also a serious examination of human relationships . . . it treats the everyday world of common experience as serious matter for fiction. This is refreshingly unusual today'
Allan Massie, *The Scotsman*

'Lynsey May's debut comes with a bite that belies its title'
Sunday Post

A NOTE ON THE AUTHOR

Lynsey May lives, loves and works in Edinburgh. She won first place in the Fresh Ink novel contest in 2020, a Robert Louis Stevenson Fellowship in 2015, a spot as Cove Park's Emerging Scottish Writer in 2016 and a Scottish Book Trust New Writers Award in 2013. *Weak Teeth* is her first novel.

This paperback edition published in 2024 by Polygon.
First published in Great Britain in 2023 by Polygon,
an imprint of Birlinn Ltd.

Birlinn Ltd
West Newington House
10 Newington Road
Edinburgh
EH9 1QS

www.polygonbooks.co.uk

1

ISBN 978 1 84697 662 9

British Library Cataloguing-in-Publication Data
A catalogue record for this book is available on request
from the British Library.

The publisher gratefully acknowledges investment from
Creative Scotland towards the publication of this book.

Typeset by 3btype.com

Weak Teeth

Lynsey May

Polygon

For Alison Thirkell and her magnificent bedtime stories

'To be born with teeth is to be born with either a curse or a blessing to mankind'
—Jeri Tanner, *The Teeth in Folklore*

1

Ellis is home first. She considers a shower. Maybe a bath. Instead, she sits at the kitchen counter in her work clothes and mindlessly scrolls through the headlines, waiting for Adrian to reply to her text. He's not much of a texter, but he's normally punctual.

She's in the mood for a quick and comforting dinner, pasta with capers and olive oil. Adrian prefers something more substantial. There are beef strips in the fridge. She's been avoiding them to spare a tooth recently turned tender. The meat is about to pass its sell-by date and she has the dentist tomorrow. Ellis takes the packet out so it can come up to room temperature. Blood swirls into the tray's plastic corners.

She reaches for the rice. At the team meeting she's just come from, no one commented on her spreadsheet. That could be a good thing. Or not. She's still so new at TravelOn she spends every day trying to be bright and helpful. It's exhausting. The work itself isn't demanding: Ellis is practised in the filling in and organising of things. There'd been plenty of that at Tee Zone and she'd been happy there, especially when they let her try her hand at the odd bit of copy. Redundancy hit her hard.

It was one of those things, obviously. Nothing personal. Except they only let go of her and Geoffrey, and nobody liked Geoffrey. Just because she's capable of everything TravelOn has for her doesn't mean she can relax.

Her phone buzzes. It's Lana, messaging about the weekend for the third time already. Adrian will not want to go. He finds her family tiresome. Ellis doesn't completely disagree, but spending time with Mum, her sister and the twins is the right thing to do. After dinner, she'll try to persuade him to come with her.

Lana would immediately have identified and befriended the office alpha. She's always been the more outgoing one, which is unfair, seeing as Ellis is the eldest.

She's choosing an emoji when the front door opens. She ditches her phone and starts preparing the rice for washing.

'In the kitchen,' she calls. Adrian doesn't reply. The regular, gentle thud of his shoes being removed and pushed into the rack is absent. She stands, listening. Nothing. She puts down the rice to investigate.

It's him, of course it's him, but he doesn't look right. He's facing the front door. Ellis stops, alert to his posture and the bad tidings it brings.

'Hey,' he says, watering down the worry trickling through her. People don't say 'hey' when there's an emergency.

'You gave me a fright. You okay?'

'Yes, well . . . not really. I need to talk to you.'

She nods, a fresh spurt of adrenaline cutting off her reply. He's been fired. He's got a gambling problem. He's been told one of the mean things she's jokingly said about him to Becca or Zoe.

She follows him into the living room. He takes the chair, leaving her the sofa they normally share.

'I didn't mean for it to happen,' he says.

'What?'

'But it has, and you need to know. I've met someone else.'

The world shifts; Ellis shrinks inwards.

'No,' she says.

'I'm sorry.'

'You . . . what? Who?'

'You don't know her. She's called Sally. We work together and, honestly, Ellis, we didn't set out to hurt you. We didn't even mean it to happen.'

'You've slept with her?' Ellis is gripping the back of her neck, fingers working against the muscle like she could tear the thought away. It won't go. 'You have, haven't you?'

'Ellis.' He shakes his head, but in a way that means he's sorry. The room crumples around her.

'But I love you.' Pathetic.

'Don't do this.'

'We can work it out. Whatever you did, you didn't mean it.'

'It's over.' His voice crimps in the middle as if he might cry. Instinctively, Ellis steps towards him. He recoils. Her heart cramps, and she stands wringing her hands and saying he can't be telling the truth as he walks out the room.

He returns before she can catch hold of a single thought, a bag in his hand. He must've packed it already. A tiny part of her brain wonders when. The rest is a cacophony of panic. She can barely hear him speak over it.

Leaving. He's leaving and saying she'll be fine.

'You can't. Where? Hers? Oh God.'

'Don't be . . . Sally would never. I've got a room at the Premier Inn.'

'No.'

'I'm sorry,' he says.

She's desperate to rewrite what's happening. Her shoulders ache to be hugged, her ribs need to be pressed to his. It can't be true.

He won't even look at her.

'How could you?' she says.

'You must've known something like this was coming.'

'When was the last time we even had a fight? We went and bought cushions last weekend. Cushions!'

'There's more to life than cushions, no matter how much you pretend otherwise.'

'What are you even talking about?'

'You know how secretive you are. How hard it is to get through to you.'

'Me? Secretive? You're the one who's been cheating.' Her voice rises to a pitch she barely recognises.

'I've got the room booked till the weekend, so if you could send me a message when you're–'

'You're throwing me out.'

'That's not fair. It's my place.'

Anger sweeps over her, cold and disorientating. It is his place, but it's her home. They've shared it for almost ten years. It's filled with things she chose for them both.

'But you're the one that–'

'Look, I'm not talking to you when you're like this.'

'You can't go.'

But he can. He does. Ellis stands alone in the living room, hyperventilating. The anger is gone, leaving a mudflat of desolation. Behind her is the bookcase she filled, under her feet the rug she picked out to hide the worn carpet they kept talking about replacing. The very air is scented with candles only Ellis ever buys. She can't stay here. She won't.

Becca's? No, Scotty has an ear infection. Zoe or Charmaine? A meeting in London and a family holiday, respectively. Lana? Never.

There is only her mum.

Adrian doesn't deserve the satisfaction of thinking he's giving her a 'few days'. Ellis is going now. She grabs the ratty spare rucksack. He's taken the good one. She barely knows what she packs. The door slams behind her. The twinge in her tooth has turned into a howl.

✱

Ellis rings the bell. It takes ages for her mum to answer the door, and when she does, her muzzy hair and crumpled jumper makes it look like she's been dragged from halfway through a film. Except she's still holding her phone and the screen only darkens as she says hello.

'Sweetheart.' Her expression switches from bemused to concerned. 'What's wrong? Come in.'

Curled into one end of the couch, Ellis stutters through the events of the last few hours. Her mum's hand flies from her mouth to Ellis's knee and back again.

'Oh God, I can't believe it. Are you sure? Of course you're staying here. I'll make up the bed. Have you told your sister?'

Ellis shakes her head. They go through the disaster again. Finally convinced it's true, her mum moves into coping mode, pushing wine on her, fetching sheets, offering to order food. Ellis lets her bustle.

Devastation circles her and she's too weak to do anything more than let tears fall down her face. She's back where she started and her mum's trying to make space for her where there is none. Ellis's room was relegated to the spare as soon as she moved out. Lana's is still Lana's. She even sleeps over occasionally, saying it does Grant good to manage without her.

Ellis can hear her mum calling for a takeaway. The gesture brings about a fresh round of tears. Even in her gratitude, she longs for her dad. He was the sort who read stories and pulled pigtails. He bestowed nicknames that none of them have uttered since. Even just being near him made Ellis feel settled. His death plunged everything into cold, dark chaos. It was Lana, tiny and ferocious, who turned on all the lights and forced their mum to switch on the boiler.

The house is hot now, and cramped. Ellis doesn't want to be at her mum's, but the place she's put so much effort into making her own is gone.

2

It's inevitable she's here, digging nails into soft belly, now that everything is falling apart. She should've paid heed to the warning squealed with each bite.

Her eyes are protected from the overhead light and – God forbid – flying speckles of tooth by a pair of scuffed goggles. Her tears pool within them.

Ellis could've cancelled, should've cancelled, except the sudden disintegration of her relationship isn't enough to override her obedience. So she submits to the scraping, the picking, the bloody suck and gorge. Finally, it's time for the gritty polish. The hygienist says she can sit up now and belatedly asks if she's all right. Ellis nods and receives a coral-lipsticked smile.

Released into the purgatory between hygienist and dentist, Ellis sways to the waiting room. It has filled in the ten minutes she's been away. Gums raw and cheeks salt-stung, she takes a seat near the door. The sweat under her collar begins to dry. She is already due back at the office. She should've accounted for the fact the dentist always runs late.

Someone is staring. She lifts her chin to look at a young girl with a thick fringe and a panicked gaze. Ellis ought to reassure her. She tries to smile and tastes the sharp tang of blood. The girl shifts a tad closer to her mother.

It's for the best. The dark-haired child may also have baby teeth that refuse to fall out, clinging to the bone even as the next set grows in behind them. She may also develop a shark's smile until those unwanted teeth are extracted so enthusiastically that they fly across the room with a sharp flick of the dentist's excavator. She too may spend her teens in braces so tight she begins to doubt the shape of her face. She too may find herself in a waiting room, miserably attending to yet another sore tooth the day after her partner leaves her.

Ellis looks away. All she can do is get through this appointment without falling apart.

*

The dentist is a locum; Dr Niall is off sick. An unexpected change of dentist is normally enough to send Ellis into a panic but this disaster pales in comparison to everything else. The new guy is whistling along to the radio when she walks in and awkwardly solicitous by the time she sits down. He introduces himself as Dr Conor.

'Just a check-up, is it? Anything bothering you?' he says, glancing at the notes on his screen.

'I think I need a filling replaced. Upper left, near the back.'

'I see we've got you booked in for a double.' There is mild disapproval in his tone. Dentists are meant to call the shots. Dr Niall always lets nervous patients book a double. 'Let's see what's going on in there.'

She closes her eyes as he heads straight in with his probe. Metal against enamel, a bark of pain as it hits dentine.

'Found it,' he says and moves on to checking the rest of her teeth. There is only the gurgle of his stomach and the chinking of his tools. It could be worse. It can always be worse. There is no point feeling sorry for herself. It doesn't matter who drives you, or sits in the waiting room, or cossets you with questions, or circles the appointment on the calendar, you are always alone in the dentist's chair.

'Right enough, a bit of discolouration around the old filling. Best to replace it. Everything else is looking nice and clean. We'll do it now, if you're up to it?'

'I'm fine.'

7

'If you're sure? We could always reschedule? No? All right then.' He holds out his hand; the nurse places a syringe in it. 'A little pinch. Open as wide as you can . . . wider. Okay, hold it, hold it. There.'

The burn is cold and chemical and welcome.

'We'll just give that a minute.' He pushes his wheelie chair away to chatter quietly with the nurse. Ellis stares up at the ceiling tiles. She shouldn't be here. She should be back at the flat, destroying things. At Adrian's work, making a scene. She should be drunk, at the very least.

No. She has to maintain.

The dentist scoots back. His breath has a coffee fug but there's no cup in the room. He must drink in secret, between patients.

The filling is taking longer than it should.

'Bit more complicated than we thought.' He leans back, drill still in hand and light reflecting on his glasses. Ellis can't see his eyes. She blinks to signal her understanding.

The ache is in the hook of her jaw, which isn't supposed to stay hinged open this way. The nurse is fierce with the sucker, and still Ellis is desperate to swallow. She tries to catch the woman's attention but she's staring across the room, thinking about her dinner or her kids or how much she likes or doesn't like this dentist's radio station and the way he sings under his breath as he works.

Ellis needs it to be over. She thinks it might be now. Now. Now. She almost raises a hand, keeps the nails sunk into her abdomen instead. Dr Conor leans back. Relief infuses her muscles. He asks for more air and swoops in again. She's going to snap.

The drill is back on the tray, at last, but when she numbly presses down on the strip he holds between her teeth, he's not happy.

The whine is part of her; it's shaking her mooring loose, eroding her structure. It's taking too long. There is tension in the room. Is it only hers? Surely it's not only hers? Just as she knows she can't keep the pain inside any longer, he stops.

'One last bite. Yes, good. That'll do. Deeper than it looked. Got quite close to the nerve there. Might be a bit nippy the next few days.' He pulls his gloves off and tosses them in the bin. Ellis sits, spits, hands back the goggles, gathers her coat and says thank you. The dentist stops typing long enough to wave. The nurse tells her to have a good day and reminds her to speak to the receptionist on the way out.

She has to pass the waiting room. The girl with the fringe is looking, waiting. There is no point in trying to reassure her: Ellis will bring no comfort.

The woman at the front desk has blonde hair like the short-bristled brush Ellis's grandmother kept hanging with a dustpan on the back of the cupboard door. They silently wait for Dr Conor to send through his notes. The computer chimes. The woman fusses over the printer then hands over the bill. Ellis holds out her bank card without looking at the total. They'll be in touch when her next appointment is due.

Ellis dribbles onto the street, unable to feel half her face. Her steps are uncertain, she is defenceless, unable to rely on a smile to save her. She takes out her phone, switches to the camera and flips the image to stare at herself. Red marks on either side of her mouth, dark pits under her eyes. Back to the home screen. No one has messaged.

She wants to report back. Her thumb trails the names of her friends. No one needs to hear about her teeth. It was a long time in the chair, too long, and the meat of her mouth is ragged. It was only a replacement though. No big deal.

The next bus is eleven minutes away, and two older women crowd the stop, chatting loudly about a boy who came off his bike. Ellis calls the office. Fabian picks up. He reminds her that Richard is on holiday so she asks him to pass a message on to HR for her.

'Course. You're sounding rough as. It's doing the rounds. My Mike was knocked out with it just last week. Get yourself a hot toddy on the go.'

'Thanks,' she says and hangs up as quickly as possible, her hands still shaking. She can't have slept for more than an hour or two, and her insides feel like they're walking at several paces removed from the rest of her. She can't face her colleagues. Ellis texts her mum, hoping to hear that she's out and the house will be empty.

3

A lukewarm glass of water with two drops of clove oil is waiting for her on the hall table. This dilution is her mum's favoured treatment for any dental ailment. The Patricks all have their own notions. They are a family of strong bones and weak teeth.

Dad used to be the one who dealt with their appointments. Mum didn't, *couldn't*, take them to the dentist. It was one thing to miss him in the waiting room, another to want his hug for every other disaster and triumph.

Voices drift in from the back garden. Lana is here with the twins. They'll be waiting for her to join them so that they can offer comfort (Mum) and gouge for gruesome details (Lana). Ellis tiptoes upstairs and sits on the edge of the bed to drink her medicinal water. She's always liked the taste of cloves.

One toddler begins to cry and then the other. Ellis sympathises with their fury. Their eyes will be pressed to mere folds, noses blanched white. Such hatred contained in such tiny bodies, it's amazing they function at all. Ellis loves Oscar and Mia. They are just so angry. Angrier than most, surely. Perhaps their rage is doubled by the mere fact of their twinship. Twice the grievances, half the attention. Or maybe they're just their mother's children.

Lana's voice cuts through their yowls. *Enough . . . ignore them . . . where is she?* Time passes. Ellis's face tingles and she thinks about lying down. Adrian may be kissing another mouth this second. He'll be at work, but then so is Sally.

It's a long time since Adrian's kisses made her feel more than satisfaction at fulfilling her duty. It had been different, at the start.

She tongues the bruised memories until the hurt is so consuming she barely registers the feet on the stairs.

Lana pushes the door open without knocking. 'Fuck's sake, thought so.' She turns back to the stair to shout, 'She's here.'

Ellis puts the empty glass down.

'Are you okay? Did you get it out?' Lana says.

'Just a filling.'

'And Adrian?'

Ellis shrugs. Lana moves Ellis's bag from the wicker chair and makes herself comfortable. Her hair is pulled back, her lips glossy. She always has glossy lips. She makes time. Lana is a master at making time.

'He's a cunt.'

'Don't.'

'He is though. Total fucking arse. Want me to go round?'

'No. God, no.'

'You going to tell me about it?'

'Maybe later.'

'Don't think you're getting away with–' The wailing returns before Lana can say more. She pauses to see if it stops. It intensifies instead. 'Damn it. Later, then.'

Ellis catches her top lip between her teeth. Feeling is beginning to return and she wishes it wouldn't.

✱

The door opens again a little while later. It's Mum's turn.

'Are you coming down for lunch? I made soup.'

'I'm not hungry.'

'You have to eat. And your sister will be taking the twins home soon. At least say hello before they go.'

Ellis follows her mum downstairs with a heavy tread. Lana and her children are spread over the living-room floor. Aside from a deconstructed train track in yellow and blue cluttering the carpet, the room is the same as always. It is still, from the bookcase to the armchairs, the space their father always loved best.

The twins are smeared with orange gloop. Lana has her phone in one hand, a wet wipe in the other.

'Look who's come to see you,' Mum croons. The twins swivel at the sound of her voice, stare for a moment, then return to their own incomprehensible conversation.

'What have you got there?' Ellis tries. Oscar looks at her blankly. Mia bangs a train carriage firmly against the track. They couldn't be less fussed about seeing her.

Lana's bowl is already empty, Mum is off fetching one for Ellis.

Adrian doesn't like soup. He always had a king rib supper on dentist days; Ellis preferred to stick to cream of chicken as a precaution. The vinegary smell would drive her wild. Most times, she'd take a single chip. Any more and he'd complain she should've ordered her own. It was ridiculous; he hardly ever finished a full portion. She should buy a can on the way home. The thought drops cold in her stomach – she *is* home.

'We're going in a minute,' Lana says.

'Mum said.'

'Here you are. There's pepper on the side there.'

Ellis takes what she is given. How many times has she held this particular spoon, which has three siblings, each slightly different and yet so alike, edges softened by decades of washing and jostling?

'Don't let it go cold.'

It swells in her mouth, gelatinous. She almost retches at the thought of blood and mucous although she knows it's nothing but sweet potatoes, onions and fresh chillies (she shared the recipe with her mum in the first place).

'Is it not warm enough? Too bland? I only used half a chilli, for the twins.'

'It's fine.'

'God, she looks like a right skank.' Lana waves her phone.

'Lana,' Mum says.

'She is though. Look.'

Ellis knows what Sally looks like. She'd spent half the night on that particular torment.

'She's had her boobs done, bet you. Botox and all.'

Ellis's grip tightens on the spoon. Her mum looks at her sister's phone, why wouldn't she?

'Nothing on our Ellis.'

'I'll message her,' Lana says.

'Don't.' It's the loudest Ellis has been all day.

'Just a wee warning.'

'Please.'

'God, fine.' She locks the screen. 'You're not letting them away with it though. Should I send Grant round to have a word? Mia, come here.' Lana grasps her daughter's fingers within the wet wipe and swoops them clean. 'Or if you want a chum from me to get your things? Don't just sit on it.'

Ellis says she won't, and, to her relief, Lana looks at the time and decides to get moving. It takes almost fifteen minutes to clean the twins enough to squash them into jackets. Ellis uses the hubbub as an opportunity to quietly take her soup to the kitchen and pour it down the sink.

Mia decides she wants a hug after all, and Ellis has to push her face into her niece's fleecy hood to hide a spurt of tears. Mia wriggles away. Lana reminds her what a bastard Adrian is and tells her she could've done better. She hasn't done better though. She hasn't.

The house is calm for a couple of moments, until Mum starts in.

'You're looking awful pale. Can I get you anything? You know your sister just wants to help. What can we do?'

There's nothing they can do. Ellis brushes her mum off and retreats upstairs. She needs to be alone.

For such a diminutive number, the Patricks are stifling.

All the grandparents and the only great-aunt died before Ellis was ten. They toppled one after another, each a tragedy over-shadowed by the felling of her father. The only other living relatives are Charlie and his daughter, Kenzie, and they are relations so distant it barely counts. Especially seeing as Charlie disappeared to America for success and glory the year Ellis got her first period.

There is only Lana, Grant, Mum and the twins, yet somehow they take up all the space.

*

Ellis is in bed. She's barely moved for hours and wants nothing more than to sleep. It feels wrong to be in her mum's tall, narrow house. She doesn't like the way the radiators tick or the feel of the spare duvet. Even the things she has always loved, like the stained-glass window in the room that was hers until it was Lana's, bring her no pleasure.

She'd been usurped when Lana was too big for her bassinet and too small to be a corridor away. Ellis can't remember minding at the time, but she minded plenty later. Resentment arrived sharp-beaked and fully fledged in her teens. She told anyone who cared to listen that she was happy to be at the other side of the house, where she could sneak boys in if she wanted to. Lana said she'd never have to worry about boys if she didn't do something about her hair. Ellis remembers trying to scrape up a decent ponytail in front of the bathroom mirror and wondering if any boy would ever fancy her.

She wants to lie with a stained-glass circle above her bed and to be back in a time where everything was safe. She doesn't want the second-best room, with no stained-glass window to soften the light and make her feel safe. But this is all she has.

Her thoughts begin to blur and grow heavy in focus. The relief spreads like egg yolk. She's jerked back by a quiet creak.

Her mum is heading downstairs, and the tiptoeing quality of her steps takes Ellis back to when Lana was such a light sleeper the rest of the household was reduced to whispers. The twins are benefiting from that lightning trigger now. Lana is no doubt at their cot with a tit out before they've even opened an eye.

The pillow is bumfled beneath her cheek. She can hear her mum's voice. Her mum never talks to people this late. Ellis holds her breath and tries to identify the timbre of the conversation. There is too much space between them to tell. She rolls from the bed and makes her way to the door, opening it carefully, but her mum's voice is still too quiet.

She pads to the top of the stairs, a flurry of potential emergencies disrupting the drone of her heart. It could be Adrian. He's been in an accident, he's hurt and unconscious, and all they could find was her old number. Never mind that she didn't hear the landline. Never mind that he's chosen someone else to look after him.

Images of disasters are blown away by a giggle from the front room. Ellis turns back; it's not a sound she associates with her mum. Further from sleep than ever, she lies back down and tries to slow her breathing. Her tooth twangs, her heart aches and a swell of foreboding darkens the night.

4

Reading in the sleepless wee hours is a torture and a comfort. She discovers that teeth were once considered totems of protection. A handful can be sprinkled, like salt, to create a protective circle. A single tooth can be burned to ward off a witch's curse. Scandinavian warriors of yore rode into battle with a string of baby teeth tied around their thick necks. Teeth are something to fear. Adrian always said she made too much of a fuss about her various fillings and chippings. He thinks teeth are just teeth. The more she reads, the more Ellis feels vindicated, but there's nothing to help her there, and it takes a long time to fall asleep, with teeth on her phone screen and sadness coiled around her insides.

She wakes to the chirp of her alarm and wishes she hadn't. Today, she has to get back to work. As TravelOn's second-newest employee, Ellis can't risk another sick day. She hadn't wanted to leave Tee Zone and she can't afford to leave TravelOn now, even if she wanted to.

She'd spent years tinkering with euphemisms for sweat, happily taking activewear samples home for Adrian and contributing to the tea kitty, thinking she was a valuable member of the team. Not valuable enough, obviously. She'd been so comfortable there, never would've thought they'd choose her as one of the first to go. Stop taking it personally, Adrian said. Or if you really think you're the problem, fix it. Shame to lose the staff discount on thermal T-shirts though.

No wonder Adrian had been so relaxed about it. He was probably already screwing Sally.

She's dreading the office. When she'd first started, redundancy-raw and determined to be quietly likeable and efficient, Adrian was one of the few topics of conversation she'd been happy to indulge in. She'd wanted them to know she came verified by another human being. She's not ready to tell them he's withdrawn his vote.

✱

Ellis arrives just before nine, slings her coat on the back of her chair and switches her computer on. Before she has time to fetch herself a coffee, an email from HR pings into her inbox. Richard is still on holiday so Gabrielle from HR will conduct her back-to-work interview. After every sick day, there's an interview. This will be her first.

She puts off heading to the kitchen for as long as she can, hoping to avoid small talk, but her body cries out for liquid. She waits until it looks like everyone else is at their desks.

The only mugs left in the cupboard are the oversized monstrosities with an old TravelOn logo emblazoned on the side. The filter coffee shimmers like oil. Ellis is at the fridge when Alison clacks in.

'How long has that been sitting?'

'I don't know. A while.'

'Euchh, no, no, no. Don't go drinking that sludge, pet.' She deftly twists the plastic filter free with one hand and opens the bin with the other. The room fills with a hot fug of decomposing fruit skins, tea bags and coffee grounds.

'Grab us some milk, will you? Normal. Can't be doing with the oat stuff. Although they're saying it's the almond one that's the real problem now. Cutting down forests to plant them, or planting forests where they shouldn't, or something. Don't know why they can't just be nicer to cows in the first place and save us all the bother. Let's see. Oh, that's no good. We'll be needing more milk than that to get through the Corfu catch-up. You're coming to that, right?'

Ellis nods. She can't remember if she's meant to be at the meeting but Alison tends to know. In-between her statement earrings is an encyclopaedic knowledge of TravelOn's comings and goings. When they first met, Ellis mistakenly assumed Alison had been there for decades. There's something of Lana about her. Not in looks: Alison is in her fifties, dyes her hair a defiant copper and wears clothes that cling and crinkle while Lana is all honey highlights and a wardrobe in heather, oatmeal and the occasional swirl of peach yogurt. Still, Alison's insistence on switching to a new filing system reminds Ellis of the time Lana decided they should give up meat (her vegetarianism lasted a fortnight – packets of soy mince lingered in the freezer for years after). What they shared was an assumption that everyone else would see the superiority of their point of view, eventually.

'Fancy nipping to the shops on your lunch? I'll be printing the agendas or I'd go. Actually, you're looking a bit wabbit. I'll get Naila to do it. You shouldn't be in if you're ill. Last thing we need is a bug going round, not with the October week planning.'

'I'm okay, nothing infectious.'

'If I had a pound coin for every time I heard that, I'd be retired already. Instead I've frittered away a fortune on Lemsips and hankies.'

'It was a thing. A family thing.' The words are out before she has time to properly consider them.

'What sort of thing?'

'Bad news.'

'Oh, you should've said. No wonder you're peaky. I've got ten minutes if you need a chat. No? Well, look here, have a fresh coffee at least.'

She tosses the contents of Ellis's mug in the sink, earrings swinging. Ellis takes the new pour with a quiet thank you.

It's good. She sips as she checks her calendar. Alison is right: she is scheduled for the Corfu meeting. First, she's on complaints, which is fine with her. Ellis prides herself on her ability to handle emails from people looking for a place to deposit their frustration. Noticing how they tended to make Naila cry and fill Alison with reciprocal rage, Ellis volunteered to take on extra.

Not long after she started, Ellis overheard Alison saying 'not everyone likes sushi' in such a pointed way that it was clearly about a person and not raw fish. Ellis looked over, and while Alison turned and caught her eye, red stippled Naila's neck. They'd been talking about her. They were right: everyone knows Ellis is a cold fish. But that doesn't mean she can't be useful.

Her phone goes before she has a chance to get stuck in. Adrian. Ellis's breath snags in her chest.

Just checking in. Haven't heard from you yet. I need to pop by after work to get some stuff.

She almost doesn't answer.

I'm not there. I'm at my mum's. Could we talk?

He's typing. Ellis glances around but no one's looking.

I thought you'd want space. I'll head home if you're not at the flat.

Her thumb keys a response before the rest of her has a chance to vet it.

I want to know how you could do this.

I'm not arguing by text.

He won't, Ellis knows that much. The bastard.

The office is open plan, and her desk faces the back wall. Everyone can see her screen. She puts her phone on her lap to open Adrian's Facebook page. It's a waste of time. He never updates his profile. It's the same smiling photo she took at the garden centre the day they bought flowers for the communal back garden.

Adrian is average-shaped. He's into cycling, especially day-long treks that necessitate a packed lunch. He doesn't enjoy reading. He likes to talk to people in pubs. He strikes up meandering conversations with all sorts, the kind that leave Ellis bored and resentful, waiting for him to stop exchanging titbits about cycle paths and craft beer. He is average, and his absence is a wound.

She taps through to Sally's page. There is one new update, attached to a photo. *Only the best cardamon buns for our team!!! #hardworkers #wedeserveit.* Hashtags on Facebook. This is the woman Adrian loves now. Who gives him what he needs. Who is as transparent as a glass of water. Who must be as boring as he is. How is Ellis going to contain all this hatred? What is there to protect her from it now?

5

Six days since Adrian spat her out, and Ellis is on her way to the flat to fetch some essentials. Lana was meant to drive her, but Grant was volunteered and re-routed from a Thursday evening pottering around his nice and sensible three-bedroom home at the last minute. He doesn't seem to mind. Ellis does.

There is dark hair curling up from the neck of his T-shirt. It's indecent. Ellis doesn't want Lana's husband with her, even though he's older and steadier and a much safer option than her sister. She doesn't want anyone with her. She'd rather not do it at all, but she can't keep rotating the same two tops.

Her stomach is folding in on itself. Ellis tried to call Adrian about picking up her things. It rang out, and she was forced to make the arrangement by text.

'You think you've got enough or shall I stop at Lidl?' Grant asks, as if mid-discussion.

'What?'

'Boxes, you got enough? We could pick up some more.'

'It's fine. I brought bin bags.'

'Let's just grab a few on the way.'

'I don't think I'll need them.'

'There's always more than you think when you're moving. And it'll be better if we do it all in one go, right? It's not like you'll want to be going back for a second round.' She doesn't reply. He taps her on the knee. 'It's no bother.'

Ellis stays in the passenger seat as he nips into the supermarket. It might've been better with Becca or even Zoe, but they'll be falling over themselves to say horrible things about Adrian, and she's not ready for it.

She wills her eyes to stay dry and massages the tender gum through her cheek. Two cars over, a family packs their boot. The children poke each other's ribs in jest and are yelled into their seats. The car drives off, and for just a moment, Ellis wishes for the sort of life she's never particularly wanted.

Lana knew what she was aiming for right from the start. Every relationship was a practice run until she met, married and subsumed Grant in the same amount of time it'd taken Ellis and Adrian to make up their minds about a new sofa. The speed of it had scared everyone but the couple. They show no signs of regret. In fact, they've achieved in four years what other people hope for in ten. The house, the marriage, the twins, the in-jokes and stability that made people envious. Lana was ruthlessly efficient. Grant – straightforward, steady and as happy chilling with family as he was with a group of pals in the pub – was the perfect match.

He strides back, a black and red toolbox with the tags still attached in one hand, a greasy paper package in the other, and several flattened boxes under one armpit. He nods for Ellis to open the door.

He thanks her, drops the package in his seat and dumps the rest in the back.

'Pastry?' he offers, pulling on his seatbelt. Ellis shakes her head. Grant fishes a maple and pecan plait out of the bag and demolishes it in four bites. Crumbs cascade down his front and settle in the folds of his jeans. Ellis waits.

'I'm addicted.' He sounds pleased about it. He balances the bag on the dashboard. 'Lana says they may as well be laced with crack, I love them that much.' He starts the car.

Grant takes a sharp corner, sending the bag of pastries skidding. Her hand flies out to catch them. The smell is thick in the back of her throat. Pancakes, French toast, Sunday mornings. Indulgence. Maple syrup shouldn't be associated with this day, this trip.

The scent clings to them both. It's still there as she unlocks the front door and turns to let Grant past. The flat is empty, as promised. It feels familiar and alien at once.

*

Grant has visited only a couple of times but seems entirely comfortable. He heads to the living room and immediately starts taping boxes together. Ellis forces herself to look around. There are tiny differences already. The TV is a few inches closer to the wall, and the blanket from the end of the bed is stowed along the back of the sofa like a fat crêpe. It clashes with the new cushions.

'I want all the plates and bowls with an orange pattern round the edge. Do you mind?'

'Grand.'

It took a whole year of watching and waiting for the right sale to scoop those up. It will be a long time until she unpacks and discovers Grant didn't think to check the dishwasher, leaving her without two cereal bowls and one side plate.

The real priority is her clothes. She half expects to find them already bagged, but everything is where it's supposed to be. Where it's no longer welcome. She pulls the dresses she never gets round to wearing from hangers and bundles reliable woolly jumpers and long-sleeved tops into her bin bags, muddling the fabrics and letting memories blur. She empties the bedside cabinet by pulling out the drawers and upending them into one of Grant's boxes. Moisturisers and jewellery tumble together. She sweeps the novel she was reading, her sunglasses and a keepsake tin in with them.

The oversized merino-mix jumper she likes to cuddle into when she's miserable is nowhere to be seen. It's only as she twirls the ends of a filled bag together that she thinks of the washing basket. Ellis baulks.

She digs through several layers of Adrian's boxers, stiffened socks and wilted jeans. The smell is unpleasant and accompanied by a note of comfort. She's been so stupid, mistaking proximity for intimacy all this time. A soft fold peeks out between two of his work shirts; she snatches it up.

The kitchen is quiet. Grant has run out of things to do. Ellis dries her eyes before speaking to him. She knows he won't clipe on purpose; Lana is just good at extracting the information she wants.

'What about the coffee machine? The toaster?' He is leaning in the same spot by the sink Adrian favours whenever he slips from helping to supervising.

'No. There's a bunch of books in the front room though.'

Grant stands with an open box as she plucks novels from the bookcase.

'Lana mentioned furniture,' he says with the air of a man determined to do everything asked of him.

'Don't want it.'

'None of it?'

'The hall table, maybe. Everything else can stay.'

She drops the last book in the box. He fetches his roll of brown tape and screeches off great strips to thoroughly seal the flaps, as if they have to survive a much longer trip than the few miles to her mum's house.

'I'll start taking these down. You give the place a last once-over,' he says.

Ellis waits until he's out the door, then grabs her razor, moisturiser and the silk dressing gown Becca gave her from the bathroom. She stops in the doorway, turns back. A new bottle of perfume sits on the shelf above the bath. The glass is pale pink and iridescent. It looks expensive and cheap at the same time. Sally all over.

By the time she emerges into the hall, the carved table is already gone and the landline that hasn't been used in years sits between four dents in the carpet. She unties a bag for her last armful of possessions and shoves them in. The rustle of plastic disguises the sound of footsteps in the stairs until they're right by the door. Ellis stands abruptly, her heart stumbling in a ragged hop-skip. Adrian's back after all.

The door opens. It's Grant. There are new pastry crumbs clinging to his shirt, and he's already bending to pick up the just-tied bags. Ellis grabs one for herself and pulls the door behind them. She doesn't want Grant to notice the thick stench of peonies, the wet tiles in the bathroom, the shattered glass neatly tidied into the bin by the sink.

Back in the car, she starts to type. Blood smears her thumb-print. She sucks it away, then sends Adrian a message saying that she's done and that she's sorry, there was a minor accident, nothing important.

*

Lana's still there when they get back. She gives Grant a proprietary kiss, peers in the boot and asks if that's all there is.

'It's all she wanted,' he says.

'It's fine.' Ellis pushes past. Lana tells her to keep it down, the twins are asleep in Mum's bed.

She's about to put some of the boxes in Lana's room when her mum says isn't it a better idea to have everything together? Ellis turns, silently walks to her room and stacks her possessions against the wall. They take up a good chunk of the available floor space. She thinks about the downstairs study, once their dad's office, briefly their mum's knitting room and now a sort of soft play area for the twins. Not a chance.

When she heads downstairs, Grant has been dispatched to fetch the shopping. He'll be back to collect Lana and the twins after their nap.

Lana wants to know everything. Ellis tells her and Mum

about the dirty laundry and the blanket but not the perfume.

'That arse. Too scared to see you. Forget him and shake things up a bit. Use your staff discount to get away. A girls' holiday in Ibiza. Don't make that face – some of us would kill for a break like that. Or why don't you go see Charlie like you keep meaning to?'

'I don't think so,' Ellis says, remembering teenage Charlie's tilted canines and the vampirish air they'd given him, irresistible at fourteen. His defection to America was a blow she'd taken months to recover from. Almost as bad as realising that Auntie Sheila wasn't an honorific title, she genuinely was a distant cousin on Mum's side, making Ellis's teenage crush even more mortifying. Stupid not to have realised, all she had to do is look in his mouth to see the family resemblance. Not now that he's had them filed, capped and regimented as a shining testament to his newfound Americanness.

'Jackson would hate it,' she says.

'I'm sure Jackson would be happy to have you,' Mum says.

'She'd put Ellis to work picking up the towels after some celebrity Pilates class or handing out drinks in a tartan skirt.' Lana snorts. Charlie's wife is a high-end party planner, and no one's more impressed with her own job than she is. Jackson and Lana had almost liked each other, but that was short-lived. Jackson is just as cutting as Lana and revels in it even more.

'I don't think so.'

'It'd be good for you,' Lana says. 'Mum, what's going on? Why's your phone lighting up like a Christmas tree?'

'What? Oh, it's nothing.' She puts her palm over Lana's old Samsung.

'Is there drama?'

'No, of course not. Actually, well, it's not the best timing obviously, but there is something I was wanting to tell you . . .'

'Spill.'

'I'm seeing someone.'

'What, like, dating?' Lana says. 'You're not.'

'I am.'

The floor rolls beneath Ellis's feet. She looks at her mum closely for the first time in, what, months? Years, maybe. There's a flush in her cheeks, her hair's swept back in a loose bun and her eyes are bright. Ellis feels deeply betrayed.

'Since when?' Lana says.

'Four months, almost. I didn't want to say anything until . . . well . . . It's silly really, you girls are all grown up. But I wanted to be sure.'

'Who is this guy? Where did you meet him?'

'His name's Trevor.' She can't help but smile. Ellis grits her teeth. 'I met him at the new dental practice I switched to.'

'Trevor? What kind of name is Trevor?'

'A very nice one.'

'So you met him three months ago?' Lana says.

'Oh, a bit longer than that. It was just after Christmas. Remember I changed dentist when my last place stopped taking NHS?'

'You picked him up in the waiting room?' Ellis says, but her mum hasn't finished.

'It was that root canal that really sealed the deal. I was back there four times in a month.'

'I remember, we had to overcook all the vegetables at Grant's birthday lunch just so you could manage them,' Lana says.

'So you did. But he sorted it right out, and I've had raw carrots practically every week since.'

'He . . . wait . . . Mum, are you dating your fucking dentist? Really?'

'Saved the tooth as well. I like to think I'd have gone on the coffee date even if he hadn't, but it helped.' Mum laughs.

'You're not.' Ellis can't keep the horror from her voice.

'I am.'

'Where does he work?' Lana asks.

'The place on the corner near Sainsbury's. They're very nice there. Good with children, they have a giant cuddly tooth called Mr Shine. The twins would love it. You should switch. All of you. I see his partner now, of course, but she's just as brilliant as Trevor.'

Ellis can't think of anything worse.

'The twins are fine where they are,' Lana says. 'Why have you been hiding him?'

'We've just been taking a little while to get to know each other. Now I'm thinking it's about time I told you about him.'

She wasn't thinking that at all. She just didn't want Ellis coming across him in the middle of the night. Oh God.

'Is this even okay? It's not against some code of ethics or something?'

'Don't be so dramatic, Lana.'

Ellis looks at her mum's laughing mouth, open to reveal two crowns, six composites, three amalgams, a bridge and one stained but sturdy incisor. How is this happening?

Grant's name appears on Lana's lock screen. She sends him to voicemail.

'Mum, I don't want to hear it. So now you've dropped this bombshell on us, we're going to meet him, right?'

'Oh, definitely.'

'Christ. That's Grant just arrived with the shopping. We're going to have to leg it,' Lana says, reading the text he's sent. 'Ellis, give me a hand.'

The twins are a sweaty muddle of arms and legs. Ellis doesn't like the way Oscar's head lolls against her forearms when she picks him up. Children are so helpless.

Lana whispers fiercely over their sleeping bodies, 'Fucking hell. What do you think is wrong with him? What's she hiding?'

'He's a dentist, isn't that bad enough?'

'She obviously doesn't think so. I'm telling you, there must be some reason we've not met him yet. Why have they been skulking around if it's all peaches and cream?' Lana hoists her daughter from the bed and starts down the stairs. Ellis follows. Mum is outside chatting to Grant.

'Find out as much as you can,' Lana says, stepping over the threshold. The goodbyes are fast, the afternoon is growing dark and Oscar is starting to whimper.

★

Ellis turns to look at her mum, who promptly asks if she wants something to eat.

'I think I'll just go and unpack.'

'I know it's been a bit of a day. I was going to wait until the weekend to tell you.'

'I'm just surprised. Like, it's a bit out of the blue.'

'For me too, love, for me too. Well, then, if you're wanting to get your things sorted, I'll give him a ring and let him know I broke the news.'

Ellis leaves her to it. Her room feels even smaller than it did before. She longs for the one she's left behind. Keeping their bedroom tidy had fallen to her, and she did it purely for the pleasure of lying in a pale, open space. The evenings Adrian spent at his clubs were a treat. How much time had she spent luxuriating in the king size while Adrian was in Sally's? Now she's in the queen bought to replace her childhood bed. The duvet cover is patterned with yellow and brown flowers and has the dusty scent of an unused guest room. It is an affront.

She pushes the black bags of clothes off the bed and thumps down in their place, phone already in hand.

There are only so many Edinburgh dentists named Trevor – he's easy to find. The man smiling on her screen has dark hair, eyes creased at the edges and a mint-green shirt. He looks just as you'd expect although the photo's definitely a few years old. He is vain. Or lazy.

She wants her mum to be happy. Lana does too. They always have. In the calm that came before the wilds of puberty, they set her up with neighbours and single dads. They made her a profile on OK Cupid and scoured her Facebook profile for cute guys. Mum had rolled her eyes and brushed off their attempts until they assumed she was happier alone. Seems they were wrong.

Wednesday evenings and Sunday afternoons. For years, those have been the times set aside for her mum. True, things had been irregular lately, especially since the twins. Ellis hadn't minded. Much. And while they were distracted, their mum has changed. She's supposed to be a constant. A fount of cookery advice, a pair of open arms.

Ellis clenches her jaw. A spark travels all the way to her eye socket. She flips her phone to selfie mode. The tooth looks like the others. Better, because its centre is a pleasing shade of cream, sculpted to ape a natural tooth. The new filling is settling. She was warned it would hurt, that her nerves will jangle. She has to be patient.

6

A tooth is a sacrifice, a charm. It is a tool for survival. It is a perfectly natural part of the human organism. It is a tusk. A hunk of bone-like substance that protrudes from the flesh. Horrifying, if you think about it too deeply. And right now, Ellis can't stop thinking.

A spa packages spreadsheet is up on her screen alongside an article about how dehydration can amplify tooth pain. Hearing footsteps to her left, Ellis hits minimise so the spreadsheet is front and centre. Alison walks by without stopping.

There are messages from Lana on her phone, asking if she's found out any more about Trevor. As if there's anything she can do. It's just like Lana to try and drag her into a fight when all she wants is to curl up and lick her wounds.

It's time for her meeting with Gabrielle. Only HR and a couple of senior managers have rooms of their own. Gabrielle's is the smallest. It has a window into the main office, but the white blind is always down. Ellis knocks, nervously, and waits to be called in.

Gabrielle's office has been prettied up with copious pictures of her children. A desk lamp, either brought in from home or specially requested, casts a buttery light on a handful of thank-you cards. Ellis wonders if she's written them herself.

'Ah, Ellis. How are you feeling?'

'Much better, thanks.'

'Good, good. Grab a seat, and let's get this tidied up.'

Ellis does as she's told.

'Fabian put you down as having a cold. Is that right?' Gabrielle's pen is black, matt and weighty. She wields it with pleasure.

'Well . . .' Ellis told Alison it was nothing infectious.

'But I have it that you were at a dentist's appointment that morning?'

'Yes, I got a filling and then I wasn't feeling so good.' Sweat prickles along the edge of her lip.

'So it was something to do with that? Should I change the entry?'

'It's not that. I . . . it's just that it's personal. He's not my supervisor and–'

'Is there something else you want to share with me?' Gabrielle says.

Maybe she should tell the truth. At least they'd know why she looks like death warmed up. Gabrielle is so poised, so perfect, and is looking at her so expectantly. The thought makes her stomach lurch.

'Is there anything we can be supporting you with? Is it work-related? I can see we haven't had your three-month review yet, but if there are any problems at all, please do feel free to share. We want you to be happy here.'

'I'm sorry if I've seemed a little distracted.'

'Something going on at home?' Her voice is treacle, her gaze as warm as a TV mom's and twice as fake. She is hungry for Ellis's failures.

Panic pulls Ellis's thoughts into a vortex. They're keeping an eye on her. They're not sure she fits in. She should tell them about Adrian, but if she does, she'll start greeting. She knows it. God. Lana would never let herself get in this mess. She'd have been honest right from the off. No, she'd not have been cheated on in the first place. Not Lana.

'It's my sister. Her husband . . . he slept with someone else. They've spilt up. It's all a big mess.'

'Oh, how awful.'

'And she has twins. They're only toddlers. She's gutted – we all are. We thought she might . . .' Ellis's eyes obediently grow damp, and Gabrielle reaches out a hand to place over one of Ellis's. She has long, pointed nails. Ellis imagines one sliding into a vein.

'How's she doing now? Will she be okay?'

'We hope so. Sorry, I feel like I shouldn't have said anything.'

'No, no. Don't you worry about last week's absence. I'll put family emergency down on the form. Any time you need to talk about it, you know where I am.'

Ellis nods gratefully. Gabrielle gives her hand one last squeeze on the way out. Everything Ellis said will be typed up and saved.

She checks her phone. Another message from Lana. Paranoia floods in. The phone was locked and silent. There's no way she could've pocket-dialled. Lana can't have heard her lie. Ellis thumbs the message open. It's a photo of a muscular grey-blue body and a set of great, chomping teeth. A pacu fish.

No deep sea creature, no animal, frightens Ellis more than the pacu. From behind, it looks just like the sort of innocent fish that might brush a leg as it paddle-dabbles around a loch. With its mouth closed, it's just a blunt-faced nothing. But when its jaws open, the pacu becomes something else. An unholy chimera, a fish with a human set of teeth.

The first time Lana sent her a photo of one, Ellis assumed it was Photoshopped. It was too uncanny to be real. But her sister sent another and then another until Ellis was forced to investigate. The trawl through a page of search results revealed more horrors: pacus had a second layer of teeth behind the first.

Lana hasn't sent a pacu picture in years. Ellis thought she'd forgotten about them, she should know better. She has to reply. If she doesn't, Lana will only send more. Ellis has already memorised the picture against her will and is imagining fingers, ankles even, clamped in the jaw of this awful beast. A body pulled under the surface. She shivers. Another message pops up.

Didn't know Adrian had taken up swimming.

Ellis's cheek twitches. Lana's on her side: that's worth the toll of seeing this fish. Guilt swims alongside its blue body; Ellis evades. Lana would swallow Gabrielle and her false concern up in two fierce bites.

*

Ellis goes for a drink with Becca because she can't think of a good enough excuse to avoid it. When Becca negotiates a night off, she's ferocious in making sure it's filled, and Ellis has already waited too long to tell her about Adrian.

She drags a palmful of moisturiser and foundation across her face and clumps on waterproof mascara. She needs to dye her hair; the mousey roots are showing. Lana staked a claim for blonde at thirteen, and Ellis has been the deepest of browns ever since. She wishes she could stay home.

The bar is busy, and Ellis hurries towards a booth soon to be vacated. She nods at the men who're leaving; they barely react. She is nobody.

Becca arrives at a clip, ten minutes after she's supposed to. The apologetic smile melts into a look of concern.

'What's wrong?'

'Good to see you too.'

'Something's happened, obviously.' Becca sits without taking her jacket off.

Ellis plunges. Becca is right with her.

'The prick, the utter fucking prick.' She is still out of breath, her indignation an erotic pant.

'I know.'

'You're sure?'

'He told me himself. He had to tell me because I'm such a bloody idiot I didn't even realise it was going on.'

'You're not an idiot. You're a trusting loving person, and he's a bastard for preying on that.'

'He's left me for her.'

'You wouldn't have been able to forgive him anyway. Shit, we need drinks.'

Ellis picks at the soft grain of the table as she waits. Becca is strong, even more so than Lana. Her fierce streak is tempered with kindness, and it's no surprise to Ellis that she has a good, healthy relationship and a baby she'd said she wasn't sure about having, but loves to the ends of the earth. She loves Ellis too.

'I got a bottle.'

Becca glugs wine into two oversized glasses and sits back, waiting. Ellis knows what she wants, and for a few minutes, she resists. She says things like 'but what about you?' and 'did you have that nursery trial day you were talking about?' until she can't hold it in any more and begins to cry in earnest. Becca comes round to her side of the booth and wraps an arm around her. She says meaningless, soothing things as Ellis tries to get hold of herself. She pulls back and wipes her nose on the back of her hand.

'Stop hugging me or I'll carry on bawling.'

Becca takes a packet of baby wipes from her handbag and hands one over. It's cool and sweet-smelling and doesn't burn the raw skin rimming her nostrils.

'At least you're at your mum's,' Becca says with a smidgen of a smile in her voice. Ellis's friends all love her mum. As they should. Her mum – Marion, to Becca – has always been perfectly lovable and kind to everyone Ellis has taken home. She remembers their names and asks about their jobs and their children and those flowers they were thinking about planting the last time she saw them. She's the same with Ellis and Lana, but when it's your own kids, niceness isn't enough. Her mum's fussing is benign, impersonal. It's hard to trust she has any idea what Ellis is really feeling.

'And it's driving me mad already.'

'At least she's got the space for you.'

'I'm lucky. Just . . . you know,' she says. Becca doesn't know.

Her own mother is nervy and prone to flights of worry that consume her so completely she forgets to check in on her own children. It's got worse over the years. She barely held Scotty, her first grandchild, for more than half a minute before starting to fret over whether she'd put the right ticket on the car and whether she'd get into bother when she tried to leave the hospital car park.

As an offering, Ellis tells Becca about Trevor. She's delighted and thinks it's hilarious that he's a dentist.

'She was petrified of them our whole childhood!' Ellis says.

'That just makes it even better. I guess she got over it.'

'It's not fair.'

'All's fair in love and dentistry. I'll top us up . . . oh.' Becca waves the empty bottle. 'I'll get another. I think we need it.'

Ellis nods, despite her queasiness. Becca returns with more wine and starts in on a list of Ellis's good qualities. All fictional. By the time another glass is empty, she's convinced Ellis's future will be rosy. Becca can't help but try and make things better. It's who she is. Her search for a bright side is abrasive, but the motive is pure.

Ellis pours, and a sob blurts out, skewing her aim and sending a thin splash of wine across the table.

Becca forces another hug on her. 'You're better off without him.'

'I know,' Ellis says, and then can't stop herself from explaining why that might not be true. Becca argues and comforts and discreetly stops drinking at some point. More than once, she reaches for her phone and stops her hand halfway there. Becca wants to check on her boys. As though they can't survive without her for one night. As though Liam isn't so capable and relaxed you could barely believe he was real. As though Scotty isn't as adorable as a three-year-old can be. As though they don't all love each other like the perfect little family they are. Ellis excuses herself and totters to the toilets.

The wine has dried her out. There's barely a dribble. She flushes and turns to the tiny mirror. Her cheeks are grey, her eyes bloodshot. She snarls at the reflection. There's a tideline of wine on the inside of her lip. The tooth on the left is aching. She's probably got dehydrated like the article said she shouldn't. It's hopeless.

Becca slides her phone away when she notices Ellis approaching.

'Everything okay?'

'Fine, fine. Scotty won't go back to sleep. He's in a mamma's boy phase.' Her pride trembles like early morning dew. 'But you, El, what are you going to do? Are you going to talk to him? Never talk to him again? What's the plan?'

Ellis shrugs and says she'll work it out, but right now it's time to go.

They start to gather their things. Becca's relieved to head home although she'd be mortified to know how obvious it is. They kiss goodbye, and Ellis feels both better and worse for confessing. Becca has said all the things she's supposed to and now she can discreetly let Zoe and Charmaine know, saving Ellis from having to. They'll try to help. None of them can fix it.

★

Ellis dreams about teeth all night through. One canine has grown to almost a foot long; she can't close her mouth. She slavers when she tries to talk. She stands at the hall mirror in her old flat, trying to file it down. She's back on the night bus, and an old woman is telling her she should be ashamed of herself. Her hand is up to conceal the tooth when part of it comes away in her hand. It's riddled with tiny holes and crumbles like limestone. The bus swerves as she tries to stand, and more tooth fragments fall down her front. She wakes, her cheek and head aching, and swallows the stale water she left beside her bed.

Her phone screen flashes. Adrian.

Are you sure you got everything you wanted? I found your university books in the hall cupboard. And what about the shoe rack?

Who gives a shit about ancient textbooks? They're worth pennies. Why is he texting now? The crook of her elbow hides her eyes.

Nothing she has is worth anything. All the bits and pieces she bought for the flat cost plenty and lost value the second she got them home. Adrian hates antiques; he's an IKEA and Habitat kind of guy so she dutifully filled the house with furniture that instantly depreciated. She never wants to see that crappy shoe rack again.

It's not just the furniture. She paid for things that seemed important and are now barely tangible. She kept the car running, until there'd been one bad MOT too many and they got rid of it. She spent money on food and clothes. Make-up, sometimes, holiday bookings for them both. She financed all the extras and it suited her. Adrian took care of everything staid and steady; she provided the colour. It was such a novel idea – being the frivolous one – that Ellis treasured it.

She is not the colour. She is flattened to grey. Adrian's supposed boringness means he is the sole possessor of everything valuable they'd once shared.

Her savings account barely has a thousand pounds. There'd been more until the redundancy. She'd grown complacent and assumed she'd be taken care of, even if the unthinkable happened. It was a flimsy legal status when a relationship died but both partners lived on. Would Sally think to get her name on the mortgage?

Becca's right: she should count herself lucky she's got somewhere to stay. Ellis feels anything but. She wants out and doesn't have nearly enough for a deposit plus one month's rent. Even if she can scrape that together, it will only leave her trapped in the relentless renting cycle she thought she'd left behind. Before Adrian, Ellis kept tight control of her money, aways choosing the sensible jobs and least risky paths. Throughout the years they spent together she stopped paying attention and all her emergency money was trifled away. All those sacrifices throughout her twenties, lost during the dullest of thirties.

Her other arm comes up to cover her face. She squeezes, and her head throbs. She allowed herself to be snared and can't see how to chew her way out.

7

Primary teeth are replaced by the secondary set between the ages of approximately five and thirteen. Wisdom teeth follow later, in the late teens and early twenties. Secondary teeth are referred to as permanent, but that's some kind of joke. They only stick around if you can protect and preserve them. Not that long ago, Scotland's young women might have all their teeth yanked out before their wedding day. A gift for the husband's family, saving them the expense of caring for those useless, vital things, when dentures were so much cheaper.

'You look like shite,' Lana says. Ellis nods; there is no denying it. They are in the café attached to Blake's Garden Centre, the twins still in their double-buggy, entertained by handfuls of soggy crisps. Mum puts down a laden tray, coffee slopping into the saucers.

'Here we go. I got this too.' She lets a catalogue slide from under her arm as she sits.

'Thanks. I'll take it back for Grant, if you're not needing it. He's wanting a new shed.'

'What's wrong with the one he's got?' Mum says, spooning up a wobbly hunk of foamed milk.

'Too small, apparently. He's been keeping his toolbox on the kitchen counter, like that's going to make me change my mind.'

'He's always been very handy.'

'That's our garden he's wanting to use up. That's space his children could be enjoying.' She flicks through the pages, pausing at a wooden playset. 'So are we going to have to rearrange your mornings with the twins, now you've got a new fancy man?'

'Oh no, we're grand.'

'Sure?'

'He works, you know.'

'I do know. Honestly, Mum, a dentist?'

'He can't help his job.'

'He can though, can't he? Maybe he should have a look at this one – she's gurning away like crazy.'

'I'm not,' Ellis says.

'Why are you pulling a face every time you have a drink?'

'It's nothing. New filling's still a little sensitive.'

'Go back.'

'It's fine.'

'You're going to drive me insane. You paid them to fix it.' Lana's teeth are just as bad, but she flipped the script years ago. It's easy to imagine the glare she gives as she lies back in the chair.

'I'm sure Trevor would be happy to have a look, give you a second opinion if you're worried? All you have to do is say the word. He'd be delighted. Shh, Oscar. Shall I let these two have a little run around?' Mum nods to the play corner. Lana agrees, and several minutes are taken up with wiping and unstrapping. Ellis manages a few mouthfuls of coffee and checks her phone. Nothing.

'You need an intervention,' Lana says.

'I'm fine.'

'Mum said you've been in practically every night. What about your friends? You need to be spending time with people who love you.' Lana's words are accompanied by a glower.

'I just saw Becca last night. And I'm tired.' There is a squirrelly feeling behind her ribs. Lana is giving her that look, the one that sucks all the energy from a room. Ellis wants to say more, to defend herself, but the internal scampering always puts a hitch in her voice, and there's nothing that frustrates Lana more than that hitch.

'That's no excuse. I'm exhausted, I have constant shoulder pain, my hips are fucked, I feel nauseous all the time. If I closed

42

my eyes and relaxed for just ten seconds, I'd be fast asleep on this chair. All you need to worry about is you. Don't think you're getting away with spending the next six months feeling sorry for yourself.'

'It's not even been a week.'

'Uh-huh, but I know you.' The words might have been a comfort, but in Lana's mouth they are a condemnation.

They keep their eyes on the faded collection of leather-covered foam shapes that the twins are doggedly trying to clamber over. Mum stands with a smile on her face, oblivious to the glares of the young mothers who want her to control the twins and clear the way for a group of impatient four-year-olds. One of the boys tries to edge Oscar out of the way; he bares his brand new teeth.

'Clear out the joint account and blow it on drinks and new outfits.'

'We don't have a joint account.'

'Ten years and you don't even have a joint account? How the fuck were you–'

She's interrupted by a screaming child. Oscar has buried his small teeth into the arm of one of the four-year-olds.

'For Christ's sake.' Lana stands to stride over. Ellis watches her whisper something in Oscar's ear. He lets go. Lana argues the crying boy's mother down, scoops the twins up and brings them back to the table.

Mum follows. 'What a little scrapper we've got. You weren't done playing, were you, pumpkin?'

'He's done now.' Lana drops Mia into Ellis's lap and starts to wrestle Oscar into his side of the buggy. Her niece wriggles and kicks, and last night's wine roils in her stomach. When Lana plucks her away, it is a relief and a sorrow.

8

Ellis sits at her desk, staring at the spreadsheet she's supposed to be formatting and thinking about the pictures she hasn't taken from the walls of Adrian's flat. There aren't many – they weren't an arty couple, or the kind who plasters holiday snaps everywhere.

There was a picture taken at Lana's wedding on the mantelpiece, one of the twins propped nearby, and a large print from the Scottish National Gallery in the alcove. It's a nice painting, picked for the cyclists rushing down a country lane. She chose it for Adrian and carried it home carefully. It'd taken three afternoons of shopping for a frame before finding a suitable one in Jenners. Then a fretful forty-five minutes trying to unroll the print and trap it beneath the glass. Adrian smiled, said it looked nice and took months to hang it. She should've done it herself, even if she'd used the wrong kind of nails.

She doesn't want the print. It's not even that she doesn't want Adrian and Sally to have it. She just wants all the time she spent on it back.

It's been a horrible week. Barely scraping by at work and going home to hide from her mum's well-meaning questions. And since she fetched her things, Adrian has messaged several times about the stuff she's left behind. He sent another one earlier. Seeing his name created a bubble of hope, quickly pierced.

I'll be out on Friday evening if you want to pick more up.

I've got everything I wanted.

You can't mean that. What about the suitcases? And the shoe rack?

I mean it.

Her phone buzzes again, setting off an answering vibration in her chest. It's Mum. Before she opens it, another appears on her screen. And another. Lana.

Ellis quickly scans the office to check no one's looking before opening the group chat.

Next Wednesday, 7.30. I'm making lasagne, Trevor looking forward to it.

Can't we do lunch? That's bang on bedtime.

Let me check.

In a separate chat, Lana messages again.

FFS, she knows that's the worst time.

Ellis runs her thumb along the bottom of the screen, thinking about all the blue ticks.

I know.

She thinks for another moment or two, then adds:

I guess Trevor works 9–5.

The message next to Lana's name says *typing*, then it disappears.

Ellis keeps her phone in her lap as she gets back to the spreadsheet. Data arrives from different holiday companies and has to be standardised before being added to TravelOn's system. It's a mindless task. A shadow falls over her shoulder. Ellis jumps and moves her arm to obscure her phone but it's only Naila.

'It's your turn to buy the biscuits,' she says quietly. 'But don't worry. I got you some.'

'You did?'

'Jaffa Cakes. They were on a deal.'

'Aw, you shouldn't have, thank you so much. How much do I owe you?' They're talking covertly, Naila leaning in towards Ellis's screen to make it look like they're discussing the document it's displaying, her heavy dark hair slipping over her shoulder.

'Don't worry about it. You can buy double next time. I'd say stock up while they're cheap and keep them in your desk, but please don't. I hate mice. Absolutely hate them.'

There have been several emails, of increasing severity, about the dangers of keeping snacks in drawers recently. The cost of pest control is growing 'prohibitive'. There's a box of breakfast bars in the bottom drawer of Ellis's desk. She hasn't checked it in a while and doesn't plan to. She's not in a place to deal with gnawed edges.

'I'll get yours next time – thanks for covering.'

'It's nothing. Just thought you seemed a bit down and could do with one less thing to worry about.'

Naila waggles her fingers and heads back to her own desk. Ellis wonders what she's heard. Anything said to Gabrielle should be in confidence, but Ellis doesn't trust people who do things supposedly for her own good. She learned that at nine years old, lined up with her classmates, everyone crying and pushing each other into thrilling and delicious fear at the news they were getting their teeth checked. Rumours flew up and down the line. The dentist was ripping out baby teeth right there. He had a needle as thick as a pencil. He left one boy with no teeth at all.

The children waited in the main corridor outside the assembly hall. Ellis's classmates went through the double doors one by one, and didn't come back out. The teachers had decided to cut crowding by funnelling them through the side door after their check-up, not considering how this disappearing act might terrify the children still waiting.

Two P5 teachers struggled to keep their combined classes calm. Ellis was silent and still. Her hands twisted into the ends of her cardigan sleeves. Some of the kids were snivelling. They got hugs and attention and still had to walk through the double doors when they reached the front of the line.

When it was her turn to cross the threshold, she couldn't step forward. Her teacher, Mrs Finch, quickly gave up cajoling and started ordering. Mrs White carried on telling milky lies about how she'd be fine, it was nothing to worry about.

When Mrs White laid a gentle but firm hand on her shoulder to push her through the doors, Ellis's black soles stayed rooted to the linoleum. Beth, who had been behind her, was ushered forward. Complaints sprouted around Ellis. Fairness trumped everything for her classmates, even fear.

Ellis didn't mean to upset anyone. She stared beseechingly at the woman who was in charge of her between eight and three-fifteen from Monday to Friday. Mrs Finch looked at her the same way she looked at the moths who'd infested the dressing-up box – like an annoyance she wanted to clap to smithereens.

Ellis's legs began to tremble. The teachers pushed and urged until she found herself in front of the dentist. Mrs Finch walked her right to the chair and waited until she cringed her way into it.

The dentist pinched her chin to pull her mouth open. Ellis closed her eyes tightly; the smell of disinfectant and mint opened up a great longing for her dad. She disgraced herself by sobbing and snotting all the way through the examination. He tutted as he wrote up her cavities.

Ellis was sent home that afternoon with a letter detailing her disobedience and the dire need for her to visit her own dentist.

Her phone flashes; it's a message from her mum. The day of the school dentist (which, contrary to her fears, turned out to be a one-off) brokered so many betrayals – her teachers', her class-mates', her mum's reaction to the note she handed over – that Ellis vowed never to forget it. You can't rely on anyone to have your best interests at heart. Gabrielle cares about avoiding trouble for TravelOn. Naila is the second quietest person in the office, looking to win the loyalty of the quietest. Lana wants a sister she doesn't have to make excuses for. Ellis is no fool.

She opens her messages. It's her mum.

Sunday lunch it is, can't wait.

She's talked Trevor into a weekend meet-the-family. Just great.

9

For vertebrates, the primary function of teeth is to tear and chew food. Fighting and/or defence is a secondary function, most prevalent in carnivores. Incisors slice, canines hold and cut, molars and premolars crush and chew.

The teeth in Ellis's mouth are the descendants of the skin plates of ancient, armoured fish. They protect, they kill, they are the first stage in human digestion. She can only see the crowns, but she knows of the roots beneath them. She's read all about the fibrous ligament attaching each to the tooth-bearing bones of her jaw. She knows what they are for and wishes they were different.

The house is quiet, Mum is still asleep and Ellis has woken with a headache for the sixth day in a row. Last night, it was a ghost that only gave a warning throb when she turned her head too quickly. Now, it pulses. The packet of painkillers by her bed is empty. Ellis finds more in the kitchen.

She wants to see her father. There's only one way she can. The brown photo album, gifted to her and Lana just after Ellis's tenth birthday, is filled with him. It'd been two years since he died, and Ellis had started to fret about not remembering how he looked. The album is as precious to her now as it was then. She takes it to the study and pushes some soft toys aside to sit down.

The early pages have pictures of her dad before he met their mum. The young man smiling and chatting and posing for the photographer could be a stranger, but as Ellis turns through the years the dad she remembered emerges. There is the late eighties beard and the soft shirts made of thin corduroy she used to press her cheek against. They'd always smelled of smoke although he never lit up in front of the girls. The trill of a cheap cigarette floating along a street can sometimes open a deep well of longing in Ellis, even though she's terrified by the photos of blackened gums found on some packets.

She pauses on a picture taken in a park and rubs a finger across the plastic sheet holding it in place. She wishes she was there again. Next is a snap of their dad with a daughter in each arm. He was quietly handsome. Ellis's elbows are pointed like his but Lana looks the most like him. She has his neat ears and easy tan. Ellis looks more like their mum's side although it's said she has his voice. Neither she nor Lana inherited his teeth, more's the pity.

Ellis closes the album, a swirl of sadnesses sweeping through her. It's been a long time since she felt anything so deeply. With Adrian, everything was distant. He complained and she listened. She'd rarely been the one to bring up problems, and not much changed when she did. It was easier to keep her unhappiness to herself. Now she knows he was hiding his feelings too, even more successfully than her.

It's different in her mum's house. Emotions rise up and refuse to be forced back down. She's stuck here. It's her own fault. Except it's Adrian's too. But what can she do about that?

She slides the photos back on the shelf and stands. The headache is waning but she is exhausted.

10

It is a beautiful Saturday, and Ellis wants none of it. She's slept in again, and Lana's on her way over for brunch, ignoring the fact it's the day before the lunch with Trevor and she's spent half the week bitching about it cutting into her 'family time'.

Levering herself up, Ellis feels a drag beneath her cheekbone. It's as if the newly filled tooth is heavier than the rest of her and needs a few seconds to catch up. The sensation is gone by the time she hits the shower. She brushes her teeth until she spits blood. She hadn't picked up the expensive electric brush that'd been charging in the hall cupboard (Adrian didn't like cables on display – everything unsightly was consigned to the cupboard), and there's no flashing sensor to tell her to stop pressing so hard on this one. She comforts herself with the sparkle of Sally's smashed perfume bottle. Ellis spits again. She needs to buy another brush and stop scraping away precious enamel.

She trudges downstairs to join her mum in the kitchen.

'Your sister was meant to be here by now.' Cheerfulness just dripping off her.

'Not like her.'

'That's what happens when you've got wee ones,' Mum says, her hands deep in the sudsy sink. Ellis rolls her eyes and takes a seat at the kitchen table. Her mum shakes her head to free the long teardrop earring tangled in her hair. She's a fan of earrings, finds necklaces constraining. Ellis regrets the youthful hours she spent poring over the Argos catalogue and searching Christmas craft fairs for pendants. Her mum had worn those clumsy necklaces a handful of times before letting them drift into the dressing-table drawer. They're probably still there.

The first siren of complaints arrives. Lana's here. She's never stopped the habit of dropping round. Ellis thought things might change when the twins were born, that family get-togethers would start taking place at Lana and Grant's place, but Lana's too territorial to let go of the family home. Ellis never liked having them all round to the flat. Mum's house felt more neutral.

Ellis stands to make tea, not wanting to be found aimless at the table. She nudges her mum over to reach the tap and catches an orange and cinnamon scent. It's a new perfume, one Ellis doesn't recognise.

A rustle of coats and the not-quite-words of the twins approach. They're in the hall. Ellis guards the kettle, waiting for it to roil. The red crescents below her eyes sting twice as much in anticipation of criticism. No one should spend the hours between five and seven crying in the dark.

'Christ.' Lana clatters in.

'How's my favourite little ones?' Mum's damp hands are immediately patting heads and tweaking cheeks.

'It's been a day already. You know how that Eleanor round the corner has been banging on about her missing cat? Guess what turned up in the Baxters' compost bin?'

'No.'

'Been there a week. She's freaking out, obviously. Wants to take them to court. The whole street is up to high doh, wanting to debate it all, and these two have been a fucking delight since the moment they woke up.'

'How did it get in? Is it . . .'

'Yes, Mum, it's dead. Beyond dead. Really fucking dead. They're lazy with the lid; it's been stinking out the street for months. I bet it was hoaching with mice and the poor thing just climbed in for a snack and the lid closed behind it. Eleanor thinks someone did it on purpose.'

'Poor thing.'

'She's a right bitch.'

'The cat.'

'It was horrible and all. Almost took Mia's eye out. Still, what a way to go.'

Ellis hands out cups of tea and offers to water down some apple juice for the kids. Lana shakes her head and starts pulling sippy cups and plastic farm animals from her bag.

'I saw Adrian on the way here,' she says.

Ellis pauses with the chair half pulled out.

'Oh yes?' Mum says in the same voice she's used to comment on dozens of teachers and school friends over the years. A tone for 'passing through' people, not 'almost a third of your life' people.

'Buying smoked salmon in the deli off the high street.'

'I thought you hated that deli,' Mum says.

'I do, but they have these amazing organic rusk things.'

'Did you say anything?' Ellis's fingers twitch against the chair back.

'Hardly. He almost walked into us and when he saw it was me, he asked how everyone was. I told him I was surprised he had the balls to ask. Then Mia pitched a fit and he ran off.'

'Don't say anything to him if you see him again.' The chair barks against the lino.

'What? I'm not allowed to even talk to him?'

'I'd rather you didn't,' Ellis says.

'You can't stop people talking.'

'Girls, come on. Don't fall out. Adrian's caused enough trouble.'

'It isn't about him,' Ellis says.

'Of course it is. He's what you're arguing about, isn't he?'

'No, it's not. Lana, don't have a go if you see him again, okay? It's bad enough as it is.'

'I kept my mouth shut, didn't I? But for what? Someone has to get him told,' Lana says.

'Please, Lana.'

'She wouldn't want to upset you, she wouldn't do that. Would she? Would she?' Each shake of Mum's head takes her closer to Oscar, whose giggles force Ellis to fake a smile. If Adrian isn't hers, she wants him gone. A wart frozen off, a cyst cut out. Lana shouldn't have something of him that Ellis doesn't, even if it's just a few minutes' worth of embarrassed conversation.

'Was he alone?' she says.

'You'd have known about it – he'd have known about it – if I'd seen that skank.'

Ellis nods and finally sits down. Oscar rests his head on her knee for a moment; it's a comfort. Mia clamours for Grandma's set of measuring cups. Lana fetches them and begins a noisy balancing game. Mum opens the bread bin. Ellis takes out her phone and begins to scroll. There is Adrian. There is Sally. Separate profiles. She flicks between them.

Lana's going through the pile of magazines and newspapers Mum keeps by the back door. She wants some for the twins' nursery box: they're always running out of collage materials. Mum is cutting croissants for the oven. Ellis can't be bothered reminding her that she prefers hers unsliced.

'You looking for places?' Lana says. Ellis doesn't stop trawling through Sally's Twitter account. 'Has he got the flat up already? Or has he got enough to buy you out?'

'What?' Ellis looks up. Her sister's sitting on the counter, flicking through a sheaf of brochures.

'Has he been earning big bucks this whole time? Would've thought these were a bit out your price range.'

Ellis scrabbles to catch up.

'Oh, those,' Mum says, pulling jars out the cupboard. 'They're mine.'

'Yours?' Lana says.

'Just looking.'

'Why? Not like you're selling, is it?'

'I wanted to see what's out there.'

'But you love it here,' Ellis says.

'I do, but I'm getting on. Are you having jam or cheese?'

'Where's this come from?' Lana flicks the brochures onto the table.

'Och, nowhere. Come and get the kids their breakfast,' she says, croissants half out the oven.

'They had their breakfast about three hours ago.'

'You know what I mean.'

'Are you really thinking about moving?' Ellis says.

Mum doesn't look up from the baking tray. 'Nothing to worry about, love. You're welcome to stay as long as you need.'

'So you *are* thinking about selling,' Lana says, swinging a grumbling child onto her hip. 'What about us? What about the twins? We love it here.'

'Girls, I'm just curious. No rules against looking. Now, who's ready for a bite to eat? Are you hungry, wee man?'

Lana glares at Ellis over the top of Mia's head. Her lips are white where they're not pearly pink.

'Are you going to strap them in or are we going with knees?' Mum says.

'I don't think there's much point trying the chairs.'

'Righto, will you do the honours?' She looks at Oscar and nods at Ellis, who bends to scoop him up. He is a watermelon and Sudocrem squirm.

Breakfast is tense. Ellis knows she should be thinking about the house but she's still fuming about Lana's run-in with Adrian. Lana can't take her eyes off the property particulars, now flecked with jam. Mum chatters away about baking and craft fairs and points out the bird fluttering by the window like it's the highlight of everyone's day. She will not engage, and so Lana turns to Ellis.

'When are you going to start looking for your own place? Can't let Mum have all the fun.'

'Soon.'

'So is he buying you out or putting it up for sale?'

'He's staying. And he doesn't have to buy me out – it's his flat.'

'It's yours too.'

'Not really. He bought it, and I just lived there. It's not like I'm on the mortgage.'

'What? Why the hell weren't you?'

'I didn't think I needed to.'

'Fuck's sake. You were there for years. How much is he giving you, then?'

'I don't know.'

'How can you not know? Didn't you sort all that out already? We went and picked up your things. If I'd thought you hadn't got it squared, I'd have made sure you waited.'

'I needed some clothes.'

'Come on, El, you never should've done that. Possession is nine tenths of the law.'

'No, it isn't.'

'It is when you're talking about the flat your boyfriend has been screwing his mistress in.'

'Lana,' Mum says.

'What?'

'That's a bit much. Ellis, you're more than welcome here, of course you are. But is he really not giving you anything?'

'It's up to him.'

'Oh, Ellis,' Mum says.

'For God's sake, what did you think was going to happen?' Lana says.

'I thought he'd be fair.'

'Maybe he will be. Maybe he's just not thinking straight,' Mum says.

'Don't encourage her. Especially when you've been planning on cutting this place out from under us.'

'Lana, I'm just having a nose. Ellis, you are all right for money, aren't you?'

Ellis tries to tempt Oscar into a bite to save her from

answering with anything more substantial than a nod. He twists in her lap, intent on returning to the floor.

'Let him down. We're meant to be at a playdate down the park in a minute anyway.'

As soon as they leave, Lana sends a text, telling Ellis to call her. She ignores it.

She retreats to her bedroom. Another message, half an hour later.

I know you've got your phone, you need to get shit sorted with Adrian. And keep an eye on Mum, something seriously not right is going on with her.

Ellis sends back a single *k*.

She doesn't need to check to know that the house is worth a lot. There have been dips and recessions and depressions, but the prices in Edinburgh continue to rise. Her mum could've swapped it for somewhere smaller and retired early ages ago. It's not like she loved working at the Post Office although she didn't seem to hate it either. Adrian once suggested releasing equity. Mum had shaken her head vehemently, not willing to trust the trend for appreciation. I couldn't, she said, I'd never forgive myself if the market crashed. Lana had agreed with her and given Adrian a look.

Ellis opens her window a crack and sits on one of the blue crates from Poundstretcher her mum picked up for her. Each is stuffed with a bin bag full of clothes. This is the first time she's stayed for more than a few nights at Christmas in years and years. She'd moved out and into a shared flat before eighteen and was proud of it. The plastic creaks beneath her. She pushes her face closer to the window, relishing the cold breeze with its hint of greens and grime. A few people wander down the street. It's peaceful, almost suburban, yet barely a twenty-minute walk to the centre of town. Plenty of people will want this house.

She already knows Adrian won't talk to her so she composes a text message.

You know as well as I do that we shared that flat. It's not fair to cut me out with nothing. Can't we work something out?

When she heads back downstairs for a glass of water, she sees that the brochures have been tidied away. Ellis drinks, her tooth complains, and she feels the foundations shift.

11

Ellis and Lana are bickering over the best way to stack the wood by the fireplace. Grant has taken the twins to the park. Technically for their benefit, but also giving Lana free rein for her initial interrogation of Trevor. The room is too hot, and Ellis wishes she'd gone to the park. Mum is singing to herself in the kitchen. As tone-deaf as they come, Mum only sings when she's alone or overwhelmingly happy. The snatches of The Lighthouse Family fill Ellis with foreboding. Lana mutters something about riding for a fall as she grabs a log from Ellis's hand, driving a splinter into her palm and making her jump.

Lana rolls her eyes. 'Let's see. That's nothing, barely a skelf.'

'It's fine.' Ellis picks at it.

'Stop picking. You didn't talk to Adrian about a share of the flat, did you? I'm telling you, you have to get on top of this.'

'I sent a message.'

'What did you say? Show me.'

'My phone's upstairs,' Ellis says, shifting to make sure her jumper covers the back pocket of her jeans.

'Don't give him an inch. Guys like him can't stop themselves. He'll find another way to screw you over if he can.'

'Guys like what?'

'Cheaters, liars, arseholes who walk all over you.'

Ellis nods and says she needs the loo. She's on her way back, wrists still cool from the water she ran over them, when the doorbell goes. She answers. The man is young. Too young. Barely mid-forties.

'Trevor?' she says.

'You must be Ellis.' He's about her height, slim, clean-shaven, good posture. Mum bustles down the hall with a joyous hello. Ellis steps to one side and watches her mum peck this stranger on the cheek and usher him in. He enters their home, bringing with him the faint smell of the pink gunk orthodontists use to take an impression, and grins his way to the living room, where Lana meets him with a glare.

'Here we are. Sit down, sit down. You've met Ellis, and this is Lana.'

'Great to finally meet you,' Trevor says, no doubt used to dealing with difficult customers.

'Wine? We opened a red half an hour ago.' Mum beams, a woman with the contrast turned up.

'A wee one. Or white, if you have it?'

'White it is.'

She leaves the room, and the atmosphere drops. Trevor swaps the plump but uncomfortable cushion at his end of the sofa for the ugly, but much softer, brown one. He's been round before.

'Mum said she met you at the surgery,' Lana begins.

'Not the most conventional first date, I'll give you that. But as good a start as any.'

'That depends,' Lana says.

Will he ever stop smiling?

'So, uh, you've been seeing each other a while?' Ellis tries.

'I suppose we have.'

His hair is slicked back, his irises as pale as a puma's. It'd be easy for someone like him to file teeth down to resemble a human's.

'You look about my husband's age,' Lana says.

Trevor grins again, teeth just visible. 'Marion says he's a stand-up guy.'

Lana's eyes narrow. 'Of course he is.' As if to prove their point, Grant arrives with two giggling twins.

'All right, mate,' he says to Trevor. Ellis gets a nod. Lana is right in there ready to wipe Mia's running nose.

Mum has set the table. Ellis sees that Trevor is hanging back, waiting to see which seat is left for him. Ellis wishes he'd crashed ahead and taken Lana's place.

She aligns and realigns her cutlery as her sister grills Trevor and Mum dishes up. They begin, but Mum keeps jumping out of her seat to fetch pepper, extra bread, another bottle of wine – that's the good thing about white, doesn't need time to breathe. She only stays still when Ellis points out that her food's getting cold.

Lana's questions continue. Mum and Grant act like this deluge is normal; Ellis is embarrassed but wants to know the answers as much as anyone. They learn that Trevor is a partner at his practice. He rides a bike to work every day, one with a fancy name that costs as much as a second-hand car. This makes him laugh. The bike doesn't endear him to Ellis. Trevor's dental nurse is a young man with skinny dreads who runs a children's music group in his spare time. Trevor shares a picture of the latest recital. Obviously he's there too, helping out. The surgery's receptionist is five years older than Mum, and Olga, the woman he set the surgery up with, is planning to propose to her girlfriend on their next camping trip.

Trevor is impeccable.

'Delicious,' he says. Mum has served a beef casserole she's been making since the girls were small. One she learned from her own mother. One Ellis used to find insufferably boring. Now she recognises its richness, the depth in its simplicity.

The plates are clear. Mum is flushed with pleasure and chases everyone back to the front room to catch the afternoon sun. They settle in the same spots as before. Trevor looks even more at home. He comments on the ingenious way the twins are working together to smoosh a stuffed cat into a toy garage.

'I know. I'm not one of those mums, but when you find out they're in the top percentile for practically everything, you have to do everything you can.'

'Keep us busy, don't they?' Grant says.

'Ready for cheese?' Mum asks. Trevor is enthusiastic. There's no way he puts away heavy meals like this on the regular; he's too trim. Ellis volunteers to fetch the cheese, tired of her mum's happiness and Lana's aggression.

There is no rational reason to doubt him, aside from his age, and that's not something he can help. Still, Ellis is in the hallway, fingers drawn to the gaping pockets of his expensive anorak. She could balance the cheeseboard on the hall table and just . . .

'Are you lost?' Mum calls.

Rather than reply and let her voice give her location away, Ellis rights the platter, pauses for the time it would take to walk the four steps from the kitchen and joins them.

Trevor claps his palms together. Ellis and Lana exchange a glance.

'Taleggio, my favourite.' He picks up a butter knife and the soft wedge of cheese sinks beneath it.

'I know. Oh, Ellis, couldn't you find the cheese knife? Bottom drawer.'

'This is grand.' He transfers a sliver of cheese to a cracker.

'You don't have kids of your own?' Lana says, knowing full well he doesn't.

'Nope.'

'Don't you want them?' Lana spears a chunk of cheddar.

'Not really.' Too casual, pretending he can't tell it's a question with no right answer. 'Got two brothers, three sisters, nine nieces and nephews and a whole host of cousins. I'm an outlier as far as my family's concerned. Benefit of being the youngest. Let everyone else get on with it, and found out I didn't have to.'

He bites firmly into his cracker.

'You're happy not to, then?' Ellis says, jealous of his ease.

'Seems we've got plenty of Stuarts to go around.'

'I can't imagine having such a big family,' Mum says with a one-Christmas-sherry-too-many touch of wistfulness.

The pink, artificial smell returns. Ellis puts her cracker back down.

✷

'He's a fucking child,' Lana hisses from the doorstep. She'd gestured for Ellis to follow her, and she had, even though it was obvious she wasn't needed for anything other than a debrief. Grant was already strapping the twins in their car seats. Trevor is still comfortably installed on the sofa next to Mum, briskly waved back down when he tried to help.

'He's not that young.'

'That smile, what's she thinking? Christ. I know exactly what she's thinking.'

'I figured the photo was out of date.'

'Apparently not.'

'He seems nice, apart from that.'

'Apart from that? Fuck's sake, Ellis. What's nice when he's going to screw Mum? When the next bright young thing comes in to get her teeth whitened and drapes herself all over him. Who's going to get hurt then?'

'You don't know that.'

'Grow up, Ellis.'

'There's probably only fifteen years in it.'

'Yeah, yeah, I know where you're going with this. If it was the other way round, we'd not even comment on the difference – men get different rules, blah-fucking-blah. This is our mum we're talking about.'

'She's so happy.'

'For now. What if he's the reason she's been looking at new houses?'

'They'll hear you.'

'Don't let that butter-wouldn't-melt act fool you. You're going to have to keep an eye out, Ellis. Now we know a bit more about him, I'll get digging.' Lana's tone is strident. She has her own home, her own family. Everything she needs. She's always known exactly what she wants out of life – a job telling people what to do, husband, home, kids (clever her, two at once) – and has advanced towards it perfectly. She jettisoned everyone and everything that didn't tally with the plan, and her ruthlessness worked. She can afford to hurt her mum.

Ellis stands at the door, not watching Lana walk away. She is picturing Mum at Trevor's mercy, his sterilised hands holding her jaw and nudging her lips open. Gently patting her throat to check for swollen lymph nodes. The image raises the hairs on her neck.

She returns to the front room, and Trevor gives her a conspiratorial head tilt. Ellis keeps her face blank and sits next to her mum. She wonders what they see in each other as she listens to a stream of chatter. They cover his new running shoes, Mum's next book group and the biography she's already bored of, the fact that his receptionist has started scrapbooking and scissors all the most interesting pictures out of the magazines in the waiting room. Ellis's phone pings. It's Adrian: he's sent an email in reply to her text. She makes her excuses and scurries upstairs to read it.

Ellis, it's good to hear from you but I have to admit I'm shocked by your message. I thought you'd be arranging to pick up some of your furniture. I am of course happy for you to take it. As for the flat, you stayed here all those years and I barely asked for a contribution. Surely you can see how much of a saving that's been for you? I never thought you were the kind of woman who'd go after someone like this. Especially when we had it all agreed.

Shock yanks the air from her lungs. She reads it again. All he's offering are some scraps of furniture, as if she cares about a fucking shoe rack.

Solicitor. Deposit. Restocked cupboard. A bed. Linen. She needs thousands and she doesn't have it. How quickly money disappears when you let it. How insubstantial everything is. She's an idiot for not protecting herself. She's always loved her own resilience and self-sufficiency. There's nothing left to love about herself now.

She reads the email again and hears his voice, but not only his; there's someone else's too. Sally's. Of course. Ellis did not hold her own and now she has been knocked loose.

12

Throughout the seventeenth century, the fifth or sixth reason cited on the annual mortality bill was more often than not simply 'teeth'. Those were the days when they knew those little off-white hunks could kill you, but not why. Ellis reads that it was only in 1960 that Dr Paul H. Keyes discovered that the bacteria Streptococcus mutans feasts on plaque, ferments sugars and creates acids that strip calcium and destroy enamel, dentine and, finally, the tooth's pulp. His research saved countless teeth and lives. It saves lives still. Without treatment, periodontal disease still strips, plunders and invades. But Ellis has been given a clean bill of health. It was only a regular filling, a little deeper than usual.

The bus edges forward. A man with an anorak on over his suit is next to her. He exhales, and the reek triggers her gag reflex. She's trapped next to the stink of quietly rotting teeth as she reads about Keyes' research.

She lets air in through her mouth, a little at a time, and scrunches down. Adrian never smelled like decay and disease. His teeth were strong and well looked after. What a paltry recommendation of a man.

She frets over the state of her own teeth and the headache that never quite goes away. Surely the nerve should've sorted itself out by now. Face scrunched into her scarf, Ellis presses her tongue against the problem tooth and gum. The pain in her head is no worse. She navigates the stalactites of her teeth to investigate the other side. Is the gum hotter than it should be?

The city passes by unnoticed. Root canals, rotting teeth, problems that breed and multiply out of sight. Her neighbour paws at his phone, breathing heavily and sending out great gusts of death. She hopes he'll get off first, but he's still there at her stop, and she has to ask him to move. She passes with her nose pressed to her shoulder and hurries down the stairs.

Ellis ties her hair back while waiting for the double doors to open. Wind whips strands loose as soon as she steps onto the street and she yanks the bobble out, taking several hairs with it. She checks the time, just enough to nip into the chemist across from the office.

Ellis knows everything she'll find in the oral hygiene section. Still, she's lulled by the aura of possibility. A woman in an unseasonable hat stands waiting for a prescription, glaring at the door the pharmacist has stepped through. A man is rifling through a rack of throat sweets.

Mouthwash. Toothy Pegs. Electric brushes. Normal brushes. So much plastic. So many promises. Exactly what she expected. Ellis spends some time, staring. She picks up an expensive brand of mouthwash designed for sensitive teeth and an electric toothbrush to replace the one left behind. Painkillers, next.

She's reaching for a packet when a body steps too close.

'One of those days, eh?' Naila says, a box of tampons in one hand and ibuprofen in the other.

'Looks like it.'

'Thank goodness for these,' Naila says, shaking the packet of painkillers and accompanying Ellis to the till. They queue together. There's no way to get out of walking to the office together now.

'Are you all right? I mean, really?' Naila asks. She is the kindest person in TravelOn. The first person there who made Ellis a cup of tea without asking. She has two cats and endless opinions about the best suitcase for a weekend break. She's in her early thirties. There's not a bad bone in her body. She is lovely. Ellis wishes she could be happier to see her.

'I'm fine.'

'If you need anything, just shout. Break-ups can be awful. My cousin cut all her hair off and moved to Australia. We were beside ourselves, but she met an electrician over there so it all worked out.'

Ellis's face freezes in horror; Naila doesn't notice.

'Tell your sister it gets better. She's welcome to come for a drink with us any time. You too, obviously.' Her laugh is warm. Ellis manages a thank-you, seething at the thought of Gabrielle whispering her lie to Naila or Alison or Jean. Maybe telling them to be kind to her. Maybe bitching about how distracted she seems and how she should be over her family drama by now. Not even thinking to tell them to keep it quiet. Oh God, was she allowed to do that? Is it illegal? But how can Ellis complain when her disaster isn't even true?

'Better hurry,' Naila says. 'Just after nine. Shout if you need anything.'

Ellis nods and heads straight for the toilets. She shouldn't have lied. She didn't mean to. And now everyone knows her business. She wants to run out the building and leave the whole mess behind.

*

Ellis escapes to the furthest away café at lunchtime. The salads are watery and the sandwiches dry, but she's never seen anyone from TravelOn come in, and she's not hungry anyway. She should be looking at flats or housing advice or the emails she hasn't answered, yet it's Sally's Facebook page Ellis refreshes and refreshes. There she is with cocktails, with a dog, wearing a pink sweatband. On a holiday three years ago. With another man, much younger and more handsome than Adrian. And Sally's younger too, of course. Not so much younger. Only five or six years. Enough for it to hurt, not enough for Ellis to believe they have no chance of lasting. Sally takes photos of her food, her flat, plant pots. Early last year she was posting once or twice a day. The flood of images has slowed to a drip. There are only a handful from the last month. None include Adrian.

Ellis knows what Naila will say, if she finds out the truth. Just like Ellis's friends, she'll try to help with kind words and hopeful suggestions. All the break-up advice Ellis has ever received is an affront. Taking up colouring or crochet won't fix this. Not that she's even spoken to most of her friends yet.

The news has trickled out and Ellis guiltily rejects their calls and replies to messages with love hearts and thank-yous. The only person she picks up for is Becca, who doesn't take no for an answer. It isn't that the rest of them are bad friends, it's just that they'll tell her she is good and beautiful and better off without him. They'll say it's lucky it happened while she still has time to start again. Better she's found out now. Good thing there are no kids involved. She doesn't want to hear it. Can't bear to hear it.

She hates everyone knowing she's been judged unworthy by such an ordinary man. A man whose words scuttle like crisp packets blown across a playground. A man who acts like he'll do what he was supposed to and then doesn't. The same man who accused her of withholding some precious part of herself (the lack at the centre, can a lack be solid enough to hold?) and who's shown her just what is at the heart of him. Her shock is unjustified. This is exactly the kind of thing a man like him might do. Except Ellis had always suspected that if anyone was going to leave, it would be her.

Sally's online pages are full of little pieces of her life. None reveal what Ellis wants to know. She gives up and searches Trevor's name instead, even though she and Lana must know everything there is to find about him online. He seems like a nice man. Can Ellis forgive him for being a dentist? Is she meant to be friends with him? Her mum had been perfectly content to keep quiet about Trevor until Ellis moved home and forced her hand. Ellis wonders if there have been other men, other flings.

She douses the glow of her phone screen and picks up her fork. It is cheap plastic, mass-produced, and as she stabs at a chunk of beetroot, a prong snaps. The sensation summons a shiver that cranks her headache up a notch.

*

Mouthwash and a new toothbrush won't cut it. She's being stupid. She calls the surgery on the way back to the office. She hates to do it. Hates the subservience in her voice when she explains she needs to come back. It's bad enough when something inarguable has happened – a filling pulled away by a dense mouthful of bread, a tooth cracked on a lurking olive stone – and so much worse when the problem is reduced to a feeling.

As always, she asks for a morning slot. Appointments first thing give her less time to work herself into a state. There are none for weeks and, no, Dr Niall isn't back yet. Ellis dithers as the receptionist on the other end of the phone taps aggressively at her keyboard. Fine, Friday at four will have to do.

Gabrielle is not pleased.

'You know we don't like letting people away early on a Friday.'

'It's all they had.'

'Sets a bit of an example.'

'I know,' Ellis says. That's rich, coming from Gabrielle – talking about setting an example when she's been spreading confidential information around the office. There's no point complaining. Gabrielle would say she was just worried about her, and everyone would believe her. Management are on her side.

'Can't you get one outside working hours? Mine opens late on a Thursday.'

'Mine doesn't. Friday was all they had.'

'I'll give you the number for mine, shall I?' She pushes her hair behind her ear, a gold bracelet slides down her arm.

'Thanks, but I don't think I can wait to get set up somewhere else. It's kind of urgent.'

'If you're sure you can't change it?' She waits, eyebrows raised, for Ellis to shake her head. 'I suppose it will be all right.'

Ellis thanks her again. Gabrielle says to leave the door open on her way out.

✱

The house is sticky with the smell of sugar. One of Mum's friends is organising a craft fair and needs a table of goodies to tempt in people who're weary of handmade cards and Fimo jewellery, so she's making fudge. The thick haze of condensed milk turns Ellis's stomach. She ventures cautiously into the heart of the operation.

'Can I tempt you?' Mum asks.

'No, thanks. I'm making a decaf. Want one?'

'If you're frothing milk, that would be just lovely.'

Frothed milk wasn't part of the plan but it isn't so much to ask. She fills the machine with water. All she really wants is to sleep.

Her mum stands by the hobs, humming. Mum will add sugar to her coffee, discounting the several fingers' worth of fudge she'll have eaten already. She never could resist scraping a mixing bowl or testing a crumbly edge, having been cursed with a self-restraint as weak as her enamel. Her sweet tooth has made her a little soft round the middle. She highlights her hair and always wears the same smoky-brown eyeshadow. Her eyebrows have paled away and it suits her. Ellis wants to lay a cheek on the back of her mum's jumper. She turns the knob and steam shoots into the milk jug. The whine goes right through her.

She places a cappuccino by her mum's hand.

'You and Trevor,' she says, 'is it serious?'

'I don't know. Serious enough, I suppose.'

'Like, really serious? Not just a fling or whatever?'

'You sound like your sister.'

'I'm only wondering.'

'He's nice though, isn't he?'

'Yeah.'

'Don't worry, Ellis. I can look after myself.'

This is where Lana would ignore the gentle brush-off and plough right on in. Ellis pauses, considers. 'Do you need a hand?' She nods at the cooling trays.

'You're fine. I've got it down to a fine art. Anyway, I've got news.'

'Is everything okay?'

'It's nice news. Charlie's coming to visit.'

'Charlie?' It's been years since he last flew back and decades since he was the boy he was when he left, but it's the young version Ellis imagines.

'And Kenzie. Just the two of them, thank goodness. It'll be good to have them close by, not shut up in the Balmoral. That was always Jackson's doing, you know.'

Charlie's wife has very particular views on what she wants from a stay in Scotland: afternoon teas, pine-scented saunas and strolls along Princes Street. Sleepovers with extended family were not included.

'When are they getting here?'

'The twentieth. You'll have to give me a hand clearing up. We'll get Lana's room ready.'

'You're not expecting them to share.'

'No, I suppose not. Kenzie's far too old to want to share with her dad now, isn't she? The study too, then. It'll be so good to see them.'

Ellis agrees, thinking of the mornings she's been wandering around in pyjama bottoms and a vest worn to a spectre.

'It's so lovely that you're here too. Oh, don't look at me like that. I only mean that it'll be nice for you to spend some time with them. Are you sure you don't want a bit?'

Ellis waves the fudge off and leaves her mum alone to enjoy the bowl's scrapings. She wants to think about this. She's not seen Charlie in years. She never made it out to visit, and the last time they came here, she and Adrian had been on one of their entirely humdrum but difficult-to-refund Spanish holidays. It was pre-TravelOn, and Adrian couldn't be persuaded to change the dates. Ellis hardly thought twice about accompanying him. She regretted it the moment they disembarked at Barcelona Airport.

She messages Lana, and the reply takes hours. It is simply: *What the fuck now?*

13

It is the day of her dentist appointment, and Ellis is running through worst-case scenarios as Richard briefs the team on the new software they're planning to trial. Ellis's phone comes out the second the meeting is over. Ice furs her lungs. Four missed calls from Lana. Four.

She hurries to the toilets and shuts herself in a cubicle to listen to her voicemails. Okay, okay. Lana's angry, not hysterical. Ellis's panic diffuses into the haze of cheap bleach. It's something to do with their mum. The house. Lana's friend Beth ran into her at the estate agents. Lana ends the message telling her to call the second she can. Ellis takes a few deep breaths, flushes the toilet in case anyone is paying attention, and unlocks the door. The loos are empty. She washes her hands, then heads straight for the kitchen to verify the milk situation (low – a given). She volunteers to fetch some. Alison says she's a doll.

In the street, Ellis calls Lana back.

'Where have you been?'

'I'm at work.'

'This is important,' Lana says.

'What's going on? What exactly did Beth overhear?'

'She didn't overhear anything. She waited until Mum left and straight-up asked him. That eejit has been trying it on with Beth for months, so of course he spills. Mum asked him all sorts of questions about the house, the market and what kind of mort-gages you can get when you're basically retired.'

'She said she was only thinking about it.'

'Looks like she's moved it up a gear, doesn't it? It's Trevor. I guarantee it. Bet he's been working on her this whole time.'

'Why would he? It's not like he's struggling for cash.'

'So? When's that ever stopped anyone?'

'I suppose,' Ellis says, walking through the door of Tesco Metro. The blast from the fridges competes with her sister's voice, and she has to ask her to repeat herself.

'Sunday morning, Mum's got that bake sale or whatever. You watch the twins, and I'll get a chat with this agent myself.'

'Are they open?'

'For bookings. I made one already.'

'Is this even legal?' Ellis grapples with the door and leans in awkwardly to pick up the milk.

'It's just a chat.'

'Maybe I could have another go asking her about it first?'

'Yeah, great. We'll just sit about doing nothing while the house gets sold out from underneath her. What have you found out about Trevor? Sweet fuck all. Did you even try?'

'I did, but she just brushes it off.'

'You let her brush it off. You always do. You've got to put a bit of effort into holding it all together. You think you can skip the dirty work and still get looked after when you need it.'

'I don't.'

'You turn up in the middle of the night, expecting her to put you up. And that's not all. Who's off researching lawyers to see if you can do anything about that flat? Who's trying to get you thinking about the bigger picture?'

'I know you are,' Ellis says.

She understands Lana wanting everything to stay as it is. Mum's house is full of memories, hot and dry like long summer-holiday afternoons. Dust motes drifting by, the rustle of a heavy Sunday paper, a biscuity scent, her dad laughing on his way from one room to another. They are pockets of time Ellis tries not to dip into too often, in case she accidentally alters them. The thought of those moments losing potency or disappearing is overwhelming. But she wouldn't ruin her mum's happiness for them.

'Just watch the kids, that's all I'm asking.'

'If you're sure . . .' She's at the till, the cold milk cartons pressed against her chest. She hands them over and reaches for her card.

'I'll be round at ten.' Lana hangs up. Ellis trudges back to work.

＊

It's the same dentist, still singing along to the radio. Ellis takes off her coat and hopes he won't recognise her. He does, and all the lilting joy of his song evaporates. Dr Conor nods her into the chair.

'All right then, let's see what's going on.'

Ellis opens her mouth meekly. He pokes and scrapes and begins to hum, cutting himself off mid-bar. Her stomach drops; she waits for the bad news. He straightens up.

'You're looking grand. I'd say it's just the nerve hasn't got itself back to normal yet. You use a toothpaste for sensitive teeth? Good. Put some on your finger and rub extra into the tooth and gum every time you brush.'

'So it's okay?' Ellis says, ignoring the toothpaste trick she's heard so many times before.

'Seems to have taken nicely, if I do say so myself. It's not unusual for discomfort to continue for a while, especially in a filling as deep as this one.'

'I really think there might be something going on.'

'Like I said, the bigger ones can be sore for a while. Just come on back again if it's still giving you bother in a couple of weeks.'

The assistant ushers her out mere minutes after her arrival. It may be the shortest appointment she's ever had. A man in the waiting room looks at her with jealousy. Ellis stops to pay, but the receptionist waves her off with a frown. It must be covered by her monthly premium. Ellis puts her wallet away and tries to feel relieved.

It's almost five, and she still has to go back to the office. There is a disaster with a Spanish accommodation database. Ellis suspects it's not as drastic as it sounds and that Gabrielle is proving a point.

She arrives to find most of her colleagues crowded round the kitchen door, clutching cheap plastic champagne flutes filled with even cheaper Prosecco. They're celebrating Fabian's promotion. She sidles up to Naila, who reveals that the database issue has already been resolved.

'Want me to email you the details?' she says. Ellis nods, and they peel away to sit at their separate desks. Naila looks a bit deflated. Ellis feels for her. According to Alison, Naila's been passed over for promotion three times already. Ellis can see why. Naila is hard to take seriously. She gets the work done, but chatters too much while she's doing it. Her smiles and inconsequential comments conceal her industry. Fabian, on the other hand, is free and easy with his boasts.

The email Naila sends has an extra line, asking if she fancies coming to the pub. She types no, deletes it and says yes. Naila replies with a smiley face and two exclamation marks.

Ellis finishes the glass of fizz she lifted from the table and heads to the loo. She's trying to examine the inside of her mouth when Jean walks in. She shuts her mouth quickly. Not quickly enough, judging by the curious look Jean gives her. Ellis washes her hands and resists the temptation to have another look. It's too dark to see anything, and the dentist told her everything was fine.

There are still quite a few people milling around the office, more than Ellis expected. She hovers until folk start collecting jackets and shutting off computers. Maybe she can still slip away. Naila arrives, a bulging tote bag over one shoulder.

'So glad you're coming,' she says.

'Just a quick one,' she says. Naila gives her a jaunty thumbs-up. Alison starts the procession towards the stairs. Several people clap Fabian on the back and promise they'll buy him a pint. Ellis sneaks a look at Naila, who's chatting to Jean about her ergonomic keyboard. What a glutton for punishment.

It's the same pub they always go to. Ellis has only been a couple of times, wary of investing or revealing too much. TravelOn's workers settle into what looks like a habitual formation. Gabrielle is there, talking to Richard, one hand on Fabian's arm. Ellis makes sure to grab a seat next to Naila. Alison stands over them.

'Vodka and lemon for you, Naila. Ellis, what are you drinking?'

'A glass of red, ta. House is fine.'

Alison pushes her way through the crowd. Naila mentions a package she'd hoped would turn up that day and hadn't. Paul from marketing leaps on the chance to rank the various delivery companies. He's deconstructing Yodel's business model when Alison returns. Ellis takes her glass gratefully.

'It's Merlot,' Alison says with a slight pause, waiting to see if it's a problem.

'Lovely,' Ellis says. It isn't, but it'll do.

As Fabian holds forth at the main table, Alison and Jean discuss baking. Ellis contributes little. The birthday cakes that appear with irregular frequency have an air of friendly competitiveness. Ellis refuses to be on the cake roster. She says she isn't capable, but it isn't that.

Naila's cheeks glow. It's Ellis's round. Alison makes sure she knows it's the fancy tonic she wants, not the normal one.

When Ellis returns to the table Fabian is mid-story. He looks up as she puts the glasses down and carries on speaking. Ellis sits and drinks. Shiraz this time, slightly less awful. Alison pours her expensive tonic into her gin and gives it a vigorous stir. Naila sips steadily. Fabian is talking about a friend who works in app design. He thinks TravelOn needs a new app. There's no development cash now, but as soon as . . .

Ellis leans in and pretends to look interested. Better than having to take initiative. Easier to smile and nod and allow time to pass; who cares if it lets him think he's interesting. She'll get away as soon as she can. Naila seems to be paying attention. Alison rattles her ice cubes. They wait and wait until Fabian goes for a piss.

'I've been saying we need a new app for years.' Alison drains her glass.

'You're very good with your phone,' Naila says.

'It's not difficult.' She pulls back the purple cover of her phablet, taking the opportunity to check it.

'I hate getting a new one,' Naila says. 'Takes me ages to wrap my head round it, then the second I finally get it all worked out, they start calling me about upgrades and it starts over.'

'You don't have to take them,' Ellis says.

'I know,' Naila replies. Ellis imagines a drawer in her flat, filled with unwanted phones, supplanted by their unwanted replacements.

'I love an upgrade,' Alison says. Her screen is littered with notifications.

A flurry of goodbyes starts at the next table. All the people who earn the most, Gabrielle among them. Her hair curls around a silk scarf. It looks so pullable. Ellis thinks this might be a chance for her to get away, but Jean beats her to it.

Naila goes to the bar and comes back with menus as well as a fresh round. Chips are ordered.

'How's your sister getting on?' Alison says.

Fucking Gabrielle.

'She's doing okay.'

'She's got kids, right? How are they taking it?'

'They're very young.'

'Poor things,' Naila says, her eyes already damp. Ellis wants that sympathy and hates it too. She's glad when Alison moves on to her own nephew, who's mid-divorce.

'He's always done his best by her. Bought her that stupid house, supported her while she went back to college. He just wants kids, you know? And she kept saying yeah, yeah and then, bang, it's over. No kids, no marriage, nothing. And she's in the wrong, obviously, but she's making it sound like it's him.'

'That's awful,' Naila says.

'I know. So she's started emailing him, and he couldn't work out why until his lawyer told him that it'll be because *her* lawyer told her to. Apparently it's how to stop the he-says/she-says thing.'

Ellis's shoulder blades winch tight. Adrian's email. So impersonal, so cold. Not an attempt to communicate, but proof he's being *reasonable*. He's getting it on the record.

Ellis feels sick. She orders more drinks.

The TravelOn group begins to fragment. Some are moving on somewhere louder. The younger girls are going to the sweets café for dessert and maybe a club afterwards. Naila asks if they fancy it; Alison says it's too rich for her blood. Shouldn't they just finish off what they've got? Ellis nods. She's had more than enough.

✳

Ellis is sour-mouthed and heavy with last night's wine. She's not drunk so much or so often in years. She cringes at the thought of the night before, not that she remembers saying anything she shouldn't have.

Mum is clattering around looking for the sewing machine she's going to loan a pal in exchange for a blow-up mattress. Charlie and Kenzie arrive in less than two weeks. Mum keeps talking about tidying without getting started. Ellis sends Lana a bitchy message about it.

I bet. He's lucky not to have to spring for a hotel. Working hol – apparently.

You speak to him?

FB messenger.

Cool.

Says Jack's too busy. Too up her arse, more like.

Ellis sends a smiley. She logs into her bank account and imagines a hotel room of her own. Nowhere like the Balmoral. Any shithole would do. Everything homogeneous and built-in. Somewhere completely neutral.

Her phones pings again. She looks down, bracing herself for a new titbit about Charlie but it's a 'hope you're getting on ok' message from Adrian's friend Anna. Ellis types a vicious reply and sits, thumb hovering over the send icon. Anna has the cropped haircut of a professional kickboxer. She makes her own protein bars, so sticky and dense they can survive a ten-mile journey in a bumpy bike pannier on a boiling summer's day. Anna has quiet, very firm opinions. Ellis has always tried to find the good in her. Now, she wants to tell her she's a patronising cow who should be making sure Adrian knows what a disappointment he is, not sending Ellis platitudes.

She closes the app. Opens it. Closes it again. She won't send it. She won't send a nicer message either. Anna might purse her lips and tell Adrian he should've handled things differently but in no time she'll be handing out her refrigerated, reusable water bottles before every walk or ride. She'll be filling one for Sally too. They'll exchange recipes for no-bake date bars. Sally will try and tempt the group with her cinnamon swirls. She'll fit right in.

There's no point replying to Anna. Adrian's the one she should be speaking to. Ellis chafes with the need to talk to him and curses herself for all the times she avoided it. Taking the long route home just for an extra twenty minutes of peace. Now, she's forgiven him all those conversational tics. Who cares if he trails off mid-sentence or if he doesn't clear his throat, so that his words take on a wet growl? She'd put up with anything to get back to normal. Almost anything.

No emails. No getting it written down for the record. A conversation. Since the first few days, when she'd been consumed with the desire to scream at him and he firmly refused to pick up the phone, Ellis has resisted. Now the blanket of her hangover obscures her reasoning.

Are you free today?

She drops the phone as soon as she hits send; it thuds harmlessly onto the duvet. He doesn't reply right away. Of course he doesn't, he's showing Sally the message. They're laughing. Her phone peeps.

Did you get my email?

Yes.

Just checking. You didn't reply.

I've been thinking about it. Can we chat, in person?

I don't think it's a good idea.

Just a coffee. Meet me at the Nero by the station this afternoon? Half one?

I don't know.

There are still some things we need to sort. Practical things.

OK.

★

He's already there when she arrives. He's had his hair trimmed. His jacket is still shiny at the collar though. Ellis knows how he will smell: mint shampoo and an aftershave thick with sandalwood. She wants to check her reflection again. Face powder might be caught on the recently developed lines under her eyes. He turns as if he can feel her presence and waves. There's nothing she can do about it now.

His smile is careful. It hovers on and off as she says hello and sits. He insists on fetching her a drink. Ellis peels away a broken chunk of nail as she waits. Be calm. Be calm.

'I got you a large latte. You look tired.'

'Thanks. I am.' She wants to take it back as soon as it's said; she didn't mean to sound so bitter.

He blows out a sad puff of air. 'I thought you wanted to talk.'

'I do.'

'All right then. You asked me to come, so I came. At least be mature about it.'

He's chilly now, the welcoming smile completely snuffed out. Ellis swallows, throat muscles protesting.

'Your email – you made it sound like I never put anything into the flat,' she says.

'You didn't, not really.'

'That's not true. I bought loads of things. I paid for all the sheets, the cushions, the curtains. Everything that needed replacing year after year.'

'You're welcome to have them all back. I'd like you to take them, actually.'

'That's not the point.'

'So what is the point? I've never said you didn't contribute, but it's not the same. You paid less than it would've cost to rent somewhere else that close to town.'

'I wasn't renting.'

'But you would've been.'

'You don't know that.'

He takes a prim mouthful of his coffee and looks towards the window.

'I can't believe you're doing this,' she says.

'I don't know what you want from me.'

To Ellis's fury, tears line her lids. She has, of course, been hoping for an apology. To hear he's made a mistake. That he regrets everything.

'I want you to be fair,' she manages.

'Stop crying.'

'You're cutting me off with nothing.'

'We agreed it all made sense.'

'I didn't think you'd fuck someone else though.'

His mouth tucks in on itself, and his eyebrows lower a fraction. Ellis knows this look.

'I fell in love. These things happen. And I told you the second I realised it was serious.'

'You . . .' The words are stuck.

'I'm sorry. But you're not blameless here. You shut me out and you know it. You were never really open with me. You keep everything to yourself and get annoyed that I can't read your mind.'

'That's not true. You're the liar. You're the one hiding things,' Ellis spits. Adrian is already pulling on his coat. 'You're walking out on me?'

'I thought you wanted to be reasonable.'

He leaves her in the café and the barely stitched wound bursts open. She cries at her table for a minute, wiping snot on her sleeve, feeling the people around her studiously looking away.

Ellis is shamed. She shouldn't have shown him how much she's hurting. She wanted to make him understand and she should know, after all these years as Lana's sister, that you can't make someone hear when they don't want to listen.

14

The last time Lana left Ellis alone with the twins, they were barely crawling. She must be gagging to speak to the estate agent. Mum is at her fair already. Ellis eats a handful of cereal as she waits. The headache is there again. She's sure it's coming from the left side. From the tooth. From her jaw. Or maybe it's just a two-day hangover and she's paranoid, primed by a lifetime of dental disasters and family failings.

Lana arrives with a flurry of instructions, kisses her children, flicks away the suggestion that they should wait and talk to their mum again rather than try to entrap some guy who fancies her friend. The door rattles shut behind her.

The novelty of being with Auntie Ellis soon wears off. She opens up her dad's former study to unleash the toys stored there. They bounce balls, make dolls walk along the edge of the desk and hit toy drums. She distracts them with a banana she finds in their stylish nappy sack. Mia smears a gloopy handful in her brother's face. They're both screaming and fractious and covered in gunk.

Ellis wrangles them through to the kitchen and, in a flash of inspiration, opens the back door. They bolt out, excitement overriding rage.

Mum's garden is a far cry from Lana's regimented lawn, and the twins love it. They dig their tiny fingers into the dirt, plucking out stones and bugs and weird, dried-out bits of plant. Every treasure heads straight for their mouths. Oscar has a smug expression. Ellis braces herself, leans down and sticks a finger between his lips to hook out whatever he's put in there. The sharp edges of his newly erupted teeth turn her stomach.

He cries for the loss of his pebble. Ellis throws it in a flower bed that was once a mud pit. She and Lana used to play in it when they weren't much older than the twins are now. They'd been just big enough to carry plastic cups from the outdoor tap under the kitchen window. Their dad had thought it was hilarious and documented the incident in a series of embarrassing photos. His bonhomie wore off during the long bathtime that followed, when Lana screamed at the indignity of having mud sluiced from her nose.

When Dad died, the garden transitioned from ambitious project to object of neglect. In the first few empty years, its hidey-holes and sunspots grew clogged with crisp packets and beer cans and the occasional pair of boxer shorts thrown over the wall. If it hadn't been for gentle pressure from the neighbours, the lawn might've disappeared entirely. Now it's merely unkempt.

The Allens on the right tend to the hedge that separates their garden from Mum's. The old wall on the left backs on to the lane and has been there as long as the house itself. The 'new' wall at the bottom was put in years later, when the young family across the back had a baby. They couldn't bear the thought of it crawling out of their sight and into the green tangle of Mum's garden. Or worse, the prospect of him pulling the old, crumbling wall down on top of him. They petitioned for something better ten years ago, and Mum contributed the bulk of the cost. She told Ellis not to mention it to her sister, but Lana found out somehow and then there was an awful row. She didn't want anyone getting one over on her mum and couldn't believe she was happy to pay. Hardly twelve months later, the young couple moved out. Lana still brings up the new wall every now and then. She can't leave anything alone.

Ellis will miss the garden, if Mum really is planning to move. The twins will miss it too. They're scooping up handfuls of dirt and dropping them on each other. The soil mixes with the banana slime under their nails and snail-tracked across their cheeks. Little grotbags. Lana will be horrified.

Ellis ducks through to the kitchen to fetch a cloth. It isn't by the sink or on the table or by the fridge. She grabs the tea towel and runs it underneath the tap. It'll do. Her phone beeps. She scrabbles for it with a damp hand, hoping for the apology Adrian didn't give her. It's Zoe, asking how she's getting on. Ellis rams it back in her pocket and looks out the window over the sink. She can't see the twins. She leans forward, scanning from one end of the garden to another. They aren't there. Ellis runs without switching off the water. There's nowhere for them to go – except the side gate. But it's closed. It's always closed. And she checked it. She checked it, didn't she?

She rounds the left corner. The gate is open. Her heart wallops. The path only leads to the front garden. The front gate will be latched, it has to be latched. Please. Latched like always. *Please.* The four or five steps down the narrow pathway at the side of the house take too long. She bursts into light. Mia and Oscar are gleefully tearing petals from the Allens' dahlias.

Ellis dives to pull them from their massacre, and they respond with indignant screams. Ellis looks around, mortified. A cab driver is parked over the road, frowning at his phone. A woman eating a bag of Maltesers glances their way as she walks by, eyebrows raised. Her judgement is clear and deserved. The twins are feral, smeared with dirt and furious tears.

The damp towel is still in her hand. She reaches down to scoop up her nephew. He bucks and squirms and says no, no, don't want to. She can't even see his face. He's got so strong. The wall is just there. She props him on it and starts to straighten her knees. Mia lunges for a particularly fat bloom. Ellis flings out a leg as a buffer between child and innocent flower. Mia thumps into her shin and staggers, laughing. Back to Oscar, but as she turns, her foot slides. She's crashing down, her hand scraping wildly against the wall as it loses contact with Oscar.

He lands in a sprawl next to her. All sound stops. No breath, no birdsong, no rush of wheels. Only the deafening grip of panic. A mighty wail erupts, freeing Ellis from paralysis. Mia opens her mouth to join him, sobs spurting from her throat. Ellis places her hand on Oscar's vibrating stomach. You aren't meant to move people. What if he's hurt his back? She might make it worse. But she can't leave him.

'He all right? Took a bit of a tumble there, eh?'

She looks up. The cab driver is hovering over them. She has no words. There is a red patch and a slight swelling at Oscar's hairline. His arms and legs beat the gravel. He's mobile, that's something. Ellis stands, grabs Mia and thrusts her into the driver's arms. She slides her hands under Oscar's small torso, pauses to see if his cries change, then carefully picks him up.

'Little France, please,' she says. 'The Royal Infirmary.'

Mia huddles close as Oscar cries in her lap. Ellis whispers to them both throughout the short trip, barely aware of what she's saying. The driver takes her tenners and leaves them at the drop-off. Ellis hurries in. She should've called her sister already. What's wrong with her?

Oscar's distress means they're rushed into a small room to be triaged. A young man checks Oscar's pupils, says something vaguely reassuring and promises an X-ray to be on the safe side. He leaves. Ellis finally calls Lana, not sure if she's meant to use her phone in here but scared of leaving it any longer.

There are a series of 'fuck's and 'what's. Ellis hears the clunk of a car door and the echo of being switched to speaker phone. Lana's questions come faster than Ellis can answer. Oscar's still wailing. A doctor walks in. Unable to divide her concentration any further, Ellis hangs up.

'What have we here?'

'He fell off a wall.'

'High?'

'About this.' She holds her hand out at hip height.

'What were you doing up there, eh, wee man? Got a future mountain climber, have we? Did he lose consciousness at all?'

'I don't think so. Unless it was only for a few seconds. Oh God. Maybe he did? It took a little bit for him to start crying.'

'Sounds more like he got the wind knocked out of him. Still, quite a cracker we've got here.' The doctor's hands move from clipboard to tiny torch and back to clipboard again.

Ellis is going to be sick.

'Righto, we'll get you that X-ray as soon as possible and then reassess.'

He leaves, and Ellis is alone in a tiny room with two distressed children and a feeling of doom. Her world expands and contracts as she lives through the moment she saw him fall over again.

Lana shoots through the door on a backdraft of fear and anger.

'Honey, are you all right? Let me see. Let Mummy see.' She draws Oscar close and examines every inch. He starts to cry again in earnest. She glares at Ellis over his sweat-dampened hair. Mia tries to get closer to her mum; Ellis holds her tighter.

'What the hell?' Lana says, each word a thrown stone.

'It was an accident.'

'Of course it was a fucking accident. What happened?'

'I was just trying to give him a wipe. He was on the wall at the front, and I was holding him and I slipped and he fell.'

'From the wall? From your arms?'

'The wall.'

'You should've been holding on. You've got to have a hand on them all the time.'

Mia begins to cry again. Not softening her expression one iota, Lana points at the mattress. Ellis puts her niece down and steps back from the bed. She could float right away. Dissipate in the clouds. She pushes her hair behind her ear. Her hand shakes.

They are finally called for an X-ray. Lana doesn't speak to Ellis except to ask her to watch Mia, who is desolate at being left behind. When Oscar and Lana return Ellis escapes to the vending machine, leans her head against the cold glass. She holds out cartons of low-sugar Ribena on her return. The twins suck greedily.

The first doctor returns, not at all surprised to see two women where there had been one. He says everything seems to be intact. No fracture (thanks to those sturdy Patrick bones) and no signs of concussion, so they're free to go.

'You're certain?' Lana says.

'As we can be. He seems perky enough so we're happy to send you home. Just keep a close eye on the wee bruiser for the next twenty-four hours. Any vomiting, unusual drowsiness or distress, pop right back in.'

Lana thanks him and strides into the waiting area, a twin on each hip. Ellis offers to phone a taxi. Don't be stupid, Lana snaps. Ellis follows her to the car park where Lana wrangles both children into their seats, angling her shoulders to make it clear she wants no help. Ellis looks round the car park, trying not to catch the eye of any other visitors or patients. She doesn't get in the car until Lana slams the driver's door.

Lana says nothing to Ellis for the whole drive. They pull up, and Lana immediately gets out and starts unbuckling the twins. Ellis moves to take one.

'We're fine.'

'Are you sure?'

'Yes.' Lana kicks the car door shut and stands, waiting for Ellis to turn away.

'I could–'

'No.'

'I'm sorry.'

'See you later.' Lana leaves her standing at the end of the driveway.

Ellis walks home. It takes over an hour. A line of blisters rises over her left heel. She's exhausted. But Oscar is fine. She only let him go for a second. Barely even a second. He's fine.

The house is empty. She switches off the kitchen tap then runs herself a bath. Her scraped hand and weeping heel sting. She cries a little.

He's fine.

She's in the living room when her mum gets home.

'What are you doing, sitting in the dark?' She snaps on the big light.

'You okay, Mum?'

'Nothing a good night's sleep won't fix. Something Oscar's not planning on any time soon – he's full of beans.'

'He is?'

'Just left, and he was singing at the top of his lungs. They're so resilient, children. Practically bounce. I'm having a sherry. Want one?'

Ellis doesn't. She says yes and trails her mum to the kitchen anyway.

'Poor Trevor. We were having lunch when she rang. I got in such a flap. I had my coat on and was about to abandon Trev without even saying where I was going. He just stood up, ever so calm, and told me to start at the start. Then he asked the waitress to box up my pasta so I could take it with me. Best primavera Lana's ever tasted, apparently. Probably just the shock talking although it is very nice. Kept her company until Grant got home.'

Lana wanted someone there. Just not her sister.

'Is she mad at me?'

'It'll blow over.'

'It was a mistake. I barely even looked away.'

'These things happen.'

'I didn't mean it.'

'Just give her some time.'

Ellis drinks the sweet sherry despite the headache cramponing its way across her temples. Mum chatters about the restaurant and Trevor and family mishaps and scrapes and scraps.

The longer she listens, the tighter Ellis's jaw clenches. Her sister hates her and her mum doesn't even care. She makes her excuses and leaves Mum in the bright kitchen with her sherry and her distorted, happy memories.

15

Milk teeth are designed to be shed. They have small, delicate roots, which will be reabsorbed into the body when the secondary set bears down. Once everything useful has been leached from the baby tooth, the cusp is discarded. A bloodied lump of pulp encased in enamel spat into a palm or pinched between two fingers.

Ellis's niece and nephew have all their teeth inside them, waiting to erupt, waiting to later fall. The blueprint is in their cells. There is no escaping the fate passed on through their mother's side of the family.

Lana never said a word about the birth itself. Grant wasn't allowed to get in touch with anyone until it was over. Labour took almost two days and ended in the C-section Lana didn't want. Forty hours of refusal until dropping heart rates forced her hand.

Her mum was notified as soon as everyone was given a clean bill of health. By the time Ellis was welcome to visit, Lana was propped up, her lips glistening with a pinkish sheen too flawless to be anything but fake. She was proud, so proud.

Ellis offered every compliment she could think of until Lana grew bored and began bitching about the other women in the ward. They were alternatively too chavvy, too stupid, too old and too selfish to be trusted.

'But look at these gorgeous things,' Ellis said.

'Pick her up then. Come on, she won't bite for fuck's sake.'

Ellis flushed and fumbled and held a tiny human who'd so recently been yanked out of another body and fretted about hurting it. The possibilities for disaster are endless.

Ellis hasn't ever wanted children enough to live with that level of guilt and peril. She doesn't hate them, like some of her ostensibly 'childfree' friends. She doesn't love her own life so much that it's an adequate excuse. She isn't jetting off on adventures all the time. She makes no contributions to art or science. She and Adrian had just had their own small lives. Still, she'd never seriously thought about asking him to ditch the rubbers. She'd been fine with just the two of them. Now they've split up, people are falling over themselves to tell her the lack of kids is 'for the best'. They mean well, but it's a horrible thing to say. It's not 'for the best' that she's spent all those fertile years working towards a future with someone who's left her.

Lana thinks everyone should have children. Everyone except Ellis.

There's another memory. The twins are three months old, not able to sit up yet and already too heavy for Lana to carry both for more than a short distance. They were sitting in a park on a Sunday morning, Grant and Adrian were off buying ice cream, and Mum had found a friend to talk to by the duck pond. The sisters grappled with babies who were too hot and didn't want to wear their sun hats or lie down or go to sleep or do anything at all. Ellis felt bad for them. How horrible to be too young to know what was wrong or how to fix it.

'Bet you can't wait until they're running around.'

'Until I'm running around after them, you mean.'

'They'll keep you fit,' Ellis said, like you're supposed to.

'I'm already fit.'

'Fitter than me.'

'I have to be now, don't I? Got other people to think about. What would happen to these two if I die? If Grant does? Who'll look after them?'

'They'll always have us. Me and Mum. She'd do anything for them.'

'Sure,' Lana said, with weary but obvious contempt. Ellis clamped her lips together and tickled her niece's sweaty belly. Mia started to cry. Lana sighed and held out her arms. The men came back with cones, and the faff of handing them out gave Ellis the chance to compose herself.

Not many months later, her mum made a comment about Lana's friend Patricia taking her role as godparent awfully seriously. Ellis asked, voice carefully casual, what she was talking about. Mum confirmed. Patricia, a woman with big hands and a blonde bob so sharp it could slash collarbones, had been chosen as parent in proxy, if the worst happened.

It hurt so much. And Lana is right: Ellis isn't the person to look after the twins. Isn't to be trusted. Doesn't want to be, any more.

It's her day on complaints. She manages three before rushing to the kitchen. She rams the plastic filter into the coffee machine. The whole thing rocks on its rubber feet, slopping water and grounds over the counter. Alison floats in to fill her mug with hot water. The peppermint tea bag rises triumphantly.

'Tell you what,' she says. 'Why don't I take over complaints for you today?'

'What? No, I'm fine.'

'You're always covering for us.'

'I don't mind.'

'I know, but we all need a little break now and then. We were chatting, me and Naila, and it looks like you're on your sixth day in two weeks.'

Alison is being kind. Ellis should appreciate it. She's meant to be appreciating the hidden depths to Alison, Jean, Naila and probably bloody Gabrielle too. But it's easier to be annoyed.

'I wouldn't want to put you out.'

'Don't worry. There's only so much time any of us can spend dealing with moaners, and you've had more than your share.'

Chastised, Ellis thanks her properly and goes to sign out of

94

the complaints inbox. She'd have preferred to deal with them herself but can't deny it feels good to let them go.

A spreadsheet of holiday destinations is open before her, each a reminder of all the opportunities she's wriggled out of. It is exhausting.

✱

Ellis changes out of her shirt and trousers and into the clothes lying crumpled at the end of the bed. She has the house to herself. She lies down in the quiet to look at Sally's Twitter feed. When the doorbell rings, Ellis hesitates, wondering if she can ignore it.

Trevor waits patiently on the doorstep, hands in his pockets. Ellis steps back from the peephole and opens up. He smiles. Two of his bottom teeth overlap slightly. It makes him look trustworthy when it really shouldn't.

'Mum's not in.'

'I'm probably early,' he says without checking the time.

'Or she's late.'

'Either way.' He cheerily lifts a shoulder. Ellis lets him in and asks if she can get him anything, hoping he'll say yes and offer her an opportunity to escape to the kitchen.

'Thanks, but I'll save myself for dinner. We're going for ribs. Would you like to join us? I'm sure we could add another chair to the booking.'

'Mum doesn't eat ribs.' None of them eat ribs, not since Mum pulled away from a Friday night takeaway with a sliver of her front tooth stuck in the Peking-sauced meat.

'That's what she said. But we went last week, and she loved it so much we're going again.'

'Oh.' Ellis picks at a stain just above her knee.

'You've probably got your own plans.'

She squints, wondering if he's being sarcastic. She does not look like someone with plans. He grins back, seemingly genuine. He could be her boyfriend and no one would look twice.

'We'd be happy to have you. I know Marion would love it.'

Mum arrives as if summoned by the sound of her name, saving Ellis from answering.

'You're not here already? Sorry, sorry.' The contents of her bags clink and discharge the room's static. 'I got tied up at the shops. There's a charity raffle in the foyer of the big Tesco, and you'll never guess but I went and won. Take a look at this.' She pulls out a bottle of Limoncello.

'Aren't you the lucky one?' Trevor says.

'Looks like I am. How are we for time? Shall we have an aperitif?'

Trevor agrees, and Ellis says she'll leave them to it. Mum reminds her there's leftover lasagne in the fridge. Ellis thanks her and tries not to picture her mother in the restaurant, teeth sunk in sticky flesh. She looks closer. The mum she's been remembering hasn't been there for a long time.

The temptation to text Lana flares and passes. It would be ignored, like all her other texts. From the hallway, Trevor sounds carefree, and Ellis can reconfigure him into someone more suitable. Closer to her mum's age. Wrinkles embracing warm eyes, hair sprouting wildly from greying eyebrows, shoulders gently rounded from a long and blameless career hunched over a desk rather than prone patients. If that had been who her mum had brought home, Ellis would've welcomed him. The reality is harder to swallow.

*

Ellis slides into her mum's room, headache following a few steps behind. It's been a long time since she last opened the second drawer of the dressing table. She finds the wooden box immediately. It fits easily into the palm of her hand. She's compelled to give it a shake, even though the noise it makes is a swipe of sandpaper along her spine.

She pops off the rubber seal on the inside of the lid and the smear of old cotton wool comes with it. Here are five baby teeth. Four off-white but intact, one molar with a brown gouge in its side. She uses the tip of her fingernail to turn over one of her front teeth, remembering the awful moment in the dentist's office when he planted his feet, pulled her mouth open, forced his probe under them and flicked, sending her teeth flying. Dad let go of her hand and got down on his knees to look for them as the dentist laughed and examined her bleeding gums. He made a joke about the tooth fairy paying extra for such feisty specimens.

There is another wooden box in the drawer. Lana's. It has only a couple of teeth. Dad was the fairy who filled these boxes. Their mum managed one tooth, the rotten molar, before sitting the pair of them down and revealing the truth: there was no castle with canine towers and premolar staircases and she couldn't do it any more.

Ellis later discovered that the tooth fairy is a relatively recent invention. The benign vision of her youth – conjured by the flower fairy illustrations of Cicely Mary Barker and the Disney version of Tinkerbell – was a replacement for Europe's traditional tooth-smuggler: a rat. It was better to believe in a beautiful winged fairy than a rodent who slipped under your pillow.

Back then, Mum didn't have it in her to be either. But she kept the boxes.

Ellis showed them to Lana when they weren't quite teenagers. Lana opened hers, flicked the tooth and said 'gross'. She narrowed her eyes at how many more teeth were in Ellis's box and flounced out. She's probably never been back.

The teeth are tiny. It's bizarre to think how much smaller her mouth once was. Stranger still to think how firmly rooted these loose things had been. How strange to keep them. Morbid, no matter how cute the picture on the lid (Ellis's had a fluffy chick, Lana's a bunny). Had Grandma hung on to Dad's teeth? Did they sit in a drawer, ready to be thrown out along with all her other junk when she died? Ellis was too young to help when that house was cleared.

Enough. She puts them away, thinking of Trevor in here, choosing a drawer for his socks or somewhere safe for that solid black Fitbit. What would he think of these mementos? None of his patients will scrabble on the floor for two bullet-like teeth, set on taking them home. Extractions go in the medical waste bin. And then? Burned? Great vats of teeth, popping like corn.

Despite herself, hunger nudges Ellis to the kitchen. She throws a sandwich together and picks up an opened bottle of wine from the ranks by the microwave. There's always a spare bottle of wine, given to Mum by her book group or a craft fair organiser or folk she'd made friends with because they were the parents of Lana or Ellis's pals and who neither of the girls had any interest in ever hearing of again.

Ellis pulls the cork, pours a glass. How has she found herself here, alone? Adrian says it's her own fault, that she didn't share how she really felt. But what if there was nothing in there to share? There is no lack at the centre of her sister, no lack of speaking her mind. Lana is complete. Grant and the twins are annexes, not structural changes. Ellis is different. Her insides have been eaten away. She is close to collapse.

16

It has been days, and her sister still isn't talking to her. She's round to drop off the twins and Ellis has been instructed to stay out of the way. Mum passed the message on with the smallest of shrugs, as if this was just another of Lana's foibles.

Ellis stands at her bedroom window and watches their slow progress up the path. Oscar has a discernible shadow at his hairline. Aside from that, he looks the same as always. Lana's still scowling. Ellis steps back into the shade and stays there until she hears her sister leave again.

Mum is mangling an unfamiliar nursery rhyme. Ellis's tread is soft on the stairs. She wants to hear Oscar or Mia asking for her, doesn't want to give them an opportunity to tell Lana she played with them. Not when she's banned from helping. She'd better get out the house.

The new café on The Shore is huge; even so, nearly every table is taken. There are hanging plants on the walls, leaflets on the tables, stone floors and wooden benches. They roast their own beans and are grinding them now. Walking past, when the place was closed, Ellis had thought the industrial-sized machine was for show. It's loud enough to shake the floor.

A woman with a high pram is blocking the way. She gives Ellis a look, wanting her to hurry up and order. Ellis pictures the woman's fingertips, hand, arm, entire self swallowed by the grinder. The girl behind the till has a sparkling lip piercing and cropped ginger curls. She looks like a very stylish thirteen-year-old boy. Ellis asks for a black coffee. No, wait, white. Coffee stains; milk counteracts the acidity.

Ellis knows how to look after her teeth. She knows and still doesn't always do what she should. She'll relax and have a can of Pepsi, suck the flavouring from salt and vinegar crisps or eat a punnet of raspberries after lunch. She'll even fall into bed, tamping down the knowledge she ought to brush before dozing off. Then something goes wrong, and Ellis bargains, makes promises, forces herself along to get the problem fixed. Once the immediate crisis has been averted, her willpower weakens again. The least she can do is take milk in her coffee.

She snags a seat in the corner, corralled by a group of women at a bigger table. They complain about their neighbours. The skinny one found a passive aggressive note on her barbecue. The one with the ostentatious bangles stood in a trail of bin juice when she walked down to get the post, barefoot. Ellis wants to pick up the jug of water being passed between them and smash it on the concrete floor. Their voices rise higher and higher, determined not to be drowned out by the birl of the beans.

Ellis has always known her sister doesn't accept her. She knew it from the moment the waffled blue blanket was pulled back, revealing angry unfocused eyes. She tentatively reached in a finger to stroke her sister's cheek. Lana began to cry. No one asked Ellis whether she wanted a new sister. Lana appeared in her life as an immovable object.

Ellis has her phone out and can't think who to call. No one grows out of things to cry about, only out of people to share them with. Becca will be solicitous and secretly appalled: what if Ellis let Scotty bang his head? Ellis still hasn't properly talked to Zoe or Charmaine. They're probably pissed-off at her for not being gracious enough about their offers of company.

What if Lana never forgives her? What if the best she has to hope for is a temporary alliance over whatever's going on with their mum and the house? And if the house goes and Mum eventually dies, what if there's nothing? Families scatter, some-times. Lana could force a scattering. She could keep Ellis away from the twins. No birthday parties, graduations, weddings.

Ellis could scream, cry, be the bigger person. She could try to force Lana to forgive her, she could wait and tell the twins her side of the story one day, but Lana would still hold all the important cards. Not because she's right, but because of who she is.

Ellis itches to text Adrian. It has been his job to listen to her fuck-ups for so long. Her unhappiness needs an outlet.

She flicks to Sally's Facebook. It's been updated with a new picture of her stupid, smiling face. Too much blusher and a pink rucksack over one shoulder. The caption says, '*couldn't be happier #blessed #weekend*'. Sally's teeth are perfect. She probably deep-throats like a champ.

A prickle of anger travels from shoulders to jaw. Ellis clenches, and the headache fires. How many days is it now? The ache in her face never seems to entirely go away, and she's still drinking and she's still crying and she's still beyond miserable, but surely that can't be the cause? The young dentist is convinced she's fine. He's the one who did the filling in the first place. He wants it to be fine.

Ellis isn't fine. She let her nephew fall. She could've killed him. She's distracted, she's in pain. This tooth has been bothering her ever since the first appointment, when she'd submitted to Dr Conor's attempt to fix it even when his attitude grated. It's not been fixed. She's not herself. Pain is more than a distraction. It changes people, blurs their boundaries.

The coffee slops and spills as she fights her way out from the corner table. She needs fresh air. Sweat springs up around her hairline. The women glare. She has to get out.

17

Ellis is plagued by her teeth. They smile, they snarl, they quietly fall apart. They ache, grow in wrong, require endless tending. They ruin happy moments and exacerbate every emotional trauma. They are her heritage and her curse.

Her teenage years were blighted by a series of braces. To no one's surprise, her bite was deemed unruly at thirteen, when the dentist tutted and said it was back to the orthodontist with her. Ellis's insides contracted. It'd be the first time since her two front baby teeth were extracted and the adult ones were brought into line with a plate. She was still wearing that plastic and metal torture device when her dad died. She did not want another.

The orthodontist was tall and thin with disdain gusting off him. Like he didn't know that no amount of brushing or flossing can change the way teeth decide to crowd through gums. He snapped off his surgical gloves to give his prognosis: several teeth to come out and she'd need at least two years of train tracks.

No one else in her class had braces. Only the older kids did. Older, unpopular kids. Her mum told Lana what had happened while Ellis lay face down on her bed, beneath a duvet smelling of crisps and sweat. Her sister came to gloat while pretending to sympathise. Ellis wanted what she always wanted: to be left alone and also to be loved beyond a doubt.

*

She was still rigid with resentment and worry when it was time to have impressions made. The plastic mould was filled with a claggy pink mixture. The orthodontist forced the concoction past her lips, pressing from side to side. It was miles too big. He ordered her to press her teeth together. She gagged. Gagged again. He told her to bite harder, it'll help. It didn't. Bite, or we'll just have to do it all again. She strained, and the thick, minty sludge oozed over the edges and she thought she was going to die.

The orthodontist didn't bother to hide his irritation; it was a set of cold fingers around her neck. She could barely breathe. She retched again, heart kicking with fear. He said, wait, wait, as he scribbled on a bit of paper, not even looking at her rolling eyes and stretched neck.

It was finally time to release her. The heel of his hand pushed against her nose, cutting off air. She kicked involuntarily. He started to pull. Her head moved towards him, and he nodded for the assistant to press on her forehead. He was going to pull them out. The tray would come out and so would all her teeth. He told her to relax. She was seconds from screaming when, with a great sucking squelch, the mould came free.

The day her teeth were to be removed was even worse. They took them both at once, despite them being on opposite sides. The orthodontist was already fed up with her and deemed it easier to put her through one large hell rather than two lesser ones. The weeks running up to the day were filled with nightmares, and the event itself muddles in her memory. What reverberates is the sound her adult teeth make when they're wrenched from the bone. They didn't want to go and they made sure everyone knew of their displeasure. Two assistants had to hold her down.

Three weeks later, gums healed but still tender, her mouth was assaulted by the glue and wire. The tip of her tongue grew raw from the amount of time it spent tracing new tracks. She spent hours at the mirror, practising expressions that kept her lips sealed.

They couldn't stay that way all the time but when they opened, it was to reveal a lisp. A small and soggy alteration to her words, discreet enough for adults to wilfully ignore and obvious enough for teenagers to seize on.

She was Ellish for the best part of four years. The name continued even after the braces were gone. Lana was overjoyed; it was such easy ammunition to add to an argument. Ellis's lisp drove the spike of self-consciousness deeper. She barely spoke for the middle years of high school and watched quietly as her friends got excited about boy bands and football and boys with popped collars. A subdued anger began to grow. She couldn't let it out where it would be made ridiculous by the swoosh of her sibilants but it escaped in sighs and small sneers during rhapsodies over the latest chart topper or school football match. The other girls noticed and drew their own boundaries.

Invitations stopped. When she tried to enter a conversation, they talked over her. Sometimes, their gazes glanced right off her face. She couldn't bring herself to move to a different registration table; she sat on the corner and listened as they chatted amongst themselves. At break time, she walked from one end of the playground to the other, pretending she had somewhere to go.

The braces had to be tightened, and the orthodontist made her feel tiny every time. The elastic bands collected small fragments of food. Her face ached in a deep, bone-shifting way. She hated everyone. Her mum didn't come to every appointment with her; she'd had to take on a second job to pay for all the things she'd put on credit when the girls were younger. The house was colder when their mum wasn't in it. Ellis and Lana were left to jibe together for whole evenings and weekends at a time.

Ellis, teeth groaning their way into order, was tasked with choosing her Highers. She'd done well in her exams (books offered some barrier between her and everything else), and her mum didn't mind what she studied, so Ellis chose all the subjects her friends wouldn't.

Both she and Lana got Saturday jobs that summer. Her sister found a hairdresser willing to take on someone not quite fifteen for a pittance, while Ellis signed herself over to a sports and camping shop run by a spry yet grumpy couple who could never remember what they'd trained her to do and what they hadn't bothered to. It wasn't the sort of place other teenagers visited, and that was a blessing.

Ellis bought a canvas satchel and a pair of hiking boots, picked from the same shelves she spent the weekend tidying. She discovered grunge, a little too late, and learned how to sew band patches onto her coats and bag. It wasn't a reinvention – everyone still knew who she was – but it was enough to help her make a few friends among the kids who hung around the art department at lunch.

The last few years of high school were less hellish than the ones before. She applied for university with straight teeth and weakly rooted hope.

18

During medieval times, some people believed that little boys and girls who didn't dispose of their teeth properly were destined to aimlessly wander after death, unable to rest. Ellis is wandering, a rattling handful of baby teeth and extractions keeping her unsettled.

Charlie and Kenzie will be landing at Edinburgh Airport any minute now. The house, which resists spotlessness, has been under assault for several days. Ellis is taking stray glasses back to the kitchen. She stops to rummage through the recycling, in case any new house brochures have appeared. Nothing. She wants to know what, if anything, Lana found out from the estate agent. There is no chance of getting more than an eye roll on the subject from their mum.

Mum is happily hoovering Lana's room. This is another charge against Ellis. Lana's room is not a guest room. Guests are meant to go in Ellis's room. If only she wasn't putting everyone through the inconvenience of needing it herself. Mum is pretending it's all grand, no problems here.

Ellis is in danger of letting the house drag her all the way back to her teenage self: needy and resentful of her own needs. She is being unreasonable and she can't tell her mum that the ache in her jaw is part of it. If she mentions this tooth, this troublesome weight, she knows what will be suggested – and she can't. Not her mum's boyfriend.

✳

Ellis is putting the stuffed bunny she found under the kitchen table back in the study when the doorbell goes. Leaving her mum to answer, Ellis stops in the doorway and smooths her hair. Their voices are loud with happiness. Charlie leads the way into the living room.

'Ellis, look at you. Come here. It's been years, huh?' He embraces her with a confident gust of airport sweat and faded aftershave. Ellis can't help but relax into it, just a little. He pulls back with a big grin. 'Don't expect any love from our girl Kenz – she's gone no contact.'

'God, Dad. Can't you be normal for even a second? Hi, Auntie Ellis.'

Charlie cuffs his daughter on the shoulder. She rolls her eyes. Kenzie's eyelashes are heavy with mascara, and her hair is twisted into a huge bun on the top of her head. She is almost as tall as Ellis.

'It's great to see you,' Ellis says. Kenzie nods and Charlie smiles. His teeth are so white and orderly, there's something discordant about them.

'Sight for sore eyes. It's so good to finally be here – what a flight. Thank you so much for putting us up, Auntie M. We're so stoked, aren't we, Kenz?'

'Yeah.'

'You're always welcome. You must be exhausted though. Why you insisted on the bus I don't know. Grant would've picked you up.'

'Sure he's got better things to do and, anyway, we got to do some sightseeing from the top deck. Right?'

Kenzie doesn't bother replying.

'You'll want a cup of tea. A bite to eat? Or do you want to freshen up first? We've put you in Lana's room and Kenzie in the study there.'

'Lovely, lovely. Except might be better the other way round, yeah? All girls together.'

'We thought you'd need the space and that she might like being down here with the TV and the stereo and all that.'

'I'm sure she would, but some of us like a place to kip near the kitchen.' He pats a modest stomach. 'Anyway, out of the two of us she's the one in need of extra space. See those cases in the hall? Seventy per cent of it's just her wardrobe. She'll be much better off spreading out in Lana's room.'

'Right then.' She turns to Kenzie with a grin. 'Shall we take your bag up?'

Kenzie nods, and they head off together. Charlie stretches.

'There's only a blow-up bed in there, sure you'll be all right?' Ellis says.

'I've had worse.'

'Jackson would never stand for it.'

'Good thing she's not here then, isn't it?' He's all smiles but there's an edge to his voice. 'I meant to message you but figured I'd see you here. I'm sorry about Adrian.'

'Mum told you?'

'The bare bones.'

Ellis nods. A silence she's meant to fill grows between them. Her cheeks flush. Charlie shoves his fingers in his hair and looks at her expectantly.

'These things happen,' she finally manages and is glad when Kenzie appears carrying a peanut butter sandwich and slumps onto the sofa to eat it. One plush shoulder peeks through her scoop-necked jumper. The fragments Ellis remembers from previous visits – skinny wrists and scrappy pigtails – are well buried.

Mum hands Charlie a plate with a selection of mini pork pies and pickles.

'You shouldn't have.'

'Hush. How was the flight?'

Charlie describes their trip like it was an adventure. His vowels are leaner and more elongated than they once were, softened in all the wrong places. The journey exhausted, he moves on to Kenzie. Her friends, her exams, her plans for this impromptu Edinburgh visit.

Mum's phone peeps throughout. It's Lana. Mum types out occasional replies in-between oohs and aahs of encouragement. Ellis's phone remains silent. Charlie is describing Kenzie's end of year project, a radical retelling of *The Wizard of Oz* that blew her teacher away.

'Stop bragging, Dad.'

'How can I, when I have such a talented daughter?'

Kenzie makes a noise of disgust and gives Charlie a withering stare. He shrugs it off.

'He's proud of you,' Mum says.

'For the cameras,' Kenzie says.

'I'm proud all the time. We all are,' Charlie says. Ellis likes the certainty in his voice.

'Lana sends her love. Mia's got a bit of a temperature, otherwise she'd be round here now,' Mum says. Charlie waves the quasi-apology away and asks her mum about the plate of tablet that came through alongside the pies. She's pleased, she made it specially. Charlie says they've missed it and looks to Kenzie for confirmation but her eyelids are drooping.

'Look at this – the energy of the youth, my ass,' Charlie says.

'We were up at five.'

'I know how you feel,' Mum says. 'Let's head up.'

Ellis and Charlie are alone. He's back but he's the wrong shape, the wrong size. America has buffed him up and smoothed him down. There's his bright white smile and the haircut that flops to one side and the tan that Ellis suspects has nothing to do with the sun. There's even something different about the way he carries himself: he looks taller and no longer quite fits in the groove worn out for him among the Patricks. Ellis offers him a nightcap; he declines.

'How's Lana getting on?'

'Good. The same.'

'She's a smile a minute on Facebook, but you wonder. Twins are a lot. I couldn't have handled it.'

'She's a lot older than you were with Kenzie.'

'Steady on,' he laughs. 'We're not that old.'

'You know what I mean.' She pulls a cushion onto her lap.

'Glad to hear she's all right. And to see you are . . . or that you will be.'

'Yeah, yeah, it's his loss.'

He laughs. 'I get it. You don't want to hear about it. But I've got an idea of what you're feeling. I may have made it sound like Jackson was just totally slammed this summer and that's why we're on our own, but it's not that. To be honest, we're not having the best time.'

'Mum never said.'

'I didn't properly tell her. Things were still . . . well, I guess I was holding out hope.'

'And now?'

'Not looking likely.'

'But you only just got that new place.'

'That was two years ago. And it was meant to be a fresh start, God love us.' The lines around his eyes look deeper than before. Ellis wants to rub them away with the edge of her thumb.

'We're on the run.' He laughs. 'Not really . . . oh boy, your face. Jackson knows exactly where we are.'

'And Kenzie?'

'She's heard more about it all than she wants to. A hundred times more, apparently. But, yeah, she has a decent idea which way the wind is blowing.'

'Shit.'

'I just want her to have a good summer while Jackson and I get our heads together, you know?'

Ellis nods, her fingers twitching to text her sister. This is news. She stops herself and, to her embarrassment, feels a prickling at her eyelashes.

'Are you all right? Sorry, El, I shouldn't be going on about it. You've got your own problems to be working through.' His face is all concern. She sniffs and smiles, says she's glad to see him and she's got work in the morning. He gets up to give her another hug. She allows a few seconds, then leaves him to his makeshift bed.

19

The house feels different already. Charlie's shoes crowd the space by the front door, and every night, after everyone else is in bed, his voice can be heard rumbling in the study. Kenzie flits between Lana's room and Mum's battered sun lounger. She's constantly online, or messaging her friends with flying fingers, or absorbed in her favourite streams. She only wears headphones when someone reminds her.

Mia passed her fever around, keeping Lana at home and away from the action. Ellis knows it'll be killing her. She swithers between telling her sister everything and nothing. In the end, she sends a restrained message explaining that Jackson and Charlie are splitting and receives a single *shit*. It's enough. Almost enough. God knows how Grant copes with the hours and days and sometimes weeks of Lana's tight-lipped animosity. She can't imagine him bustling like Mum does, or growing solicitous like she is. There's more to him than it looks. Or less.

Mum announces that the second Lana and co. have shaken off this bug, she wants everyone round for a traditional lunch, the kind that stopped when Granny P died. Maybe for Ellis's birthday? Ellis is not keen. Charlie is delighted.

'You'll meet Trevor,' Ellis says to Charlie. He's making a salad. Mum's at her book group.

'I've been looking forward to it.'

'You have? What's she said about him?'

'Hmm . . . that he keeps fit, that he likes his food. That he's got a cousin who was a hair's breadth from competing in the Paralympics and changed her mind at the last minute because she didn't want the only pictures people would find if they googled her name to be her in that patriotic pig's breakfast of a uniform. He'd like a dog but is worried he wouldn't have enough time to look after it properly. He's not that good at numbers, even though you'd think he would be. I don't know why you'd think that though.'

'Mum only expects everyone else to be good at numbers because none of us are. You know a lot about Trevor.'

'To be fair, I think she was looking for any excuse to sing his praises. What? Should I be polishing a pitchfork?'

'He's fine. It's just . . . Lana thinks . . .'

'She's obviously not going to like him.'

'It's not that. We're worried about Mum.'

'Auntie M's a peach. I'm sure this Trevor knows that.'

He's saying what she wants him to and still a territorial footstep resounds in her chest. Marion is her mum. Hers.

'He better not hurt her,' she says.

'You sound like me whenever I think about Kenzie dating. Drives me mad. Mind you, if anyone's a heartbreaker, it's my Kenz.'

'True.'

'Not that I blame you for being extra cautious, considering.' He splatters mayonnaise over a pan of cooled new potatoes and doesn't look up. He wants the ins and outs of why it all fell apart, but Ellis can't think how to spin it. All these years and she's not even got a good anecdote out of it.

'I know I'm not meant to say anything bad about Adrian, just in case you get back together or whatever. But I've gotta say, I never thought he was good enough for you.'

'Maybe you could tell him that.'

'I'd love to. I could hire a plane with one of those banners – *Adrian Whatsyourface Nowhere Near Good Enough*,' he says. Ellis gives in to the itch of a smile, passes him the spatula he's looking around for.

'You never used to talk so much,' she says.

'That's America, baby. This is ready. Kenzie.' His yell is unself-conscious. They wait. Nothing. He tries again, his hands under the tap. Ellis offers to fetch her.

The upstairs hall smells like it used to – heated hair and perfume and girl. Ellis pauses outside Lana's door, discombobulated. She raps again, a little harder, and the door jerks open. Ellis jumps.

'Auntie El, you okay?'

'Sorry, fine. Your dad wants you. Dinner's ready.'

Kenzie flashes her straight smile and nods. It makes Ellis feel like she's stepping between times, both younger and older than she's ever been.

20

Ellis has already had more teeth out than average. Saving as many of the rest as possible is one of her top priorities. And yet, she puts off subjecting herself to Dr Conor again. She lets days pass. Puts off thinking about all the things she should think about. Isn't it enough, just to survive?

Ellis worries the dentist has missed something. She considers the pain. Rates it. It's not the worst, but it is persistent. She has experiences to draw on. Tender gums in the early stages of gingivitis, stabbing pain when sugar invades a cavity, dry sockets after each lower wisdom extraction. This is more than just an unsettled nerve. She thinks of telling Dr Conor he's missed a problem but feels exhausted. Soon, she'll ring up and ask for another look. But if she leaves it a while longer, maybe Dr Niall will be back.

She's leaving the office, headache waxing, when Becca calls. She almost doesn't answer. It will be about her birthday. Ellis would cancel it if she could.

'What's the plan? Shall we have a posh lunch or something? Afternoon tea? We could head to the Haven and dump Scotty in the play corner while we stuff our faces?'

'Not sure, love. Can I get back to you? Mum's planning a family thing and Lana's not got back about it yet. It's all a bit flakey.'

'Course. Oh damn, I'd better go the now – my rusk biscuits are not smelling right. Pass my love on to your ma, will you?'

Tersely, Ellis promises she will and hangs up. She doesn't want to be another year older. She doesn't want to be alone. She's full of frustration. She's also on her way to Adrian's office.

She's not going for him though. It's Wednesday, the day Adrian's pale ale club meets. He'd negotiated an early finish with his boss so he could get to the meetings in time for the stovies and oatcakes meant to line their stomachs before the real business began.

Ellis checks her watch: she needs to get the timing right.

She takes a seat on the bench by the railings, bang on time to watch the slow dribble of people from Adrian's building. She recognises several from a round of utterly charmless dinner parties, a venture that quickly fizzled out. None of the hosts enjoyed themselves enough to issue a second invite.

A purple jacket catches her attention, but the woman in it has dark brown curls and Sally is emphatically blonde. It's ten minutes after home time for Adrian's company. Ellis wonders if Sally has the day off. Or worse, has also left early to take part in the pale ale club. She burrows her hands into her pockets and presses her palms against her thighs.

Ellis is turning and overturning the idea of leaving when Sally appears in the doorway. There is no question it's her even if she's not as smooth as her pictures. She's barely five foot three – there's nothing in the slightest bit threatening about her. She's wearing a long, creamy cardigan over a pale pink dress, and Ellis is pleased to see a hint of rabbit to her bite. She's fussing at the clasp of her handbag. She is prey, not hunter. Yet, somehow, she's bagged the prize.

It would be easy to take a fistful of that fluffy golden hair and use it to drag Sally's head down to the pavement. Or Ellis could sidle over and ask if she's always been a cheater. Or she could just stay sitting here, a maelstrom of feelings battering her ribcage.

Oblivious, Sally trips her way to the bus stop at the edge of the railings. Ellis freezes. She didn't expect Sally to get the bus. She didn't think about the position of the stop and the bench, how clear the line of sight is. Adrian walks. Maybe Sally does too, when they're together.

Sally twiddles one of her earrings. She's the kind of person Adrian wanted all along. Sunshine in a bottle. A painted cottage, not a haunted house. Ellis was an accidental detour, a depressing cul-de-sac it took him too long to back out from. She should be happy he found his road. Ellis is not happy.

Sally looks up from her rose-gold iPhone. Ellis wills her not to turn around. Sally knows what she looks like. Of course she does. There are photos. Or, if Adrian has already consigned those to the bin, there's always Facebook. Or LinkedIn. Either way, Sally knows. All women check out the ones who came before. Ellis holds her breath. Sally looks back down at the screen.

What does Sally think of her? Is she smug about the laughter and frown lines that have become permanent? She must be pleased that Ellis isn't particularly thin (although slimmer in the last few months) and that she's an uninspiring B cup. Maybe she's smug, thinking Ellis should've taken better care of herself. How was she to know that Sally's conventional prettiness is what Adrian wanted all along?

Sweat fugs up her underarms. Ellis is trapped, waiting for Sally's bus to arrive so she can escape unnoticed. Sally smiles at her screen. Dimples. Actual fucking dimples appear. Inside her pockets, Ellis's nails dig into her thighs.

A bus pulls up. A short eternity has passed. Sally squeezes her way on board graciously. People shuffle to make way for her. The very ease with which she finds a seat irritates Ellis. As soon as the bus turns the corner, she stands and walks away on stiff legs.

The desire to tell someone throbs through her. She needs to lance the abscess, and the only person who could truly help her do that is Lana.

Becca would hold her hand with an unbearable show of compassion, asking why she's torturing herself like this. Charmaine and Zoe can't be expected to understand. Everyone at work believes it's Lana who's been dumped. Charlie would think she's mad. Only Lana would nod and say, 'You're sad because he ended up with some Barbie softcore bitch? You're going to sit there throwing yourself a pity party because he wants a doll? Shut the fuck up. And tell me what time she finishes work so I can go and accidentally spill a mocha over that stupid cardigan tomorrow night.' Ellis would vomit up every single despicable thing she's thinking and still feel like the bigger person, because Lana thinks worse. Lana does worse too. But she won't do it for Ellis right now.

Ellis doesn't need her. Doesn't need anyone. Sally didn't see her. No one knows where she's been or why. She just has to never do it again, and she'll be safe.

✳

Charlie's on the phone in the living room, Kenzie's gone to the cinema and Mum's with Trevor, obviously. Ellis pours a glass of wine and stands at the back door, looking at the garden without taking it in.

'Can I join you?'

She nods.

'Anaesthetic?' Charlie says.

'Pretty much.' The collection of wine bottles beside the microwave is noticeably smaller. She should buy some replacements.

'Sorry,' she says. 'I'm crap company.'

'Don't beat yourself up for feeling bad.'

'Why not? You seem to be functioning like a proper human being.'

'Glad it looks that way. But to be honest, I'm a bit lost right now. Maybe it's hard to tell quite how cut-up I am about the whole thing because I've been mourning Jackson for actual years already.'

'Is that meant to make me feel better?'

'I don't know. Grab a seat?' He gestures to the sun lounger and ducks into the kitchen to fetch a chair for himself. The evening is just warm enough. The wooden slats remind Ellis of the bench outside Adrian's work. She blushes and rubs at her cheek to hide it.

'Were you already having problems the last time I saw you?' she says.

'Oh yeah. We could hardly look at each other.'

'You covered it up well. Lana did mention . . . but you two were so . . . and Jackson is so . . . you know.'

'Yep, she's a lot. It's one of the things I like most about her. I thought she wasn't afraid of anything, but of course she is. Everyone is.'

'Do you miss her?'

'Loads.'

'Is it her you've been talking to at night?'

'Sometimes. More often I'm just catching up with some of the people from back here I should've stayed in touch with. Old friends, work folk.'

'Good idea, you should see them if you can. How long are you guys staying for?'

'Probably about as long as you can put up with us.' He grins, teeth so white they flare. It's been so long, and still a candle flickers for the older cousin with his vampiric smile. It's not the same. And yet.

'Did it hurt? Getting those done?'

'I can't lie: it was a total bitch. Took ages too.'

'But it was worth it?'

'I suppose so. Definitely made me feel like I'd made it. American dream, American teeth.'

'I've imagined what it would be like, having enough money to get someone to knock me out and fix everything that's wrong with mine.'

'If only it were so easy.' He stops there, distracted by Kenzie sticking her head out the back door.

'There you are,' she says accusingly. Charlie asks how she

enjoyed the movie. She screws her face up, says it was a waste of money. She should've listened to Lana and seen the other one. Ellis hates that while she's at work, her sister's been round giving Kenzie film recommendations. Showing off her perfect family. Ellis wants to be the favourite cousin.

Charlie persuades Kenzie to help him make dinner. Ellis stays out in the garden, nursing her last inch of wine. Talking to Charlie is easy. Too easy.

21

A chocolate chip muffin with a candle stuck in its middle sits on the kitchen counter. Ellis reaches for the coffee. Her mum hurries in from the garden with a handful of bluebells when the machine begins to burble.

'You're up already. Happy birthday, Elly,' she says.

Ellis nods. She's up at exactly the same time every weekday.

Mum pops the flowers into a jam jar and puts them beside the muffin. Ellis allows herself to be kissed and waits while her mum scrabbles for a lighter in the overfilled drawer by the oven. She gamely blows out the tiny flame and bites into her treat. She prefers not to eat before ten and normally breaks her fast with a satsuma or an apple (sliced, to avoid the intrusive vision of front teeth snapping against taut, waxy skin).

The journey to work is scattered with digital well wishes. Becca sends a gif. Charmaine's text says it's been too long, call as soon as she fancies a drink. Zoe has attached a video. Ellis opens it with the volume turned down low. Zoe sings 'Happy Birthday' into the camera, which jiggles along with her girlfriend's laughter. Ellis kills the clip before it ends and sends a *thank you, you beautiful gem. Give Maz my love.* Charlie sends a gif of a cartoon birthday cake dancing. It's kind of depressing.

She arrives at TravelOn a few minutes early and is glad to find the office empty. She gets settled and opens her emails. There is one with a lot of exclamation marks and also a picture of a dog that is supposedly smiling. Naila's fond of such memes; Ellis doesn't have the heart to tell her that the animals are baring their teeth as a warning.

Ellis sends a few more thank-yous and opens Excel. She normally books her birthday off. This year, she couldn't think of anything she actually wanted to do with the day and didn't bother.

Having resolutely refused to be part of the baking rota, Ellis expects to get away with it, but at eleven, there's some fussing in the kitchen. A few minutes later, a wan chorus of 'Happy Birthday' rings out. They baked a cake for her anyway. A pity cake. Jean made the sponge, which everyone agrees is the fluffiest they've ever had. Naila supplies a package of napkins patterned with balloons. Ellis's cheeks go numb with the effort of smiling. She takes the knife, and it trembles only a little as she sinks it into yellow peaks of buttercream.

'This is beautiful. I could never make something so lovely.'

'You deserve it,' Naila says, which is a lie everyone goes along with. Ellis forks cake into her mouth, wishing for olives or pickled onions. The frosting is meltingly sweet. She eats as much as she can, listening to the chatter around her as her saliva ducts squirt their disapproval. After the allotted ten minutes of socialising, Gabrielle from HR leads the drift back to work-stations. She wishes Ellis a happy birthday before pointedly shutting the door to her office.

Ellis thanks Jean again.

'My pleasure.'

'Most people would just be saying that, but our Jean really is born to bake. I keep telling her she should start a sideline,' Naila says as she stacks plates. Ellis agrees. Jean tells them not to be silly and preens as she stores the meagre leftovers, then presses them on Ellis to take home with her.

Ellis and Alison load the dishwasher.

'I know you don't like a fuss, but we all need an excuse for some cake and a chat every now and then.' Alison pats her on the arm. Ellis feels patronised and also pleased.

She spends the rest of the day looking at the Tupperware container of cake on her desk, wondering if Adrian will message.

She'll be angry if he does and even more so if he doesn't. Just before lunch, Lana sends a picture of the twins sitting beside the oversized Happy Birthday badge bought for Grant's fortieth.

Ellis receives it with a pin strike of relief and immediately compliments Oscar and Mia on their adorable expressions. She is being forgiven. Silently, the way Lana always forgives. Lana sends a thumbs-up. Ellis decides to capitalise.

Did you find out anything from the estate agent?

He's desperate to value the place. He wanted me to talk her into it. Would I fuck.

Ha. That all?

Bad enough.

Anything we can do?

Lana reads the message and doesn't reply. That's as much as Ellis is getting. Buoyed but disappointed, Ellis logs into Facebook to like the birthday comments people have left for her. There are fewer every year, and none of Adrian's friends or family wish her happy returns. This is no surprise. It's crazy to think she once believed Adrian's mother, with her soggy pies and weekend watercolours, was an integral part of her life. Ellis is no one to them now.

The app shows her a memory from her last birthday. The picture was taken by Anna, champion of reusable water bottles. There's a genuine smile on her face and a card in her hand. She barely recognises herself.

She's a blur. A person at a distance. Every time a little bit of herself sneaks through – the desire to eat alone at lunch or to say no thanks to the cake made for her – she quashes it with guilt. Who even is she, with no one to remind her how to behave?

✱

Becca is waiting outside the office with a gift bag dangling from her wrist. Ellis hurries over.

'What are you doing here?'

'You didn't think I was going to let you away with ignoring your birthday, did you?'

'Should've known better. I'm not wearing a hat though,' Ellis says, giving Becca a hug and suppressing the impulse to check over her shoulder for emerging colleagues.

'I promise no hats or balloons this year. Come on, we're going to Huevos. And before you say anything, I called your mum, and she's saving your stir fry for tomorrow. Tonight, you're having a bloody drink.'

'When did you get to be so pushy?' Ellis gives her shoulder an affectionate nudge.

'Always have been, you're just getting it in more concentrated doses now that three quarters of my non-working hours are taken up with Peppa Pig.'

At the restaurant, Becca places the gift bag in front of her.

'You shouldn't have.'

'I was going to light sparklers but I wanted to live to see your next birthday.'

Ellis digs through the crumpled tissue paper and pulls out a couple of mini gin bottles and a glass with 'bitch' written on it in glittery cursive.

'I know it's not really your style, but who doesn't need a drink and a reminder of how awesome they are? Please count this as a holdover present until I actually get the chance to shop in places that aren't the supermarket or IKEA. You almost got a giant cuddly owl, so count yourself lucky. Are we getting margaritas? That isn't a real question by the way: we are.'

The drinks are overly sweet, and there's too much salt around the edge of the glasses, but as she drinks and nibbles tentatively at a bowl of popcorn drizzled with tabasco, Ellis's muscles begin to ease. She tells Becca about the cake. They snort into their glasses.

'I can just see your face. Did they sing? Perfect. What about the rest of the day? How's it at home? Enjoying having Charlie there?'

'It's a little crowded, but okay.'

'Don't play coy with me. I remember you going on and on about him that summer. You'd have loved him moving back then.'

'You're being gross. He's family.' Ellis dips her fingers in the glass of water she should be drinking to dilute the tequila and flicks a sprinkle of drops at her friend. Becca laughs, then pulls her serious face.

'Distant, as you took great pains to tell me. Wouldn't have stopped you then, just wondering if it would stop you now. But just take your time – we're too old for messy rebounds.'

She hates it when Becca does this, makes it sound like they're in it together when the problem belongs absolutely and inescapably to Ellis.

'I'm done with men.'

'No, no. Have a little hot sex with a new guy for all us poor souls stuck with the same one forever.'

'Can't I just skip it?'

'Not allowed. You have to get back in the driver's seat. But with the windscreen wipers on, if you know what I mean? No fuckarounds and sad sacks.'

Becca is dangerously close to the level of drunk that will attract exactly the kind of guy she's warning Ellis away from. After a certain number of drinks, she tends to think everyone wants to talk to her. Ellis isn't in the mood for that kind of night.

'I'll keep that in mind,' Ellis says. 'Medium-sleazy only.'

Becca pouts. Tipsy Becca is also capable of taking the merest pinprick of an offence and worrying it into a gaping wound.

'I know, I know. You're just looking out for me.' Ellis accepts another glug from the pitcher. She loves Becca. Loves her so much that she's fine with hating her sometimes too. Most of Becca's tics are born of generosity, which doesn't always make them easier to bear.

Ellis bites down on a nacho and winces. Becca pats her arm sympathetically. She understands as well as she can, considering she's only ever had two fillings.

'Got a date with your nice dentist booked in?'

'Dr Niall's off. They gave me a new one. Nowhere near as nice.'

'You don't have to see him if you don't like him. The dental world is your oyster. What about your mum's boyfriend?'

'Becca, don't even.'

'Or the one Liam's mum recommended?'

'Oh, him. He killed himself.'

'He didn't!'

'Yeah, couple of months ago. I checked him out after you said. Anyone who makes Liam's mum happy is worth a look. I did some googling and found rumours that he'd been a bit handsy with his female patients.'

'Shit. She said he had kind eyes.'

'Maybe too kind. He hanged himself over a bank holiday weekend.'

'What am I going tell her?'

'Just be sure and let her down gently.'

'Great. Maybe she can start seeing this Trevor guy. Is it still going well? Is he nice?'

'Too nice.'

'Your mum deserves plenty of nice though, right? You like him?'

'I don't think I can actually *like* him, on principle. He seems all right, I suppose, apart from smelling like a dentist.'

'Bet you love that. Remember when I worked in that fudge shop? I smelled delicious.'

'I know. And I remember when you said you tasted even better than you smelled and you got Fred O'Neill to lick your neck at the Mission.'

'Oh God, I did.'

'And worse,' Ellis says. Becca looks so pleased with herself that Ellis smiles and reminds her of all the other boys she persuaded to have a nibble on the dance floor. They delve into a trove of old memories and root around in walks home with heels off, toes poking through ripped tights. Bonfires at the beach, sand floating in their bottles of beer. Conversations with strangers where everyone was laughing and laughing at nothing.

All the wildest nights were when Ellis was single. Nights where her loneliness was shot through with hope. She thinks of that hope wistfully now and knows that all Becca's hugs aren't enough to sustain her. Ellis needs blasted by a fiery attention. She needs someone to temper her. She needs a new man to burn away Adrian's rejection. She toasts her friend and thinks that she doesn't want to be living through those nights again.

22

The day after her birthday is a hungover blur. Alison winks over a pile of printouts. Naila asks who it was that met her with a present. Ellis stays upright and in one piece until home time, then starts falling asleep over the postponed stir fry. Her mum says they'll save the presents for the weekend, seeing as she's still suffering the effects of coming home fleeing, and she should go and have a nap.

She wakes with tidemarks under her eyes, scrapes the scurf away with her fingernails, and joins Mum and Kenzie in the living room, where they are half watching a programme about people competing to throw the most elaborate dinner parties. Ellis alternates between Sally's Facebook page and her own, where likes are still dribbling in on the post she made thanking people for their birthday wishes.

Charlie, bored with the show and his daughter's insistence they finish it, is in the shower. Soon he will be back, a dram or a cup of tea in hand, ready to wind down for the night.

Adrian liked to get everything in order of an evening. Bedtime was a process. He pottered for so long – soaking oats for the morning, plucking at stray hairs, distracting himself with this or that – that she'd often fallen asleep by the time he humped his way under the covers. Her passing out with boredom while waiting for a shag was probably an early death knell. Whose fault was that? His for taking so long or hers for not caring enough to stay awake?

Charlie walks in, still damp from the shower and smelling a little like ice cream. He sits by Ellis and, feeling the heat peeling from him, she squidges discreetly away.

'Dad, did you use my vanilla and cocoa butter bar again? God, you did. It's a total waste on you. You don't have enough hair.'

'Kick a man where it hurts, eh?' he says, but he's smiling.

'Which one is that, dear? There's so many,' Mum says.

'It's the big creamy-coloured one with the black flecks. The blue one is a blueberry bubblegum shampoo. The sparkly one with the salt chunks is a seaweed-infused body scrub. The teal one is a facial cleanser, with lavender and litsea oils.'

'I'd mix them all up in no time. Twice I got my shampoo and conditioner back to front. I bought that silly brand with the black and white bottles the other way round. As bad as cheese and onion in blue bags. They look really pretty, all your what-have-yous.'

'Shame they take up so much space though, isn't it?' Charlie chips in.

'Who cares about shelf space when they're stopping tons of plastic being dumped in the ocean? I've saved loads of bottles just in the last six months.'

'Uh-huh, so now you just buy twice as much, as long as it comes wrapped in dried kale or whatever.'

'At least I give a shit. You're the reason we're in this fucking mess. Sorry for swearing, Auntie Marion,' Kenzie says.

'That's all right, pet.'

'To be young and full of righteousness again,' Charlie says.

'If you're not part of the solution, you're part of the problem. You know how bad it is? We're all drinking plastic every time we pour ourselves a glass of water. Teeny-tiny bits of plastic just swimming around in our guts. Our insides are gonna end up completely coated, and none of the nutrients will get through, and it won't even matter because the oceans will be on fire anyway.'

Kenzie has that strange, consuming passion of teenage girls. So overpowering and so selective. No sympathy for Charlie or anyone else who doesn't behave the way she thinks they should, but sudden, swampy tears for animals, people who've been cancelled online for spurious reasons and elderly couples holding hands. Mum gets more sympathy than Charlie. Ellis isn't sure where she lands on Kenzie's scale. It's exhausting just being in the same house as her.

Ellis decides she'll also have an evening shower.

She tips her head back and lets the water beat her face. A little slips into her mouth, and she straightens, thinking of plastic fragments sneaking down her throat. She examines the soaps. The pink sparkly one might've been carved from a crystalline cave; the teal one reminds her of mint sorbet. She tries to remember which is which and decides to give each a go. The exfoliating bar is her favourite. Then she slathers a blob of her mum's conditioner in her hair and rubs a handful of Radox over her arms and legs, masking the exotic smells.

Ellis normally picks up whatever is cheap, with a bias towards things that claim to be refreshing or revitalising. Adrian is the same. Sally will be all violets and roses and creamy lotions. Sickly sweet like the perfume she left by the sink, begging to be smashed. Sally is pastel and sugar-spun, all her darkness locked inside.

Ellis clambers damply into bed with her laptop and googles her younger cousin. How different Kenzie is to the way Ellis was when she was that age. And how similar. It doesn't take much digging to find Kenzie's sparsely populated YouTube channel. Her videos are all make-up tutorials. Ellis hits one of the first ones, with the sound turned down low. The video is less polished than the ones Ellis has seen pop up on her Facebook feed. There is a formula: bare face, wry smile, little shrug, waggle products at camera, apply with great intent, repeat. Pout and pose in a new look. Not everyone narrates; Kenzie does. All her videos are a few months old and none have more than fifty views. That won't do.

Ellis skips to the start of the channel and checks auto play is on. She turns the sound down and lets the videos chatter in the background to bump up the view counter as she follows her well-worn social routine. Nothing new from Adrian, nothing new from Sally, nothing new from any of the friends they now have in common. Nothing new to worry about. She flicks from page to page and thinks about the heat emanating from Charlie's side of the sofa, the soft, sweet smell that'd been coming off him and which was buried in her own hair now. Kenzie's face plays on another tab.

23

Ellis is on peeling duty. Mum is smashing digestive biscuits for a cheesecake and a chicken roasts in the oven. Charlie and Kenzie have been dispatched to the shops to pick up juice and nibbles. Sun blazes through the kitchen window, and between each thump of the rolling pin, Mum tells her about the chairs she's borrowed from next door. Ellis has not thought about Adrian or Sally for at least half an hour.

Charlie and Kenzie return with packets of tiny salted pretzels that make them giggle. Trevor arrives with a huge bunch of flowers. Lana, Grant and the kids are hot on his heels. Everyone is siphoned into the living room with drinks. Lana comes through to help, says the briefest happy birthday, takes over the gravy and starts needling Mum about the house.

'But you love this street.'

'I've been here thirty years. I've outlived all my favourite shops. The café on the corner has changed hands four times since we moved in, and I still miss Jasmine's scones.'

'What are you on about? You can get scones a hundred places.'

'It's not the scones. Anyway, it's just a case of knowing your options. Especially now you girls are grown up.'

'But you know how much it means to me, the twins growing up in the same rooms we did.'

'You know we almost had to give this place up when you were about their age?'

'But you got it for a song.'

'In today's prices, but it was expensive to us then. Your dad loved it though. So we scrimped, we saved. I cut vouchers out of newspapers. We ate from the reduced aisle every night. The boys from the supermarket would roll their eyes when they saw us coming. Do you know, they kept the bargains in the stock room until after I finished paying, just to be mean. We talked about downsizing. Then your poor dad solved the problem in the short term by going and dying on us. So I stayed. We stayed. I wanted you girls to enjoy the house he fought for. It was a struggle, even with the insurance.'

'But you're all right now?' Ellis says. Mum nods, clasps Ellis's waist briefly on the way past.

'If you're wanting to downsize or whatever – which makes no sense at all considering the menagerie you've got here the now – why don't I look into you renting it out so you don't have to give it up altogether?'

'Who'd want all that bother when I could sell up and move somewhere a bit cheaper? If I did that, there'd be money left over. For all of us.'

'It's not the money – Grant and I do just fine.' Lana's serious voice slices like a scimitar.

'Of course you do. Let me in to check the chicken.'

It's almost time to eat. Charlie and Trevor are summoned and asked to carry the table through to the front room where there's more space. Its folded panels bang against their legs. Lana sets out the placemats. Ellis piles potatoes into the green dish with harvest vegetables carved around the edges.

Ellis hasn't properly enjoyed birthdays since she was very young. There's too much pressure, not enough reward, but the house is so busy it feels more like Christmas. The kind of Christmases her friends had. Except she's the only one getting presents. Lana hands over a book about reaching your full potential. There's a soft, black woollen jumper from her mum and a very expensive-looking candle from Kenzie and Charlie. Trevor reveals a bottle of fancy vodka; Lana narrows her eyes, preferring him to have been idiotic enough to show up empty-handed.

Squashed round the table, everyone is quickly overheated. Grant is telling them about one of the lads he works with. This is the thing Ellis has always liked best about Grant, the way he'll talk about his mates and their problems like there's nothing wrong with having them. Kenzie is enamoured with the twins and doesn't mind them smearing food all over her. The chicken is praised. Over seconds, Lana fills them in on the dead-cat situation: no lawsuit but a neighbourhood WhatsApp group close to imploding. Ellis takes a second helping of green beans.

It's strange to have three men in the living room. Ellis looks at them passing each other beers and politely wielding the gravy boat. They are so normal, so alien. Her life has long been lacking in men. The male friends she's hung on to have dwindled as they found other people to pair up with. For years, Ellis has only really spent time with other people's husbands or Adrian. What happened to them all? She's twisting her glass of wine when she feels the air shift. Ellis looks up. Lana is scowling.

'Right then. And how long is it you're staying?'

'Not sure, to be honest. We're having a nice time, aren't we, Kenz?'

'You don't have to get back for work?'

'We're flexible.'

'So you didn't tell Mum you were on the verge of a divorce when you invited yourself over?'

'He didn't need to. You didn't need to, love – we're happy to have you.'

'Lana, come on.' Charlie looks at Kenzie.

'I'm not an idiot, Dad,' she says, but her voice is not as steady as it usually is.

'I hope you've not been hiding anything from her,' Lana says. 'I've had it up to here with secrets in this family.'

'There's nothing to hide. There's also a time and a place, and maybe this isn't it, you know?'

'And there's being upfront about what you're up to from the outset, *you know?*'

Trevor sits, eyes darting one way then the other, unsure of what's going on. Kenzie is tense. Grant's unfazed. Ellis swallows tightly.

'Well, there you go. Sorry, Auntie M. I guess I should've filled you in,' Charlie says with his newfound American expansiveness.

'It's not a bother, honestly. I think it's time for pudding.' Mum holds out a hand, and the tableau breaks as everyone rushes to pass their empty plates. The cheesecake comes out, and 'Happy Birthday' is sung with various levels of enthusiasm. The conversation turns to films. Kenzie is quizzed about what her friends are watching. The sense of celebration has gone despite all the effort to recapture it.

Ellis helps with the clearing up, both hoping for and dreading a moment alone with Lana.

'Are you all right?' she says.

'Why are you asking me that?'

'Just, you know, with Charlie. I thought it was Trevor you were worried about.'

'As if he wasn't enough. I just can't stand seeing someone else take advantage of Mum.'

The inside of Ellis's bottom lip is clamped between her teeth; the comment is directed at her too. She exhales.

'If you want Mum to keep the house, isn't having them here perfect?'

'What if he's trying to stake a claim?'

'Lana, he's not.'

'Then why lie? When's he going back? Why's he sucking up to you so much?'

'He's being nice.'

'Nice, eh? Why's he really here?'

'To get away from Jackson.'

'You think he can't do that in America? He's got you wrapped around his finger, pretending you're in same boat when it's not the same. You should see him when you're not around. He's chipper as fuck.'

'He's had lots of time to process,' Ellis says quietly, straining to hear the voices in the other room. She wants to tell Lana to shut up and knows it would only make her louder. 'It's been hard for him.'

'You're such a sook. He's not here looking for friends or to connect with the folk he abandoned a million years ago. He's got an angle. You think he's got all this time off because his boss is a sweetheart? Bullshit. America's not like that. You barely get two days' maternity leave, and holidays are like gold dust. Divorce is expensive. Everything is expensive. He wants something.'

'You don't know that.'

'I know a lot more than you. And all this, I can't stand it.' She gestures towards the living room. 'And don't think I've forgotten what happened. I know who I can trust.' Lana slams down the green dish. Ellis anxiously picks it up to check for cracks. The harvest vegetables remain intact.

By the time she's filled the dishwasher, her sister is gone and everyone is frazzled. There has been some other parting shot that Ellis missed, and no one wants to fill her in.

It isn't the first time Lana has fallen out with everyone. The teenage years were the worst. There was the Christmas she accepted a Saturday job at a designer shop in Glasgow, and Mum put her foot down and forced her to phone and tell them she couldn't do it. The boyfriend Ellis accidentally offended. Their mum's idiocy in expecting Lana to come to the holiday cottage with them two days before the start of summer holiday, meaning she'd miss the quali (not even her year's, just her boyfriend's).

Everyone works to put the house to rights, and Trevor insists on taking Mum to the pub for a quiet one to cap off the week.

Ellis is grateful and heads to her room. Kenzie needs some time with her dad.

Charlie hasn't mentioned money once. He acts like someone who's doing well. He'd changed their flights more than once already and never complained about the cost. Kenzie's iPhone is so large and flat that it must be dear. But. They do normally stay in a hotel. Maybe it isn't all Jackson. Maybe that's where they'd rather be but they can't afford one. He's not working. He's spending a long time on the phone, talking to people he never meets up with. He could be broke. It doesn't matter. Does it? Bloody Lana. Ellis doesn't want to be wondering whether he's here for a cut.

Ellis hasn't said to anyone, certainly not her sister, that if Mum does decide to sell the house, there's a good chance that the resulting gift for her daughters might be enough for a deposit on a flat. A studio or a one-bedroom, if she's lucky. That would be something. Not that she'd want to lose this house for it.

And she'd thought, just for a little while, that Lana was over the thing with Oscar, but she's obviously still holding it against her. Ellis's phone is on silent; she pulls it out thinking of her sister. There's a voicemail. Adrian. Her heart skitters.

She sits on the bed to listen. He says hello in a way she never thought she'd hear again. He sounds like he always did. And then says he wanted to let her know he's taken her off their life insurance policy. She should look into setting up a new one as soon as possible.

It's not the fact of it that's devastating, but the casual, genuine concern in his voice. As if he really thought she needed to know. The phone call is a service, not an insult, and yet there's something else about it. Something she notices but can't pin. She hangs up slowly, deliberately, and lies down.

The headache is back, heavier than ever.

24

Tooth enamel is one of the human body's permanent cell types, of which there are only four. That means they don't renew themselves after a set number of years. When they go, they go. Either on the pre-programmed date of their destruction, or when they're destroyed by outside influences.

Charlie wasn't crying. He was too grown up at seventeen, apparently, and Auntie Sheila had been sick for a long time. He was used to looking after himself. Had to be when his dad hadn't been seen in over a decade. That's what Ellis and Lana said, aged fourteen and almost thirteen. They were in Ellis's room, hiding from everyone. They had a pack of cards out but no one wanted to start playing.

They could hear the adults talking and some children squabbling. It was all wrong. There was a gentle knock on the door, and Lana was ready to send whoever it was away, but it was just their mum. Ellis moved up the bed to make space. Mum looked very tired. Ellis reached for the bag of wine gums they'd been sharing and held it out to her.

The taste stayed sharp in Ellis's mind. Sharper still was the moment her mum's face froze. Tentatively, she spat a gelatinous lump of wine gum affixed to a harsh jag of grey metal into her hand.

'Oh dear,' she said. She fumbled in her pocket for a Kleenex and wrapped the horrible mess up. The teenagers watched, aghast. None more so than Ellis, who had handed the sweet over. It was only a minor tragedy in a decade of bigger ones, but it was awful to think of her mum comforting everyone else with a freshly opened hole in her mouth to match the one in her heart.

Afterwards, Ellis helped clean up. The platters of food had been decimated. She asked how people could be so greedy. Mum said people ate at funerals to remind themselves they're alive. They're defying death. Those closest to the tragedy, like Charlie, wouldn't want to eat. Couldn't. Everyone else would do it for them until they could be tempted into doing it for themselves again.

Ellis remembered the piles of food that arrived after her dad died and nodded. She thought Charlie was handling the whole thing so well. Better than anyone could, or should, expect. Better than Ellis and Lana ever had.

Hardly any time later, he ran away to America and reinvented himself. It worked. He looked and talked and smiled like someone who'd put the hardest things behind him.

∗

Ellis dreams of running her fingers up her leg, past the silky damp at the back of the knee, along the cable of muscle edging her thigh and towards that soft, inner plane. Her fingertips glide until they are arrested by the crags and ridges of the molars sprouting from her skin. The teeth are humped like barnacles, rooted in the femur and impossible to scrape away. Her hand is frozen, resting on the intrusion. Danger. Men will be pulverised between her thighs, blood will run down her calves, and she won't be able to scrub herself clean. Particles of the dead will rot and dissolve in the gaps of these teeth. Her thighs are cavities.

She wakes, uneasy, and presses a palm to her damp skin. The feeling of solid dentine can't be so easily dispelled. She imagines her legs shifting, the teeth scraping and barking against each other. Ellis puts a pillow between them and starts to count to a hundred. It's one of the tricks she uses to stop the worst thoughts from taking over. It only works when she's awake. Ellis's dreams are like teeth – erupting, ready to wound.

At ten past seven, she admits that it's time to get up. It's Monday, and she will not be calling in sick. She pops a couple of paracetamol from the blister pack. They leave a pressure in her throat after swallowing.

She doesn't have to speak to anyone until she arrives at the office. Alison says she looks like someone the cat dragged in. Ellis apologises and offers up the tense family get-together as her excuse. A few minutes later, Alison sends through a link to a counsellor, saying she did wonders for her neighbour, maybe Lana would benefit? This is Ellis's own fault. They are trying to cheer her up because they think her sister is semi-suicidal, rather than outrageously angry with her. She replies with a thank-you.

By lunchtime, there are two messages from Naila. They contain multiple smiley faces and links to a wine and paint group and an aerial class. Naila wants the best for Ellis and, by extension, Lana. It's easy to want the best for people when all you have to do is send perky emails. Naila's suggestions fill Ellis with dread. She hates the thought of twenty women trudging to a foosty converted church hall with maroon walls and splintered floorboards, winding themselves up in ropes slung from the rafters and imagining themselves flying across the big top in spangled knickers.

Jean – staid, solid Jean – once announced to the office that she'd mastered the drop-down shimmy at her burlesque evening. Alison said she should come along to her pole dancing class, it does wonders for your waist. Naila's laugh fluted into embarrassment, and everyone else seemed to think it was a perfectly acceptable way to spend an evening. How strange to pay to try and be sexy. But it's not just stuff like that. What about Jean's cakes? How many of the women Ellis knew believed that, really, deep down, they were performers, artists or world-class bakers who just haven't had the right opportunities? Ellis wants to weep at the worthlessness of it. And she's grateful to Naila for sending the hopeful little messages on anyway.

Ellis's problems are never the ones people want her to have.

There was the dentist she saw as a teenager who was convinced she was bulimic and refused to offer any advice. The enamel on the back of her teeth was worn so thin he assumed she was sticking her fingers down her throat or finding an alternative use for her toothbrush. It didn't matter how many times she promised she didn't make herself throw up, he would not be convinced. He told her she'd need crowns if she carried on. They'd have to file the stumps of her teeth down. Wouldn't it be better to stop what she was doing? There was no point helping a girl who wouldn't help herself. She left in tears.

Now, she really has created a monster. She's going to have to make up a happy ending for Lana. Someone's going to piece it together, if she doesn't. She's not ready to walk back her lies. She feels dreadful. If she tells them Lana is fine (she's taking Grant back? She's met a new person with the same name?), Ellis will be expected to also be fine. She's not fine. She's a fool, she's alone and she's ashamed. Ashamed of her tears, her teeth, the things she can't help and the things she should've done something about a long time ago.

Ellis inspects her face in the reflection on her computer screen. The ache is so pressing, so constant, that she expects to see swelling but her cheek is concave. Gaunter than normal. She clenches her jaw, and the needle jabs again. She still looks like herself, but she knows something is wrong. To say it would be to admit it. She can't mention the pain at home, can't bear the thought of being pressured into Trevor's surgery. Having him examine her is out of the question. Even visiting one of his colleagues is too much. It's bewildering to think of her mum being so intimate, so vulnerable, with him. It should be comforting that Mum's fear of dentists has softened so utterly. Instead, it feels like a trick or, worse, an insult. Doesn't she realise that she passed on not only the genes that ruined their chance of a naturally nice smile, but also a terror that ate away at their ability to accept treatment?

She calls the dentist's and is told Dr Niall will be off for an extended period. She says she can't wait, she'll see the replacement again if she has to. Morning only though. There's a cancellation on Monday they can slot her into. If they run to schedule, she'll only be fifteen minutes late for work. She sends a message to Richard and copies in Gabrielle. Her boss wishes her luck and asks if she saw the email about Iceland. The HR manager extends her sympathy: it's the third appointment this month, right? Everything okay?

Gabrielle wants the gory details. Or she thinks Ellis is covering for something. Ellis can't protest the truth without becoming more embroiled in her lie. She sends a reply to the question about Iceland and a separate thank-you to HR. It'll have to be enough.

*

Over dinner, which Ellis partakes in for the sake of setting a good example, Charlie and Kenzie relate tales of museums and H&M. Trevor's there too, and it's all very jovial. He and Charlie get on annoyingly well. Ellis feels like a cold spot in a sunny room. She dumps her half-full plate by the sink and mumbles an excuse. Her bedroom is stuffy. She tries to read about a mortgage scheme for first-time buyers but the clauses and restrictions make her eyelids droop. Her stomach rumbles and she resigns herself to scrounging for leftovers.

Charlie corners her in the kitchen. Now that Trevor has scooted off home, Mum and Kenzie are in the living room, making labels for the huge batch of coconut ice cooling on the counter. It's destined for another fundraiser organised by one of Mum's friends. There are splatters of red food dye by the sink. Beneath a layer of cling film, the bumpy white top of the confectionery cools. Ellis shudders.

'You all right?'

'Tired. Was up half the night.'

'Bad dreams?'

'Yeah,' Ellis says, thighs briefly tensing at the memory.

'Tell me.'

'Why? You going to try and interpret them? Tell me that dreaming of never-ending staircases means I'm leaving my ambitions unfulfilled or something?'

'Well, not exactly.'

'You've got so American.'

'I know. But I'm not going to apologise for being interested in people's feelings.'

'So bloody American.'

'I reckon I've picked up the good bits. Come on, let's get a drink and take it outside.'

Talking to Charlie is the wrong kind of pleasure. Something that she has to pay attention to. Like when the joy of eating makes Ellis forget about various tender spots and she stuffs her face only to be pulled up short by a crash of pain. It is a reminder to be cautious. Charlie's an old friend who's like family, except he is actually family, so he's off limits. But he does make her feel good.

Ellis can't face more wine, so she fetches the vodka Trevor gave her. They mix it with apple juice that's just on the turn.

'There's a fizz to it,' Ellis says as they settle in the garden.

'It's not terrible.'

'Not completely, but it's a sad kind of cocktail.'

'Jackson says it's not a cocktail unless there are three ingredients, minimum. Accoutrements don't count.'

'She would.'

'It was cute.'

'Cute's not a word I associate with Jackson.'

'She'd hate to think it was. Look, there's something I need to say . . .'

Ellis takes a careful sip and waits.

'I wasn't all that upfront about what was going on before we got here. I didn't mean to lie to your mum or anything – it's just, well, it's always complicated, isn't it? And I still feel like we're dealing in half-truths.'

Ellis nods, gestures for him to go on and tells herself it's a relief that he has nothing to say about her. He tops up his drink and embarks on the story of his wife, a spiky New Yorker with bleached hair, a serious stride and eyes like jackhammers. She also has a father who beat her up on several occasions between the ages of eleven and fourteen when buzzed out of his mind. By the time Charlie met him, he came across as an amiable old hippie who'd dabbled with a few things he shouldn't have over the years.

In their first few months together, she was a picture of confidence. She had a good job and wasn't afraid to move on to an even better one. They ate out, they made each other laugh, they accidentally began a child of their own and decided to keep it. He moved in. They exchanged rings. He got a green card after years of applying. And despite all this, Jackson couldn't stop the hardening that had started in her teenage years and showed no sign of stopping. Her carapace got thicker and tougher until Charlie saw no way in at all.

'Fucking hell. Did you know about her dad?'

'Not for a long time. She said from the start that the relation-ship with her family wasn't conventional, and I spent ages trying to figure it out. Picking at all these little clues. I remember making a comment about what a good grandad he was, and she totally flipped. It all came out then. It took me a while to get it, because he comes across as the gentlest guy. Obviously, me pointing that out really didn't help.'

'God.'

'Later, I went to therapy on my own to see if I could find a way for us to get on track. A lot of therapy. But by then, Jackson was done with it. In some ways, I can't blame her, because they went to family sessions back when her dad first decided to get clean, and the guy just took her dad's side completely. It's gutting. The right therapist, a good one, could help her be a much happier person.'

'It's so sad. Poor Jackson.'

'I know. That's why I've wanted to keep trying. Even a couple of weeks ago I would've tried again, if she'd been up for putting the work in. There's only so much you can do to save a relationship when one half just isn't there.'

'Does Kenzie know?'

'As much as she needs to know, but some things are just her mom's. It's not for me to tell. Not yet, anyway.'

'So you were trying to protect them? That's all?'

He nods and smiles just a touch, revealing a small sliver of white in the darkening garden, and Ellis, God forgive her, is envious of Jackson.

25

The weekend stretches before her. Charlie and Kenzie asked her to head into town with them but Ellis woke headachey and heavy with dread. Her mum's out too. The house is briefly her own, except of course it isn't.

Ellis wants to sit in her dad's study and is discomfited by the way it smells of Charlie. He's pulled the rumpled duvet over the blow-up bed. Toys are bursting from the chest under the window, her mum's sewing machine is packed onto a shelf, Charlie's clothes are half in and half out the suitcase, and the desk is covered with a guddle of books, toiletries and chargers. She's poking through coins and fluff emptied straight from his pocket when the doorbell goes. Ellis hesitates, considers hiding.

Too embarrassed at the thought of being caught, she goes to answer the door. A man with a phablet in a natty leather wallet looking for Mrs Patrick.

'She's not home. She'll probably turn up soon.'

'I'll just get started, if you don't mind?'

'Where did you say you're from?'

'Walkers. Shouldn't take more than ten minutes. We're just hoping to get a feel for the place.'

This is serious. Ellis thought if she ignored the brochures and Lana's niggling, the whole thing might go away. Mum kept saying it wasn't anything to worry about, even when she was off secretly organising a visit from some smarmy agent.

The man *hmm*s his way around the hall and front room with confidence. He takes out a laser pointer and begins measuring the distance between walls and typing the results into his phone. Ellis follows, working up the courage to send him away. Before she manages it, her mum arrives with a jumble of shopping bags.

'Sorry, I'm late. Traffic was crazy. A lorry dropped all these sacks of rice, and it went everywhere. The pigeons are halfway to heaven,' Mum says, pushing her hair back from a sweaty cheek with a shoulder. 'A woman scooted out her front door with three empty containers and filled them right up. The bus was just stuck, watching it all. Have you had a cup of tea yet?'

'You're all right, ta,' he says, giving Mum a dismissive sort of look. Ellis clamps her jaw. Her mum doesn't notice.

'I was planning on giving the place a whiz-round before you got here,' she says. 'You're going to have to use your imagination a little bit. We've got a few extra bodies staying at the moment but it scrubs up nicely.'

'That's fine. I'll just get some pictures and–'

'Oh, you won't be wanting to do that when we're in such a mess. But you'll be able to give me an idea of what we're looking at in the meantime, right?'

He lowers his phone in a pantomime of reluctance and sets off with the pointer. Ellis sits in the rocking chair and listens in as they tour the rest of the house.

'Can I get out to the back garden this way?'

'Yes, yes. Just give the key a bit of a jiggle . . . No, wait. There you are.'

The bags bump onto the table. She's unpacking her shopping. Ellis has her phone out; there's a half written message to Lana. The man's voice intensifies again; she strains to hear.

'. . . wall. Do you remember when it went up?'

'A good ten years ago.'

'And what was there before?'

'A much older wall.'

'In the same spot?'

'I'd have thought so.'

Ellis creeps into the hallway, ear angled to the kitchen.

'Uh-huh, there's a drainage spot right up against it.'

'Is there now.'

'We should have a look and see which house it belongs to. Could be a bit of a boundary issue there. Although, if the neighbours haven't noticed and aren't complaining, there's a good chance that can be the next owner's problem.' His laugh, a simulation of mirth, stops as sharply as it started. 'Apart from that, it's looking just smashing. Obviously, you'll need to have a proper surveyor in, but you're looking at four-seventy, four-eighty easily. It'll need a bit of love first though. New carpets. That stained glass needs replacing. Maybe a vinyl, if you want to keep the aesthetic.'

They're back in the hall. He reminds her to call as soon as she's ready for the next step. Mum sends him on his way with a merry goodbye.

'I thought you weren't going to sell,' Ellis says, chasing her back to the kitchen.

'All I'm doing is finding out my options. And I'm not having another argument about it. You and your sister are driving me up the wall.'

'What's Lana been saying?'

'Not now, Elly. I have a million things to do and I'm meeting Trevor in half an hour.'

She sidesteps Ellis's half-hearted apologies and hurries upstairs. Ellis picks through the mess on the kitchen table. There's butter and milk for the fridge. More sugar and essences for the cupboard. Ellis puts them away, thinking about her dad. He hasn't been part of the house for a long time, despite the armchair in the study, the bathroom wallpaper, the books on the upper landing. Ellis wants him to be there, and he isn't and the house is her mum's. It's up to her to sell or not. That is the truth, no matter how it makes Ellis feel.

26

She arrives at Niall & Ballantyne's while the day is still cool. The street bustles with commuters but it's quiet in reception. The woman asks her to update her forms. Ellis does as she's told. Fills in everything they know already and ticks 'no' to all the medical history questions. There is nothing there that describes her. All her problems are in her mouth, her heart or her head, evidenced by the fact that she's reflexively written Adrian's address at the top of the sheet. Blue ink scratches over it. Her mother's details snake around the corner of the page.

Dr Conor welcomes her with his customary cheer. He has a different assistant, and the room holds an easy note of Earl Grey. Ellis takes her seat and, before tipping her head back, states her case. Continued pain, a headache, sensitivity, a feeling of mild disconnection when she stands or sits. Reluctantly, he agrees that the tooth shouldn't still be hurting after all this time. He nods her into a supine position and, after tapping at the offending molar, says they had better take some X-rays to be sure.

Silently, the assistant adjusts the seat. Ellis is now upright. She is given a vertical strip of plastic-coated metal attached to a strut with a long, insulated cord trailing off the end. It is surprisingly heavy. The metal goes behind her teeth, and she has to hold it in place with a firm bite. The dentist and assistant leave the room. She clamps her jaw, the plastic gouges the thin flesh under her tongue. Hold it, hold it, Dr Conor says from the other side of the door. Her eyes water; the pain digs deeper. He darts back into the room and swings the X-ray machine's arm so that it can capture the other side of Ellis's skull. He tells her to bite again. Ellis bites. There's a well of blood in the hollow below her tongue, surely. Humming fills the room as the dentist clicks, clicks.

It is over. They open the door, all smiles: that wasn't so bad now, was it? She removes the metal and hands it to him; there's a small red smear at the base. She shivers when her teeth appear on his screen. They are horrific, prehistoric. The roots are slanted and the cusps are splattered with white blotches, each a filling dearly paid for. The dentist leans in and obstructs her view.

'Good news. Look . . .' He taps the X-ray with his pen, pointing at the tooth he recently filled. 'I can't see anything going on up there. The composite looks snug. It's exactly as we thought. The nerve has been agitated and keeps being reinflamed. All it takes is a little bad luck, sometimes. Do you use toothpaste for sensitive teeth?'

'Yes. And I've been rubbing it in, like you said.'

'Excellent, excellent. Ibuprofen can help with inflammation. I'm not seeing much evidence of swelling but as long as you don't have any stomach problems, it can't hurt to have them a few times a day for a bit.'

'Are you sure? It's really been bothering me.'

She sees him scroll backwards through her notes. Pages and pages.

He makes a little noise in the back of his throat before replying. 'Let's just carry on keeping an eye on things, all right? You know where we are.' He scoots his chair back, and it's time for Ellis to go. She pays for the X-rays. Her plan covers one set per year and these are extra.

It's good news but she doesn't feel good. She's been so sure that there's something going on. A distraction, a distortion. A reason she's been so off kilter. She was hoping for some sort of quick solution and a clean slate. But at least there's no root canal, no extraction – just painkillers and time.

✳

Ellis walks home after a desultory day trying to clear her inbox. She hopes the house is empty and she'll finally have a chance to look for the deeds. One of Zoe's previous girlfriends had a terrible time with a boundary problem when she was trying to sell her dad's house. He'd relocated to China, leaving her to deal with a nightmare of blurred property lines and an access issue. The neighbours had hated him. They wanted to build a barbecue by the back patio, and opened a dispute that meant Zoe's friend either had to deconstruct a wall, take the neighbours to court, or give up selling the house at all. Ellis can't remember how the saga ended, but she knows at least two sales fell through.

She should let Lana know. Except it took Lana weeks to fill her in on what she found out the morning of Oscar's accident. The official line is that the whole situation is Ellis's own fault, and now, ages after the fact, she's feeling petty.

The front door is unlocked; someone's home. She sticks her head round the kitchen door and finds Kenzie sitting alone at the table.

'Your dad around?'

'Haven't seen him.' Kenzie swipes at her phone.

'I thought he might . . .' Kenzie doesn't look up. 'Get up to much today?'

'Nah. Auntie Lana and the littlies were round. We made edible playdough.'

'Oh,' Ellis says, jealousy sinking in like hot butter.

Kenzie's still looking at her phone. The nail tapping at the toughened screen is lime green and squared-off at the tip.

'I like your nails,' she says.

'Thanks.' Kenzie looks up, eyes bright below heavy lashes.

'You do them yourself?'

'Mostly.'

'How do you get them so perfect?'

'It's just practice.' Her fingertip strokes the screen more slowly.

'I don't think so. Look at mine.' They look. The last of the nude polish Ellis applied before Adrian dumped her has finally flaked off, revealing pale blotches caused by something to do with calcium. Or stress. Her left pinkie is ragged, and the right index has split just enough to snag on her hair.

'I could . . . you know, do them for you? If you want?' Kenzie's eyes are back on her phone. Ellis's fingers curl automatically. She straightens them out. She doesn't want to be touched. She wants to keep sitting with Kenzie. The second one wins. She says yes. Kenzie is up and moving in seconds.

Ellis sits and waits. Her cousin is such a mix of things. She dips in and out of styles and moods and yet still comes across as genuine. Authenticity is more malleable than when Ellis was her age. Kenzie's outfits aren't a statement of allegiance. Yesterday, she looked like a sweet country star, with waved hair and a tight flannel shirt. Today she's all black eyeliner and lace. She cares about the environment, owns multiple sleek silver electronic devices, and is comfortable with her contradictions.

Kenzie's travel bag rattles as she places it on the table.

'First, I'll trim and shape them, and then I'm thinking something dark. Or maybe a warm grey. What do you reckon?'

'You're the expert.' Ellis shifts in her chair and holds out her hands when Kenzie nods for her to. Her cousin's fingers are soft, her grip firm. She gets to work with a tiny pair of scissors.

'Look at all this stuff. You should be charging,' Ellis says.

'Mum says you shouldn't make the thing you love your career. You'll just end up hating it.'

'She does?'

'And you should never stay somewhere you're not happy for more than six months. Makes it harder to go for the next promotion or whatever.'

'Mmm.' Ellis wonders what heights Jackson expects Kenzie to scale. The snipping completed to Kenzie's satisfaction, she pulls out a large metal file.

'You like your new job, right? Do you get cheap holidays and stuff?'

'Sort of. There's a staff discount, but it's tiny. You do get to see all the deals as they come in though. First dibs. Not that I've seen anywhere to jet off to yet.'

'Too many people fly. I wanted Dad to get us a boat over, but he said it was too expensive and that I'd probably end up killing him if we got stuck together for that long.'

'Boats are better?'

'Mostly. Depends on the boat.' She blows on Ellis's fingers; tiny fragments of nail sprinkle over the tabletop. 'Really the best thing is to only travel to the other side of the world if you're planning to stick around for a while. Minimal impact.'

'Are you? Planning to stick around?'

Kenzie pauses, the file poised. 'Did Dad say something?'

'No, I just wondered. I mean, I hope you like it here and everything, but I can't imagine it's all that exciting. I daydreamed about living in America when I was your age. New York, California, LA. Somewhere glamorous.'

'You should've come. Dad would've been stoked to have you.'

'Probably should've. I wanted to stay close to Mum. And then I went to uni and fell in love with an idiot and then found a job and got together with another idiot and there was just never a good time. One of those things.'

'You could always come next year. Now hold still, I'm going to do the base coat.'

They stop speaking as the colour is slicked on in precise, unwavering strokes. It feels good.

Kenzie's attention flicks to her phone. This is her summer holiday. Ellis hopes she isn't hating it too much and feels bad for first of all not wanting them to visit, and now not wanting them to go.

'There. Stay like that for another couple of minutes and don't smudge it.' Kenzie sits back and smiles. She has a beautiful smile.

She doesn't offer it up often, she knows what it's worth. Her tiny bottles clatter back into her bag as Ellis thanks her. Her nails are smooth, grey, matt and strong. They look like they belong to someone else.

∗

The house is quiet but it's still not empty. Ellis looks for Charlie, but he's nowhere to be found. Mum's making iced biscuits. Kenzie is going to help bag them up later. For the moment, she's off messaging friends in Lana's room.

'Fancy giving me a hand?' Mum holds out a piping bag. Ellis joins her. Leaning over the biscuits, her face feels heavy. Mum talks about the charity her friend is raising money for and about the plants they're thinking of picking up for Trevor's waiting room and Lana's trip to the hairdresser. They don't mention the fact that the sisters still aren't speaking. When it comes to Lana or anything else difficult, Mum doesn't ask, and Ellis doesn't tell.

Icing flows from the nozzle like toothpaste from a tube. Ellis's bag is pink; she wishes she had the blue batch. She carefully finishes the biscuit she's doing then pauses, takes a deep breath.

'You know it's not okay Lana acting like I'm some sort of reprobate for what happened with Oscar. I said sorry a million times.'

'You're not still upset about that?'

'I am. A bit.'

'She didn't mean anything by it.'

'Why are you always sticking up for her?'

Mum looks at her over the table, eyebrows crimped. 'I don't know what you mean.'

'Why can't you just agree with me? She's being mean.'

There are only a couple more biscuits to ice. Mum fusses with a packet of rice paper motifs, hands half over to Ellis.

'You know what your sister's like,' she says. It's the most she ever says.

Pressure builds behind Ellis's eyes.

'Thinking about it,' Mum says, 'he should probably go with cacti. That way they won't have to worry about them over the weekend.'

Ellis refuses to sanctify this changing of the subject or to have an opinion on the type of plants Trevor has at his surgery. She carefully pushes the pictures of rainbows and stars into the icing. As the discs dampen, they stick to her fingers. Mum says how handy it is, having her and Kenzie around to help. There's another three fundraisers in the calendar already. Ellis nods, thinking what a waste of money it is and wondering how her mum got swept up in all these fairs and bake sales.

The smell of vanilla drives Ellis back up to her room to sit on the creaking plastic crate at the window. She looks down at her fingertips and the pale pinks, blues and yellows that have seeped into her skin and muddied the clean job Kenzie did on her nails.

27

When Mum and Kenzie head out to deliver the goodies, Ellis moves quickly. She knows where all the important papers are kept. Each of the three deep drawers of the hall bureau are filled with folders. Some are crisp plastic and contain congratulations for a new phone contract and heating bills over the last few years. There is one marbled box file, cardboard softened at the edges, that's been there since Dad died. If she is to find anything relevant, it's likely to be in that.

Ellis takes the whole box to her room. There's nowhere to sit but the bed, where stour falls from the pages onto her sheets. There are birth certificates, bank statements with pathetic amounts of money in them, an old wallet for travellers' cheques with nothing in it and, finally, a mortgage confirmation letter and, under that, the deeds. Ellis flattens out a photocopy of the house, chopped off at the knees. Another page with the top floor. There is the room she sits in. There is the adjoining wall. There is the garden and the boundary line. It doesn't look like it does in real life. The circle marking the drain is on the wrong side. Ellis taps the papers together and gets out her laptop. After a few false starts, she ends up on the Ordnance Survey site looking at the maps of the street. She finds their garden and its boundaries. They match the ones in the deed. Not the reality she can see out the back window.

Just as the agent had speculated, the wall Mum paid for is a problem. In trying to help out the previous neighbours, she's accidentally turned a bit of their garden into hers and taken their drainage along with it. The mistake could cause a hold-up. If the couple who live there now decided to care about a few feet of land. If they could be made to care. This information is priceless, for someone willing to exploit it.

Ellis bookmarks the map and takes pictures of the deeds and the line-drawn house. She wants praise. She wants acknowledgement. Here is a way to get Lana on side. To snarl up plans for a house sale for months or even years. Or complicate real estate listings, at the very least. Ellis could do it. She might do it.

Ellis is expected to break the stalemate between them. This is a golden opportunity. But why should Lana get what she wants? Why should their mum? Why should anyone? How desperate Lana is for them to keep this place, when she has her own home. Even though, one day, she'll have the two-up, two-down belonging to Grant's parents, where his ostentatiously stoic mother gave birth to him on the kitchen floor. It's not enough. Lana always wants more. She always gets more.

There is a sound from downstairs. Ellis holds her breath, listening. Heavy footsteps to the kitchen and the tap is on. It's Charlie. She packs everything away and barks her shin against one of the plastic crates. This fucking house.

She tiptoes down to the hall and opens the bureau, box file clasped guiltily to her chest. She slides it back where it belongs.

Charlie's putting on a wash, his presence filling the kitchen. He has no worries about belonging.

They nod to each other as Ellis switches on the coffee machine. He starts to tell her about the meeting he's just had with the friend of a friend and a website they might work on together.

'Based here?'

'Well, it'd be global eventually.'

Charlie's already starting to lose some of the leanness he arrived with. His calves don't have a sharp edge any more and the tan is fading from his cheeks. Scotland is returning him to an earlier version of himself. Not rewired then, only reupholstered. Ellis passes him a mug. Their fingers don't quite touch; a small thrill flickers in her stomach.

'Charlie, is it really over? You don't think you and Jackson will find a way to work it out?'

'Sometimes there's just no way back. You wouldn't forgive Adrian, would you?'

She shakes her head, not mentioning how much she's wanted to tell Adrian she'd forget everything if they could just go back to how they were.

'Neither of you cheated though,' she says.

'There are other ways you can grind a person down.'

'That's what she did?'

'We both did. I just recognised it first.'

Ellis nods, thinking how unfair it is that people like Jackson and Adrian get all the love they could ask for and don't even recognise it. She clenches her teeth, and the left molar sends a flare of distress.

They're sitting at the table when Ellis gets an email. Adrian has finally replied to her message reminding him that she doesn't care about insurance but she does think she deserves to be compensated. Except he hasn't. His email is a directive. He wants her to sort out getting 'her things' picked up from the flat. Her phone cover creaks but she can't seem to relax her grip. Bastard.

Charlie asks if she's okay, and she shares the highlights.

'And you don't want to?'

'I picked up what's mine already. This'll be the crap he can't be bothered taking to the charity shop. He's trying to fob me off.' Ellis can't bring herself to explain the full extent of her anger. Charlie already sees her as someone who's been cheated on; she can't bear to reveal how little consideration Adrian thinks she deserves.

'I could go with you.'

'No.'

'I wouldn't mind.'

'I appreciate it. I just don't think it's necessarily the right thing for me to do. Why should I sort it out for them? I don't want all the things Sally has rejected.'

'Then just refuse. Let him deal with it.'

'I've tried, but it's not that easy,' Ellis says quickly.

Her mum and cousin are back. Kenzie thumps her way upstairs but Mum is drawn right to them. Ellis doesn't want to tell her what Adrian has said just yet but Charlie fills her in before Ellis can think of a way to stop him.

'Is it a lot of stuff?'

'I don't even know what he's on about,' Ellis says.

'It's just with Charlie and Kenzie here and everything – and we're so happy you're here, sweetheart – there's not a whole lot of space.'

'Ellis doesn't seem to think there's much to come.' Charlie says.

'Still, I don't know where we'll put it,' Mum says, unwinding a silky scarf Trevor gave her.

'Right. Thanks, Mum.' Ellis walks out, ignoring the perfunctory attempt to stop her. The low burble of Charlie and Mum's conversation follows her upstairs. She will not give Adrian what he wants. She deserves more than the things he's decided she can have. She won't reply. Not until she's checked her rights again.

28

It's Becca's birthday, and Ellis has to go. There is a debt to be repaid, and if Ellis tries to find a way out of it, Becca will feel the sting. She's a sociable, big-hearted soul who can't understand why a night out is anything but a tonic, after all.

Ellis washes her hair, uses Kenzie's body scrub bar and pulls a dress from one of the bin bags. It smells of the fabric conditioner she normally buys. Her mum prefers a different brand. The dress is also deeply creased.

The iron lives in the cupboard under the kitchen sink. Charlie's at the table, tablet glowing before him.

'Mind if I?' Ellis says. The dress and a towel hang over her arm. He nods quizzically. 'I can't be bothered getting the board out.'

He shifts his tablet, and she lays the towel on the edge of the table, noticing crumbs and marmalade smears too late.

'Nice dress. You going out?'

'My friend's having a few birthday drinks. Probably won't be a late one, unless she's left her husband home to look after the kid.'

'Girls only, then?'

'Angling for an invite?' She's joking, but he looks eager.

'I wouldn't want to put any pressure on . . .'

'Oh, right. I mean, I don't see why not,' Ellis says, pressing the iron around the dress's small buttons, creating creases where there were none.

'I promise I won't embarrass you in front of your friends.' He grins, and Ellis remembers the once-crooked incisors.

'I'm leaving about half past.'

She dresses quickly. It's good that Charlie is coming. It's smart to give people something new to gossip about when you're in a crisis. Still, she feels conflicted. She half wants to keep him separate, at home, where he's only hers.

He's waiting by the door with his jacket on.

'Come on then,' she says.

They walk to the bus stop at the end of the street. It's a warm night, and Charlie talks about how nice it is to be in Scotland where darkness falls slowly in summer. She interrupts him to check if he's got change for the bus.

'Should do.' He pulls a handful of smash from his pocket and holds it out for Ellis to inspect, as if he's forgotten his own currency. Despite herself, she picks out the right combination of coins and holds them while he funnels the rest away. The heat from his pocket transfers to her palm. It reminds her of long-ago sunny days, when she was entrusted with sweetie money from her dad.

'You look really nice,' Charlie says.

'You too.'

'You don't have to lob a compliment back every time, you know. Sometimes you just gotta take what someone says and accept it.'

'Yeah, yeah. This is us,' she says, nodding at the number 10 about to draw up beside them. She does think he looks nice. The sensible haircut he arrived with is growing out and the crinkling round his eyes is softer now that he's growing paler. He stares out the window, looking for streets with stories attached and pointing out all the ones he remembers. Becca's friends will love him.

Once off the bus, Ellis sets off at a clip.

'What's the birthday girl's name, again?' Charlie says, dodging this way and that to stay abreast as they weave through a crowd of tourists.

'Becca. Just to warn you, she's probably going to be fleeing already. Breastfeeding turned her into a lightweight.'

'I remember those days,' Charlie says. Ellis *hmm*s and walks faster, but is glad to have him by her side when they push their way into the heaving bar.

Becca is at the centre of a bloom of friends and doesn't notice Ellis until she's only a few steps away.

'Ellis,' she yells. 'You're here, you're here.'

'I'm here. Sorry we're late.'

'You're grand. And who's this?'

'Cousin Charlie,' Ellis says firmly. She knows Becca knows who it is and also that she's the right level of tipsy to want to make mischief.

'Happy birthday, Becca. Sorry for gatecrashing. Is that a G&T? Can I get you another?' he says.

'You sound so American! Great, yeah . . . I don't need another one but why not? Line them up.'

Ellis is gestured into a seat a few spaces over. She tries to remember how much she told Becca about Charlie, back when they were younger. She hopes not too much, which is a pointless hope because she's told Becca pretty much everything she's ever meant to keep to herself. Too many drunk, hungover, bored and exuberant conversations have passed between them for secrets to survive.

Charlie returns with drinks and is introduced to the circle. Ellis barely needs to say a thing, and it's a relief. The iced drink shoots pain from her jaw to her eye socket. She sips carefully. Both Charmaine and Zoe come to hug her and say kind things, and it's not as bad as she expected. She says sorry for going silent on them. They forgive her, offer a smattering of advice and, after a short while, move on. She should've called them earlier.

People switch chairs and share stories; Ellis stays still. It isn't the kind of bar Adrian drinks in, but at one point, her eyes automatically search for his sloped shoulders. She wants him to see her having fun. She decides on a cocktail; Charlie insists on paying.

She doesn't know all Becca's friends like she once did. There are mums who've appeared from various baby and toddler meet-ups, all cherry-picked from their particular groups. Some are obviously meeting each other for the first time, and the only thing they inarguably have in common are their children, so conversation keeps coming back to nappy rashes and nurseries. Ellis drinks quietly, smiles. Katherine, one of Becca's university friends, is doing the same, glass gripped tightly. She's drinking wine. It seems the latest – third? fourth? – round of IVF hasn't been successful. Ellis moves to Katherine's side of the table, swaying just a little.

'Did Becca tell you about my break-up?' Ellis says. Katherine nods warily. 'Did you hear he was cheating on me with, like, his secretary? The actual secretary. Can you believe it?'

Relief eases the tension around Katherine's mouth. 'No, what a fucking bastard.'

'I know,' Ellis says.

'You caught him?'

'He told me. Threw me out, basically. I lived there ten years.'

'He can't just throw you out.'

'Turns out, he can.'

'That's ridiculous,' Katherine said, invigorated. Ellis knows the anger has little to do with her predicament (Katherine has always made it clear she's not Ellis's biggest fan) but it is gratifying.

'Yep. Replaced with a younger, prettier version, just like that.'

'No. You're gorgeous. Bloody gorgeous. Don't let him make you feel like that.'

'Should've married him after all, probably. Didn't want the dress and all the fuss. He was fine with it. Thought I was lucky. Probably he just never gave much of a shit in the first place.'

'There's got to be something you can do.' Katherine puts her glass down a little too forcefully, better-off for being reminded that she's not the only one having a shit time. Laughter interrupts them. Charlie's encouraging everyone to share celebrity stories, and one of the women is explaining how she tried to time her shifts to coincide with Hugh Grant's coffee breaks when he was filming near her café. He smiled at her once, then studiously avoided her every day afterwards. Or maybe she imagined it. Another woman lives practically next door to Dylan Moran. Charlie has met Heidi Klum, Leonardo DiCaprio and Helen Mirren. He doesn't mention that these encounters all took place through Jackson. Katherine drifts off to get another drink. Ellis sips and smiles and isn't required to do much more. Soon it's time for bags and coats to be untangled from the backs of chairs.

Becca squeezes her tight and says she's so glad she came. Ellis is glad too. She's drunk in a good way. Contented. Not even bothered that they've missed the last of the normal buses and the night bus is only every forty minutes. Charlie says she has nice friends, and when she points out that most of them are Becca's, he reminds her to take the damn compliment. She bats him on the arm and asks him to look out for a taxi. He tells her to Uber, she says she's not into it, and they argue for a while about steady jobs and benefits. An orange *For Hire* sign approaches, and she swings her arm out for it.

They bundle into the back seat. Charlie jokes with the driver about yellow cabs. Being with him is easy. He has memories of her that no one else does: of when she was young and they both had squint teeth and they played in the muddle of the back garden. He was there on the summer holiday after Dad died, where every fish and chips by the sea was salted by tears. He sat through countless Disney movies and never laughed once during her brief shell-suit phase. There were no childhood secrets to be unearthed. Making herself known to a new person would be exhausting; wouldn't it be easier with someone who knows her?

Ellis zones out, checks her phone. There's an email from Adrian that she triumphantly ignores and a message from Becca.

Good to see you smiling. Careful tho. Thanks for the pressie.
Scotty awake, so drunk. Mmmbad mum!

Ellis sends love and kisses back and puts the phone away. Charlie's still talking to the driver. The street blurs beyond the window.

✳

Mum knocks on Ellis's door and opens it immediately. Ellis is jerked from a murky, enamelled dream.

'There's a man with a van downstairs. He says you're expecting him.'

'Shit.' Her breath is bilious.

'Were you?'

'It must've been Adrian.'

'For goodness' sake, I thought you were going to work it out.'

'I'll be down in a minute.'

Ellis waits until Mum shuts the door (a little too firmly) before dragging on cold, crumpled jeans. The front gate clangs. She heads down the stairs, one hand on the wall.

'Ellis Patrick? Adrian said you'd be waiting.' The man thumps a box onto the paving slabs as punctuation.

'Eh, sorry,' she says automatically. She should've read his email.

'I've got another job at ten.'

'Right.' She squints at the van's darkened interior. Her plan of looking through it all to send back anything she doesn't want withers in the face of this surly man in a too-tight T-shirt. Everything will be staying for now, even though she can already tell there's nothing she wants.

Mum hovers at the front door, frowning at the number of boxes being humped into the garden. The man can't be persuaded to take a cup of tea. Ellis is not offered one. She is in the bad books.

Kenzie nudges her way outside, freshly made-up although still wearing the joggers and T-shirt she sleeps in.

'Intense. It's like the show at the Modern Art Gallery I saw with Dad last week: *Life Unpacked*.'

'In ruins, you mean,' Ellis says.

'This isn't looking too hot, that's for sure.' Kenzie rubs the wilted leaf of a potted palm between thumb and forefinger. Picked up one optimistic Sunday, it obviously hasn't been watered in a while. Adrian is too busy slicing her out of his insurance policies to look after the plants they bought together. There is a solid lump somewhere beneath Ellis's collarbone. An ambergris of grief. It's taking all she has not to throw up on the shrubs.

'That's it, then,' the man says, placing one last bag just inside the gate.

'Did . . . is it paid for?'

'You're sorted,' he says and leaves before Ellis can tell him she really isn't.

They start to move everything indoors. Kenzie shifts boxes with ease, Mum with a face like fizz. There is no space for the side table or the rocking chair or the awkward chest of drawers that surely belonged to Adrian's parents. He's even sent the bike Ellis only rode a handful of times. She's scared of cycling in the city, and nothing Adrian said quelled her fear. The bike lived in the tenement's stairwell. She has no idea where the key for the padlock even lived. It's the sort of thing Adrian remembers.

'This is yours?' Mum says doubtfully. 'Do we have to keep it inside?'

'Wherever.'

'There's hardly room for all the rest of it, let alone a giant great bike.'

'Just leave it in the garden. I'll sort it.'

'What if it rains? I suppose we'll have to put it round the back for now. Help me with these drawers, would you? I'm not

166

sure when Charlie will be back. I mean, if we'd known all this was coming . . .'

Ellis silently takes hold of the wood and prepares to lift. They get no further than the hall. She promises that when Charlie returns, they'll move it to her own room. She'll make space, somehow. Mum squeezes the rocking chair into the living room's only empty corner and pronounces the shoe rack (who sends a shoe rack?) useful enough to live by the front door.

'I was going to keep it all together until I can get to the dump,' Ellis says from halfway up the stairs. Kenzie is sitting on the bottom step, reabsorbed in her phone but thoughtfully waiting to see if she's needed.

'You can't throw away perfectly good things,' Mum says.

'The charity shop, then.'

'What if you change your mind?'

'I thought you were worried about space.'

'It's not like you're going to be here forever.'

'Oh God, what are you actually wanting? It's not like I asked for this. It's not like I planned it. You know what, I don't care. Do whatever you think. I'm going back to bed.'

She shuts the door firmly, far too angry to go back to sleep. She shouldn't have drunk so much last night. Becca's birthday has ruined her chance to throw Adrian's gesture back in his face. The carefree feeling that accompanied her home the night before has been buried by all this useless tat.

There's no space for Adrian's rejects. Her room is ridiculous as it is. The whole house is leaning that way. There are all Lana's leftovers (as if she doesn't have a three-bedroom house near the Jewel to move them to). Toys for the twins took over the study long before Charlie was set up in there. Now he and Kenzie are spreading out all over the place. Then there are the bits and pieces left over from when Dad was alive. The bookshelves and picture frames and armchairs that are falling apart and that Mum walks around pretending she barely sees. It's not fair.

She kicks a box without conviction then bends to open it. Photos. Fucking photos. She tries another and finds a stack of magazines and a pile of bills from before she went paperless. She checks the rest of the boxes. The bowls that Grant didn't fetch from the kitchen are not there. She has filled her mum's house with stuff she doesn't want. And she didn't even get her fucking bowls back.

Ellis thinks of the deeds she's talked to no one about. Her mum's drawers have teeth and the bureau contains bits of paper that could cut a potential house sale out from under her. Ellis should tell her so she can move the wall. She should tell Lana so she can stir up trouble with the neighbours. She should tell someone. She ignores the jumble of possessions all around her, gets into bed and tells no one anything.

29

Ellis arrives home to the sound of her sister's raised voice. Drawn to the disagreement, she walks straight towards the kitchen, pausing at the door.

'Why? Where?' Lana says.

'He's got a share in the little cottage in Inverness.'

'Of course he does. Looks like Trevor's got everything he could possibly want, doesn't it? Will there be other people there?'

'It's only a wee place, two's your lot. And what does it matter, anyway? We're planning some nice walks and dinners, not a party.'

'You're going off on your own with him?'

'Lana, I'm sixty-three years old. I'm not asking your permission to go anywhere.'

'Fine, go and get yourself murdered in the middle of nowhere,' Lana says. Ellis hovers in the doorway, unsure whether to intrude. Oscar and Mia are chewing at jigsaw pieces. Lana's hair is twisted into a tight bun, secured by one of the bands she keeps in her purse, never around her wrist.

'Well, thank you for that vote of confidence. Me and Trevor are going to have a lovely time in the countryside, isn't that right, sweeties? And maybe Granny will bring you back a little something from up north? But first, it's about time we got the garden watered.' She leads the twins away.

Now it's just Ellis and Lana.

'She likes him.'

'Course she does. He wants her to,' Lana says.

Ellis spins the jam jar lid one way and then the other, thinking about the estate agent. Lana starts packing up the plastic cars littering the floor, tossing them into a red crate.

'And what's all this crap?' Lana points out to the hall and the shoe rack by the door.

'Just some stuff. I'm getting rid of it.'

'So you really are moving right on in, then? Making yourself comfortable.'

'It's temporary.'

'Just like every fucking thing that goes wrong with this family. Everyone gets upset and doesn't do a bloody thing about it and then, bang, that's it. Stuck that way forever.'

The cars crash into the crate. She slams it onto the floor.

'That's not fair,' Ellis says.

Lana gives her that look: brows down, white in the eyes, mouth pushed forward. Ellis is twelve again, fifteen, nineteen. Gangly, snaggle-toothed, rejected.

'If you're so mad at everyone, why are you always here?' she says.

'I belong here as much as anyone.'

'Obviously. But you're always raging before you even walk in the door.'

'Least I'm honest about what I want.'

'Even if Mum doesn't sell the house, why would you definitely get it? I'm the eldest.'

'Oscar, Mia . . . *hello*.'

'So you were just going to waltz in? Move in the second Mum dies? Were you planning to buy me out or just take it?'

'You never even wanted to live here.'

'You don't get to decide what I want.'

'And you don't get to tell me whether I can come round, just because you've fucked things up and Mum let you move back in.'

'It's not my fault Adrian's a bastard.'

'They all are. And I'm done paying for other people's mistakes.'

Lana's sitting in her mum's chair, head dipped. Ellis's chest expands. Lana is hurting. She's got a thin shell like everyone else; here's a crack. She reaches out and lays her palm on Lana's shoulder.

'I'm so, so sorry about Oscar. I should've known–'

Her sister jerks away. 'What's wrong with you?' she says, picking at the smear of jam Ellis has somehow left there. 'I heard you the first time. It was an accident. I get it – doesn't mean I have to pretend everything's fine.'

She stands up and stalks out the kitchen. Ellis blinks, eyes stinging. She's thrown herself on her sister's spikes so many times over the years, her blood spots every carpet.

✱

Becca has come to meet Ellis on her lunch break, even though her office is a fifteen-minute walk from TravelOn. Becca does marketing for an arts in the community charity and, thanks to all the extra hours needed during festivals and holidays, she has some flexibility the rest of the time. Most of that flexibility is saved for Scotty now, so her visit gives Ellis a twinge of trepidation.

She is right to be cautious.

Becca barely gets pleasantries out of the way before launching in. 'Remember when you broke up with that idiot Oliver? Remember how bad it was? How upset you were for months and months. And you kept getting back together with him, despite the fact – and I'm sorry for saying this – he was a total arse.'

'I know. He had a real inferiority thing,' Ellis says, looking around the café. They're in the quiet, unpopular place well off the Main Street. No familiar faces in the queue – it's safe for now.

'Yeah, I know, and you saw past it and recognised the good

in him and loved him anyway. That's great and all, but he still acted like an utter div.'

Ellis murmurs an agreement. Peels the wilting lettuce from her sandwich.

'And you were better off without him, way better. Except you didn't seem to think so.'

'It was stupid. I knew he wouldn't change.'

'I'm not having a go at you for that. What I'm saying is that you were heartbroken. Proper gutted. And then you got over it and you started pulling yourself together, and it was great to see. And then you met Adrian, like, immediately.'

'It was a good six months.'

'Since you broke up, maybe, but you'd only just started coming out of it. Emotionally, it might as well have been a day. Things are different now, and I just don't want to see you not giving yourself a chance.'

'Right.'

'Please just be careful, won't you?' Becca is doing her concerned face. Ellis is fed up with being a recipient of the concerned face.

'Careful . . . right.'

'It's not that I've got anything against Charlie, exactly. He's turned out pretty good. It's just a bit complicated, isn't it? You need a fling and some time to yourself, yeah? Not a big old family drama.'

'I hear you,' Ellis says. Becca's warning is fair. She knows all Ellis's weak points. Ellis has not spent much time single. Never happily. Never purposely. Before Oliver it was Max, before Max it was Keith, before Keith it was her disaster of a first boyfriend Frank.

She doesn't tell Sally that she looked Oliver up, weeks ago. He works for the sort of poetry publisher he used to rail against. He still does shows, occasionally. Not with any names she recognises. He never seems to be top of the bill, and for that

Ellis is glad. He would poke fun at her job, and it's exactly what he would expect of her. She wonders if he ever looks at her Facebook page. If Adrian does.

'Anyway, how was the wee man when you got home? And how bad was the hangover?'

'It was killer. Absolutely killer. Worth it though.'

'Totally. And no fall-out at the nursery gates? Did that woman with the ironed hankies and the pink gilet throw a fit for not being invited?'

'Oh, Samantha. No, she's at her in-laws this week. She's not so bad, you know. We've had a playdate since that thing with the hankie. You know what it's like, any port in a storm.'

Ellis blinks, and moves the conversation on to the chat she had with Katherine, and then, when they're almost out of time, drops in a lame joke about Adrian and the furniture. Becca reacts angrily and Ellis finds it irritating rather than gratifying. She says she'd better get back to work. They hurriedly finish up and Becca gives her an extra squeeze before they walk their separate ways.

Ellis doesn't appreciate the idea of an intervention. Especially from someone so ready to change their tune about a woman in a pink gilet. And yet. Ellis knows what Becca's talking about. She's been looking to Charlie to help settle something in her. Charlie knows her. Knows things about her. He has snapshots of her as a teenager, sulking on a beach or laughing as she loses yet another game of Monopoly. He knows her in more lights than one, and she wants to bask in them all. But is that familiarity enough? Does she really want Charlie?

Ellis can't trust what she wants. There's too much advice flying around. She's buried under suggestions and well wishes. Your partner is meant to make you feel happy, excited, supported, understood, intrigued. They're meant to feel like home and also as thrilling as freshly popped champagne. Relationships are also hard work, complicated, and not to be taken for granted.

All couples argue. If they're right for you, even arguments won't feel like arguments. Let it all out. Say what needs to be said. Forgive. Know when to walk away. Talk. Give it a rest. Bare your soul. Don't get above yourself. You're worth more.

Adrian has shown her what she's worth. He suggested she drove him to it, that's how awful she was to be with. The embers of guilt are ready to flare with the slightest rush of oxygen. She knows she isn't perfect. Is far from perfect. That she has daddy issues. Ellis is hard-pressed to think of a friend who doesn't. Her life is littered with late-night confessions about fathers who hit or criticised or cheated. Or died before you had a chance to work out who you are.

Ellis knows how to talk about that moment of abandonment with a raised eyebrow and an ironic laugh. Her knowledge that the issue exists doesn't do anything to change the way she hangs on to relationships, even when they're dissolving. Even when the acid is sluicing in, stripping her down. She knows she can't let go because she hates to be left behind. Validation is the only thing that matters, even when the need for it makes her pathetic. It's her dad's fault. It's her own fault. No matter how many times she's opened up to Becca or Zoe or Charmaine or all the other women who've drifted in and out of her life, the relief delivered by their wine-parched tongues has been short-lived.

Her computer takes a moment to burr back to life. She has three emails from Naila. From the bottom up:

The restaurant sheet on the spring breaks Excel has an issue, it's meant to go to web team today do you mind having a peek?

You're on lunch. I think it will be ok.

I fixed it, hope you're good :)

Shit. Ellis opens the file and scans, heart tripping. She resents the idea she made a mistake. She suspects she made a mistake. She did. She sees it and she sees where it's been sorted out. She sends Naila a thank-you email and looks up to see her read it. Naila turns in her seat a fraction and smiles. She won't tell anyone.

Concentrate. Just three hours until home time.

Naila corners her by the printer to check she's all right.

'Just a headache. Thanks for catching the wonky column in restaurants. I don't normally miss stuff like that.'

'It happens. You're awful pale. I've got fizzy vitamins in my desk if you'd like one?'

'No, thanks.'

'I'm sure your sister wouldn't want you to neglect yourself.'

'I don't think she gives a shit,' Ellis says with a touch of venom.

Naila blinks. 'I know it can feel that way. But she'll want the best for you, even if she's having a hard time.'

Naila thinks Lana's husband has left her and she's practically suicidal and that Ellis should be protecting her above all else. Ellis is failing to hold the threads together.

'You're right, you're right. It's just hard. She's so angry.'

'Some people are like that,' Naila says, and she looks sadder than Ellis has ever seen her. The impulse to reach out and hug Naila takes her by surprise. The printer begins to whirr and Fabian is on his way over.

'Thanks, Naila, I really appreciate it,' Ellis says.

Naila smiles with pleasure.

Ellis keeps the spreadsheets open and visible on her computer as she runs through her social media cycle, which now includes Lana and Charlie. Facebook is throwing up ad after ad for tooth whitening and invisible braces. She's invited this torture on herself, but can't stop searching for stories of dentists who miss glaring problems and the various catastrophes that can be caused by undetected dental issues.

There is something wrong with that tooth. She knows it. It could be anything. She might need an extraction, the first since her wisdom teeth came out in her twenties.

A red notification pops onto her screen. Naila has sent her a friend request. Ellis clicks on the link without thinking.

Naila's profile picture is a selfie. The header image is a sunset with *You're a small speck, the world has space for you* in an ugly cursive font across the skyline. Ellis closes the app. She would rather die than post an inspirational quote.

Naila is being kind because she's a nice person and wants to help. She believes Lana is in crisis and Ellis's mess is only fallout. Being so upset for the sake of her sister is noble. Being so unhappy over her own betrayal isn't. Naila wants to be her friend and she has no idea who she's being so nice to.

30

Ellis heads to a bar straight from work. Before leaving, she shuts herself in a cubicle and slaps on some mascara and lipstick while sitting on the toilet. She won't go home to Charlie and Kenzie and her mum.

She chooses a place she's walked past many times and never been in. A parmesan fries and local brewery kind of bar. She orders a gin and tonic and takes a seat near the window. This is an experiment. Years ago, a guy she worked with told her women had no idea how hard it is for men. If she wants a guy to go home with her for a night, all she has to do is turn up.

Ellis sips her drink and tries not to take out her phone. The people around her must be looking at her, noticing that no one is coming to meet her. Pathetic, they're thinking. Tragic.

She drinks slowly. The ache below her cheekbone eases. Her stomach growls. She doesn't want to order fries and eat them alone. She drinks and stares out the window as sweat rhythmically rises and cools on her temples.

A young man approaches. She assumes he wants to know if he can take the spare chair beside her for his table. Instead he asks how her night is going.

'Fine.'

'Good, good. That's great.' He can't quite focus; his lips are moving without words. Ellis wants him to go away. He starts to tell her about his ex-girlfriend and leans closer and closer as he does. The girl lied and cheated and laughed at him when he confronted her. How could she even do that? Ellis can't tell if he's looking for a conquest or someone to salve his freshly skinned ego. His phone begins to ring. Ellis points it out to him, he stares at the screen for several seconds then walks away to answer it. She's glad when he doesn't come back.

The night progresses. People have arrived and left in the time she's been sitting there, diligently drinking. The woman behind the bar has been replaced by a younger guy. Ellis weaves her way to him and orders a double. Someone turns to smile at her as she passes. His right incisor is grey – a wasp sting of disgust pushes her back to her window seat.

The man who sits down next to her asks if she's having a good night and what she's drinking. He's the right age; his teeth look fine.

'I always thought gin was rank, could never work out what it was about it that my mum and aunties liked so much,' he says. 'Took me way too long to work out two things. One, gin is fine; it's the tonic that's minging. Two, tonic was all my mum was ever giving me. She poured it in my wee glass with its World Cup logo, tee-heeing away. I thought they were giggling about how naughty we were being. Laughing at my expense though, weren't they? I still buy her gin every Christmas, mind.'

'It'd be pretty depressing if she'd been giving you actual gin, to be fair. I like tonic. It tastes like I think it's supposed to. Medicinal.'

'So you take the drink they call Mother's Ruin and make yourself feel better about it by adding tonic? Fair enough. It's looking good on you, after all.'

Ellis tips her glass towards him. He lifts his, and they clink. They swallow. Ellis considers leaving. He asks if she's waiting for someone and she says her friend stood her up. Babysitter troubles.

'Lucky for me,' he says. 'I'm just here with a few mates.' He waves vaguely behind him. Ellis sees a couple of guys looking over. They seem normal. Men in their late thirties and early forties wearing T-shirts. One has a sad quiff, so thin it can barely support itself. It should've been shaved off months, years, ago. There's no one in his life to tell him to.

'They're missing you,' she says.

'They'll manage. Will I get us another?'

He does. They chat, fall silent, then chat a little more. She gets them another round. The bar's noisy now, and they have to lean in to each other and yell. He works in a bank; it's fine as jobs go. He's out with everyone because they've been on a training day and there was money left over for a couple of pints. He's not watched anything good on the telly for ages. He wants to know what she likes to do, and Ellis can't think of anything apart from drinking. He laughs; their glasses clink again. She says it's getting late, to see what happens. He asks for her number, and she recites it. Moments later, her phone begins to ring.

'That's you got mine now,' he says, grinning. It's a test. She hadn't even thought about giving him a fake number.

'Thanks,' she says.

'I want to ask you back to mine, but it feels a bit forward.'

'So you don't want to ask me?'

'Nah, I do.'

'That was you asking me, then?'

'Suppose it was. Fancy a drink without all the background noise?'

'Suppose I do.'

He downs the last inch of his pint and asks for two minutes while he makes sure he doesn't owe the kitty anything. She makes a show of organising herself, covertly watching him say goodbye to his friends. One claps him on the back, another takes the twenty he's holding out. Ellis checks her phone battery (fifty-two per cent, enough) and that the taxi number is still top of her pinned contacts. The numbers hop and skip around the screen. She needs a glass of water. He's walking back towards her. She's going to see this through.

*

His flat is the only sensible option. Her mum's house is beyond ridiculous. Besides, if anyone's getting an escape route, Ellis wants it to be her.

The journey to his place is patchy. She's laughing and then asking an earnest question about the last time he was in a cinema, fascinated by the sensation of her heels hitting the ground. If she thinks about it too hard, she veers to the side. He nudges her back onto the pavement good-naturedly. She is wasted.

He lives in a perfectly normal new-build flat somewhere in the depths of Newhaven. There's a dark kitchen, a grimy bathroom, a cramped living room and a bedroom door he doesn't open right away. They settle on the sofa, and he magics up a bottle of vodka.

'Cheeky nightcap?'

'Go on, then.'

He fetches glasses. He's been gone ten seconds, and she can't remember what he looks like. There he is. He's fine. Two tumblers and a bottle of ginger ale in his hands. Looks aren't important – this is an experiment. She is bold, she is triumphant, she is pleased with herself – even as the walls sweep in and out like the skin of a wind-battered tent.

The sofa smells of summer sweat. The ginger ale is flat. Conversation falters, and as she paddles about for something to say, he lunges for her. Or maybe he approaches slowly and carefully, and she only notices in the last second. Either way, his face is a surprise. She meets it with feigned enthusiasm.

There is an earnest moment when he pulls back and asks if she really wants to do this. If she isn't maybe just a little too drunk, actually. A distant spark tells her that yes, she's far too drunk, but she douses it by reaching for and downing the last of her vodka. He smiles.

Her top comes off, then his does. He's more tanned than Adrian. The hair on his chest follows a different pattern, and his upper arms feel smoother. She's still dry as a bone as they grapple their way to the bedroom. She mumbles something about the booze dehydrating her to make them both feel better. It's true. Her mouth clicks when she opens it, and her skin is parched, so she's relieved when he pulls a bottle of bubblegum-scented lube from a drawer. He applies it enthusiastically and then it's happening – she's fucking someone else.

There are a few flickers of pleasure, but mostly she feels the weight of him and the uncomfortable squeak of under-lubricated condom against flesh. She's on top. It's making her nauseous. They swap. The angle isn't right but it's working for him. She grips the edge of the mattress. He sweats and shudders to a stop. She's suffocating. He rolls off to deal with the condom. She can see its heft but still worries whether he's satisfied. Cares more now than she did while they were at it. He looks unbearably sad. She rubs her leg against his, and when he turns towards her, says she's going to pee.

The toilet stinks. She tenses her throat once, twice. Swallows. It's no good. She's going to throw up. The liquid is tinged with green and splashes hot against the porcelain. Wave after wave. She vomits until black dandelion seeds float across her vision. Finally, she can rock back on her heels and wait for her heart to slow. She stands, wobbles, sits for a piss. Cold water on her face, a fingerful of toothpaste swished around her mouth.

He's propped up in bed, wearing a different T-shirt and a concerned smile. 'You all right? I wasn't that bad, was I?'

Ellis is impressed by his resilience. She smiles. 'Sorry, should've had dinner.'

'I suppose neither of us was planning a wild one. Not regretting it though. I got you some water and Alka-Seltzer, if you can stomach it.'

She flounders, thinks of getting home, and sits gingerly on the edge of the bed. He shifts down and asks if he should put the light out. She says yes, drinks the fizzy water in the dark and listens to his breathing as it deepens.

★

He's out of bed before she is. Ellis can hear him rattling dishes. She creeps to the bathroom. Her face is the wrong colour, and she can still taste bile at the back of her throat. She is toxic. This was meant to make her feel better. Or at least in control. She can't remember his name. He'll have told her at some point. She's seen his cock, she must know his name. He's making toast. It's time to get home.

'There you are. Fancy a slice?'

'Better not, I should get going.'

'Fair enough. Not feeling too clever myself.'

He crunches away as she gathers her coat and shoes then walks her out. They mumble a few words, his goodbye hug is brief, and she's relieved and hurt by how easily he lets her go. He waves once and shuts the door behind her. Ellis pauses on the stairs for a few deep breaths.

She doesn't recognise the street and has to use her phone to find the nearest bus stop. Thirteen per cent battery left. Lucky. The sun is out. Ellis feels sticky. The bus is busy, when it comes.

She arrives home gasping for a cold drink. Charlie and Mum are sitting at the kitchen table with coffee mugs, surely waiting for her.

'You're home,' Mum says cheerfully. 'Good night?'

'It was fine. Just out with Charmaine.' She walks to the sink and fills a glass.

'That's nice.'

Charlie says nothing. Ellis can't look at him. This is why she did it, she had to do it – and she can't face it.

'You're looking a bit peely-wally.'

Ellis says nothing, just locks herself in the bathroom where she pukes the water back up. It's still cool, not having been inside her long enough to reach body temperature. She showers, lathering herself in her own innocuous shower gel. When she emerges, there's a cup of peppermint tea waiting for her on the banister. Charlie. She takes it to her room and tries to feel defiant.

31

Work is work is work. The office smells of day-old tights and suit jackets freshened with aftershave. Her computer takes a full minute, longer, to boot. Her chair still bears the imprint of someone else's arse. She's not substantial enough to even leave an impression on her own seat cushion.

It's been half a week, and Ellis has heard nothing from the experiment. His number is still in her recent calls. A number that will remain nameless, unless he rings and reminds her what he's called. She's glad he hasn't rung. She doesn't want to deal with him. She might have liked it if he'd wanted to deal with her, but now isn't the time. He is her first and only one-night stand, and also a means to an end. She and Charlie haven't mentioned her night on the town once, yet it is palpable. The line she's drawn is messy, and every time she's tempted to try and rub it out, she reminds herself that Charlie can't love her.

The painstaking proofing of a romantic weekends in Portugal brochure is interrupted by another birthday. Greig, one of the programmers, is turning thirty. Ellis signed the card when Naila left it on her desk and remembered to bung a couple of pounds into the envelope. Jean has baked a chocolate cake heavy with plums and hazelnuts. Someone else brought cookies. Greig looks delighted.

TravelOn staff are clumped around the central banks of desks. Naila, Jean and Alison are standing by Ellis. Naila's scraping the last pieces of icing from her plate, Jean's basking in compliments on her baking, and Alison's showing pictures of her grand-daughter. Ellis eats, although she'd rather not. She's thinking of Charlie, she's looking at Greig, and murmuring answers to

Naila's questions about the weekend. Nothing will ever change. The office will celebrate birthday after birthday. Ellis will watch. They'll eat the baking and another occasion will slide past. She'll be worn down to nothing. There's no escape from sweeties. TravelOn runs on biscuits and cake. The house is her mum's fudge and the chocolate Kenzie keeps buying great slabs of.

All this sugar, and Ellis is sushi. That's who she is to them: someone they wouldn't choose for lunch. Even if she were part of a Boots meal deal. She doesn't blame them. They're talking about the office plant (dying), the parking (dire), Alison's grand-daughter (teething) and then, to Ellis's horror, the conversation moves on to teeth in the more general sense. Naila asks if she's still having bother. Ellis shakes her head awkwardly, so Alison picks up the baton.

'Did you know you get all your dental treatment free when you're pregnant? The whole time we were trying – and it took quite a bit of trying, let me tell you – I made sure I didn't go. So I finally fall pregnant with Sadie and take myself along to the dentist, and he's just appalled. Appalled. And I can tell he doesn't want to do half the stuff, made me wait until the second trimester for the root canal, but I had the certificate so he had to book me in. It was the same when our Jason came along – got it all done for a song.'

'What a good idea,' Naila says.

'Now I tell everyone, if you're planning on weans, be sure to get yourself booked in sharpish. They won't do cosmetic stuff, but the rest's fair game.'

'If I ever manage to find someone and get as far as talking about children, I'll remember that. Not that it's looking likely,' Naila says.

'Nonsense,' Alison says. 'What about the birthday boy? He's got a nice set of lugs on him.'

'He met someone on Tinder. They've got a second date at the weekend,' Naila says.

'Well, then, you need to swoop in Monday with a bit of lippy and ask how it went.'

'He'd not be interested.'

'He'd be a fool, then. Isn't that right, Ellis?'

'Right.' Greig and Naila would be a perfectly nice match. Perfectly nice.

'And how's your young man?' Alison says.

'What?'

'Your Adrian. How's he coping with the family troubles?'

'He's fine,' Ellis says, mouth teeming with bacteria. 'I'm just going to . . . this is lovely by the way.' She holds up the plate as she backs away. It's too much. If she stays, she'll say something vile about Adrian, about Lana, about poor Greig, about the way Alison thinks everyone should do what she says, about the way Naila swallows every laugh halfway through, as if there's something wrong with being happy.

Ellis sits down as her colleagues continue to mill and chat. She uses her work phone to call Niall & Ballantyne, hoping Gabrielle will assume it's a work call. She asks to see a different dentist.

'We like to keep continuity,' the receptionist says, words like snipped mint.

'I know. Dr Niall's my dentist, so if he's going to be back soon–'

'Not until the winter.'

'That long? Then someone else, please.'

'Would you like to report a problem or a complaint regarding Dr Conor?'

'No, I'd just really like a second opinion.' Ellis's face flames, but her voice stays steady. This appointment will cost her almost thirty pounds. She spent ninety-five on the initial filling, more on the X-rays: she won't justify herself any more. The woman relents. Ellis makes an appointment. She looks across the room. Gabrielle is towering over Greig with a great big birthday smile.

★

She waits until the end of the day. The door to the HR manager's office is open. Ellis knocks quietly. Gabrielle looks up from her computer and nods.

'Ellis, how are you? I've been meaning to chat to you.' She gestures for her to come in. Ellis sits. 'Informally, that is. I'm just so happy to hear things are going better for your sister.'

'I . . . yes. But, what do you mean?'

'My cousin Maria was showing me pictures from a barbecue on Facebook – her little girl was wearing the cutest pinafore with ducks on it – and I realised it was at your sister's house. Can you believe that Maria's husband works with Grant? Isn't Edinburgh just like a little village? Anyway, I wanted to let you know, in confidence of course, just how pleased I am to hear it.' Gabrielle's face is open, expectant. 'I always think it's better just to get all these little crossovers out there in the open. It's silly to pretend we're not all connected in one way or another, right?'

Fuck, fuck, fuck. She had a barbecue. A summer afternoon Lana will have filled with food and drink and ways to impress her guests. Family not invited. Ellis's ears fill with static. Gabrielle knows she's lying. She must. Ellis meets her eyes. No, she's fishing.

'They've been trying to work it out,' Ellis manages. 'For the kids.'

'So glad to hear it. When there are children involved, well . . .' She gives her shoulders a shimmy. 'Maria said it was a bit strained but they look like an adorable family. Your sister must be very strong.'

'She is.'

'But anyway, you wanted to see me?'

Ellis bites back a quick spill of rage and tells her she has to go back to the dentist. Gabrielle is surprised. Ellis says she'll only be a little bit late and she'll stay on after work to make up the hours.

'If you must. You know, I can't help thinking there's something wrong with a system that pays people for finding problems. What's to stop dentists making things up to charge more the next time?' Her laugh is a pinged wine glass.

Ellis wishes her mouth wasn't a crime scene's worth of evidence. There's no point wishing: the Patricks have weak teeth.

Gabrielle tells her to have a good evening and be sure to pass on her compliments for those adorable twins. Ellis nods and nods and backs out of the room.

If Lana finds out what she's said about Grant, she'll kill her.

32

It is ridiculous. There is nothing to gain from seeing her replacement walk from the building and make her way to the bus. Yet still. Ellis is there, sitting in the hotel across the road from Adrian's work, watching Sally leave. It feels better to know she could do something if she was desperate enough. Sitting doing nothing is a sign that she's not desperate. She's got some control.

Sally leaves the building. She's not smiling. She doesn't look angry either. She walks past the bus stop, fawn handbag swinging, tote bag bulging. Full of Tupperware, no doubt. Sally makes healthy lunches to balance out her pastries. She's organised, wholesome, scheming. Ellis stays until Sally is long gone, then leaves her half-drunk coffee on the table.

★

Kenzie is knocking on her door, wanting to know if she can borrow Ellis's bike the next day.

'Dad's moaning about a sore tooth he's got, and I want to meet some friends in town.'

'Friends? From here?'

'Yeah.'

'Where did they come from?'

'Uh, the internet.'

'You're off to hang out with people from the internet? Who are they?'

'You sound like Dad.' Kenzie rolls her eyes a little. 'I met them on Twitter, and we've been chatting about climate stuff for weeks. They're cool.'

'What age are they?'

'I don't know. About the same as me. Chill, I'm not being catfished.'

'Your dad doesn't mind?'

'What's he got to mind about? He's the one who dragged me over here and told me to have fun.'

Kenzie has her phone out now, using the camera function to check the way her fringe swoops to one side.

'You didn't want to come visit?'

'It's not that I didn't, but not exactly like I did either.'

Ellis chews at her lip. 'The bike's yours if you want it. God knows I'm not using it. It probably needs oiled or tightened or whatever you do to bikes.'

Kenzie laughs, thanks her and lollops off to shut herself in Lana's room. She is so fierce and so fragile in the next moment. Like a daddy-long-legs that will break into pieces with an overenthusiastic swipe or a tiny bird who might die of fright while a clumsy human tries to offer comfort. How does Charlie stand it?

Ellis considers herself at the same age and suspects she was mainly just the fragile half. Her rebellious years were an embarrassingly tame period in her early twenties, when she ventured far enough out from her shell to pass her heart around to anyone who would take it. Then, once bruised by careless handling, she shut it back up inside herself and settled.

Kenzie said Charlie has a toothache, and Ellis feels cheated by that too. What's the point in him spending all that money on veneers and crowns if he still gets toothache like everyone else? Wasn't the whole thing an investment in invulnerability?

She sits in the dark with her laptop balanced against her thighs. She wants to know how much Charlie might've spent on teeth that still give him pain.

A reality star gurns in a dentist's surgery, baring the stumpy pegs inserted into her jawbone, ready for the false teeth to be attached. She's wearing a tight green dress cut low at the front as she proudly shows off her ravaged mouth.

Ellis's daydreams, already fractured, begin to crumble. Even all the money in the world couldn't fix it. The solution to her problems isn't to hide a pegged smile within her own. Charlie's beautiful crowns cover his own teeth, which have been reduced to the same monstrous points.

A couple of hundred years ago, people filled the gaps in their smile with animal teeth, filed down to resemble their own and attached with metal plates. All that careful carving was barely worth it, because with the majority of the enamel removed in the reshaping, the teeth would quickly rot. They might not even last a year. Human teeth lasted so much longer, fitted better, made it easier to chew and curse and suck. So dentistry turned to corpses. Surely the convenience was worth wearing a dead man's smile for. Who cares if the ghost of the tooth's owner lived in your mouth, tainting everything that passes over your lips?

How lucky Charlie is to have pretend teeth that no graves were robbed for. Although who knows what damage producing the porcelain and the procedure itself does to the environment? What we're willing to sacrifice for vanity.

What would it be like to kiss someone with pointed stumps under their pretty porcelain? She's not sure she'd want to.

✱

Lana's smiling, the twins laughing. Ellis hits the button, and the picture changes. Lana and Grant now, looking into each other's eyes. A photo of their immaculate back garden. A close-up of Lana's hand holding Mia's. Or maybe Oscar's. She shuffles on, looking for the barbecue, while she picks at a plate of over-crystallised fudge her mum judged unworthy for the craft fair it was meant to go to. Ellis's mouth is flooded with a bitter sweetness as she clicks.

Her sister's voice makes her jump. It takes her a second to realise that Lana is in the house as well as on the screen in front of her. Ellis stabs at the mousepad to close the tab and quickly folds the laptop shut.

'We're on the waiting list but they're not promising anything. Still, three mornings a week will make a big difference. And, of course, you'll still be fine to have them every Wednesday, right?' Lana says, barely pausing when she sees the kitchen isn't empty.

'Right, right,' her mum says in that distracted way she has.

'Because if you don't think you'll be able to, I'd rather you told me now.'

'You know I love having them.'

'It's the scheduling I'm trying to work out, not how much you like spending time with them.'

'But you know I do.'

'So you're planning on being nearby for the year then, yeah?'

'Whatever suits you best.'

Ellis's phone rings. She takes it to the hall to answer, not wanting an audience.

The voice on the other end is recorded. A scam. She hangs up, looking at her reflection in the hall mirror and remembering all the time she used to spend examining it and pulling faces during phone calls with Becca. How alien it seems, being tied to a house phone. She returns to the kitchen.

Lana has the laptop open in front of her. The sight snags Ellis into stillness. Mum is sitting on the other side of the table. Lana's cheeks are tight with contempt. She's worked it out. She's worked something out.

'Creeping on Facebook now, are we?' Lana says.

'I was just looking.' Her voice is wrong.

'God, your face. She's a stupid bitch, and Adrian's a fucking idiot – stop wasting your time.'

Ellis exhales slowly through her nose. When she clicked away from Lana's page, she landed on Sally's. Thank God. But Lana's tapping on Ellis's keyboard like it's her own. Typing words into the search bar, which will autofill to all sorts of things Ellis doesn't want her to see.

'Can I have that?' she says.

'Anyway . . . Mum, look at this, two streets over, rented out for nine hundred a month.'

'I wonder how much of that is going on repairs and fees and tax.'

'Give me it.' Ellis steps closer.

'I'll just be a second, fucking hell.'

Ellis leans over the table and grabs the laptop.

Lana snaps straight. 'What the fuck?'

'You should've asked.'

'It was just sitting there. What the fuck is wrong with you?'

'Girls,' Mum says.

Ellis forces herself to take the seat next to her mum and places the computer in front of her, one palm on the cover. There is the tiniest smear of pink on her sister's cheeks.

Now it's Lana's phone that's buzzing. She ignores it for a full thirty seconds, glaring across the table. Finally, she pulls it out, checks the number, then walks out the kitchen. The front door slams a few seconds later.

Ellis rubs her eyes.

'Don't worry, she's just upset,' her mum says.

'She's not the only one.'

'It's just a laptop,' her mum tries. 'No use crying over spilt milk.'

Ellis picks up the computer and leaves her alone at the table. Why can't her mum take her side? Just once.

Ellis jangles. Her face feels wrong. The left side is throbbing. Lana doesn't know. She was only looking at house prices. But it was so close. Barbecue pictures are one thing, but the thought of her sister popping into her emails shoots liquid fear through her centre. What if Lana read the jokes she and Charmaine shared about women with babies? The message Ellis sent to Becca when her mum had suggested a girly holiday with her daughters? The way she and Adrian used to refer to Lana as Margot when she was being strident? What if she found the draft to the solicitor, asking how much it would cost to investigate a border dispute between neighbours? Enough fuel for years. Enough to obliterate the original violation. No one should get a glimpse of what other people really think of them. Especially not someone like Lana, who already sees offence everywhere.

33

Ellis feels the burn of acid reflux. Too little sleep, too many coffees and glasses of wine. She is in Tesco looking for something soothing to eat and a packet of Rennies. She scans the aisles, wary of spotting someone who knows her. She's not in the mood for a tilted head or, God forbid, a hug.

There's a discount on bumper packs of American pancakes. They are his guilty treat. She passes them by. Her thoughts curdle by the yoghurt aisle. She chooses without thinking and calls Becca on the way out.

'You busy?'

'The wee man just got himself comfy with some *Hey Duggee*, so I'm all yours.'

'I just wanted to buy Adrian pancakes.'

'Screw him and his pancakes.'

'I know.'

'Don't beat yourself up. You were together a long time and you were so good about fitting round his stuff, it's going to take a while to shake it off.'

'I didn't fit round his stuff. We fitted round each other.'

'Hmm, you did more of the fitting though,' Becca says. Ellis can hear a knife thwacking a chopping board. It's slow going. Something hardy. Sweet potatoes, probably.

'A little, maybe.'

'You bought a fleece two months after you got together.'

'He wanted to go walking and I didn't have anything.'

'I'm not having a go. Just saying you were pretty accommodating.'

'Not any more than normal. I never had a personality transplant.

Not like Charmaine and Roddy.' Ellis stops at the end of the street, her back to the wall. It's easier to concentrate standing still.

'God, that was a nightmare. But she was just a kid then.'

'That's no excuse for buying bongos and flowery harem pants.'

'He wasn't even fit. But yeah, okay, I'm not saying you full-on abandoned yourself, and thank God you didn't start droning on about chakras or whatever, I couldn't have taken it. All I mean is you've made space for him and it'll take a while to get it back. Do things for yourself.'

'I do the things I want all the time.'

'Real things? Or little things like making sure you get the teabags you want?' There's humour in Becca's voice. Tea's been a running joke since they had a screaming match over which brand to buy on a package holiday to Crete.

'Not drinking pish is important.'

They laugh. Ellis remembers to ask questions about Becca's day and Scotty, makes her excuses and carries on walking.

You can't help but be moulded by the people you spend time with. She was with Adrian for more than a decade. Of course she accommodated. Of course new bits sneaked in – things that weren't there before. That soft bobbing of the chin Adrian got from his grandma that she catches herself doing. The way she says 'oh no', born from the time he dropped a burning wok and exclaimed in an uncharacteristically high-pitched way. The things she didn't bother thinking twice about because they'd decided on an answer together, at some point. But maybe it was more.

Adrian wears jumpers from M&S, has an unassuming hair-cut and says 'well, now' if one of his friends says something he disagrees with, and still he seems to get everything he wants. He's a quiet guy. And yet. Without raising his voice, he cordoned their life together. If she talked too much, he grew silent. If she enthused about a long-distance trip, he said that was all right for some people. If she mentioned her dad or anything else that hurt, he'd look at her until the words dried up. Then he'd ask why she'd gone quiet, was there something else?, and would refuse to hug her if she got teary. He knows what he wants life to look like. Ellis slotted in. She'd been happy to. And what about Sally? Does she do the same?

*

Mum makes sure it's Trevor Charlie sees. How can he say no, when he's staying in her house? When they're both so happy to help? When Charlie doesn't have a dentist of his own already? He's in and out by the end of the week.

'It was a breeze. I didn't even need a jag. Two minutes with the drill and done.'

'God's sake, Dad. It's not like you won the lottery,' Kenzie calls out from the corner of the garden, where she's helping with the weeding.

'Feels like I did, pumpkin.'

'I told you he was an excellent dentist,' Mum says.

'I believed you before but I one hundred per cent believe you now.'

He hugs Kenzie exuberantly as he talks, trying to show her his teeth. She wriggles away.

'I'm going to end up with issues.'

'Never. You're a well rounded and robust young woman.'

'Are you calling me fat?'

'No twisting it around on me, there. You're just perfect. Right, Ellis? Auntie M?'

They hurry to agree. Kenzie rolls her eyes. Ellis is starting to see that the teenager's confidence is a crust full of potential fault lines. Her constant emotional shifts force cracks, and with each comes the chance that the lava beneath will bubble up and scar the surface.

'Fine,' Kenzie says.

'Love you too, sweetie.'

'Oh, and Auntie M? Trevor wanted me to tell you they've had lots of compliments on the cacti.'

They're all so bloody pleased with themselves. If Lana was here, she'd deflate that smugness. Everyone would be reminded of their limitations. Ellis wants to ask if Trevor fixed his fake tooth free of charge but keeps quiet. It'd backfire, and everyone would start telling her she should see him too. Ellis can't bear the thought of Trevor's gloved hands near her mouth. The same hands that touch her mum. Repulsive.

'Perfect timing,' Ellis says. 'Another couple of weeks, and you'd have had a big old American dental bill.'

'True, true.'

'I guess not everything's better over there.'

'Lots of things aren't,' Charlie says.

'You'd never have thought so, the way you talked about it,' Ellis says.

'You'd hardly want me whinging and whining all the time. It wasn't all easy though, especially the early days. But who sends home pictures of the ramen you're eating nine days out of ten when you can snap a hotdog stand instead? I was hardly going to tell you how sick I was of boiling water in a saucepan because a kettle cost a bomb. I knew how lucky I was to have the money Mum left me and . . . I wanted everyone to think I did the right thing, not that I was lonely as hell.'

'I didn't know you were lonely,' Ellis says, thinking of all the invitations he extended and all the times she thought she might visit and didn't. She was busy or scared or with someone who wouldn't want to travel. And she hadn't forgiven Charlie for leaving in the first place.

'Well, I was. I can't stomach instant noodles any more, but I got this wee monster out of it.'

He hugs Kenzie again.

Feeling unexpectedly overwhelmed, Ellis makes her excuses and leaves them by the wall Mum helped pay for. The one she'd not registered as a potential problem and that Ellis should probably tell her about.

Ellis heads for the living room and switches on the TV for the distraction of noise. Kenzie slouches in a few minutes later. She asks if she can change the channel. Ellis nods. Kenzie's always watching romcoms she pretends to hate while busily taking notes for her own grand romance. She finds a show that's just started. Ellis watches the love interests simpering and presses her fingernails into her palm.

Her notifications chime. Naila is sending her pictures of kittens again. She's sent some sort of meme nearly every day since Ellis finally accepted her friend request. It's endearing. It's enraging. She tries to be grateful for them.

The kittens prompt Ellis to start her social media rounds, which now encompass Kenzie, Jackson, Oliver and several other exes, as well as Lana, Adrian and Sally. It can take a while. Sometimes the loop starts again at the beginning as soon as it ends. She stops on Sally's page. A post about how much she loves her salon with a picture of bountiful blonde curls. Of course she wouldn't use box dye. Sally's the sort who loves sitting in a chair, having things done to her, being pampered while she witters on about her holidays, hopes and dreams. She'll have told the hairdresser all about her new boyfriend – Ellis's betrayal snipped and styled into a romance like the saccharine story entrancing Kenzie.

She fumbles to close the page, but in the instant it disappears, she hits a blue thumb. She's liked it by accident. The page is open again. She hits to unlike. It doesn't respond. She hits again just as it updates. She likes it again. Unlikes. Likes. Unlikes. Sally won't have seen it. She might've seen it. Sally might be lying on the bed Ellis bought watching the like being bestowed and removed over and over.

Ellis caught and erased this accident, but if she's done it once she might've done it before. Shaking, Ellis searches whether it's possible to see all her own likes. So easy. She types *photos liked by me* into the search bar on her own profile. A picture of pancakes held up by Sally's manicured hand is top of the list. A picture from six months ago. And another, a more recent post about supporting local businesses. Ellis has liked that too. She takes them back but it's too late. Sally has seen them. Sally has to have seen them.

Fuck.

34

It's a different room this time, smaller. The dentist is a woman, maybe in her late forties. Her hair is in a tidy plait. A gold necklace glints beneath her white collar. Nude nails, a steady smile. Ellis says hello and sits primly on the edge of the reclining chair as they talk through the problem.

'I see. If you wouldn't mind lying back?'

She examines. Ellis hopes. The dentist is thorough. She takes a blue strip from a sealed packet and asks Ellis to bite.

'Feel anything? No?'

She moves the strip; it touches Ellis's lip ever so lightly. The tickle makes her shiver.

'Again,' the dentist says with a smile. Ellis bites. The strip moves again, for another round. And another. The strip is swapped for a fresh one, and they repeat the process until she makes a satisfied sound.

'There, that'll do nicely. All right, let's get you up again.'

The chair rights itself beneath her. What to do with her hands. She clasps them in her lap. The technician takes away the disposable bib. Ellis thanks her and grips her fingers tighter.

'I think there are two things going on here.'

Ellis listens, hope twitching inside her.

'One, while the tooth looks sound, it has an awfully large filling. We've had to replace most of the pulp. That isn't a problem in itself, but what we have to be aware of is that the composite is softer than the tooth itself. So when there's a thin outer shell, like we have here, it's likely to be taking the brunt of any bite. All the crushing power focused onto one, small area can be very intense. And when a nerve is already inflamed, well.

Obviously, we don't like to mess with a healthy tooth if we can help it, but it could be that we need to file down or remove a little of the corner, so the pressure is spread more evenly. I've had a good look at your bite and can see what might be the problem edge. So having a go at that is option one, but I'd rather try something else first.'

Ellis is light-headed. The room is too bright. The filling can't be softer than the thing it's meant to repair. She expected it to hold when the tooth couldn't.

'So, two, I want to check how many stressors you have going on at the moment. I see plenty of evidence of grinding. You haven't noticed? It's happening most nights, I'd say. Lots of people grind their teeth in their sleep, especially during periods of stress. And even if you're not noticeably grinding during the day, just clenching can be enough to set things off. Have you noticed that? Your upper and lower teeth shouldn't ever be touching, unless you're actively chewing. Will you do me a favour and look out for it? I know it might sound like a small thing, but it's not. I'm going to give you a mouthguard to wear while you're sleeping. During the day, it's down to you to keep those teeth apart.'

'You're positive it's not something more serious? I've had infections before and I can't help worrying.'

The back of the woman's hand is on Ellis's forehead. It's such an instinctive gesture, Ellis doesn't have time to be surprised by it.

'You're a bit warm, but it's hard to tell at this time of year. You could ask your doctor to have some bloods taken for your peace of mind. And in the meantime, let me give you this generic guard. Wear it at night, starting tonight, and we'll get you booked in for a fitted one in the next few weeks. You might find it makes all the difference.'

Ellis holds out her hand. The plastic guard settles there like a butterfly. The dentist is so happy to help her. The dark thing inside still throbs.

Ellis is home sharp. She kicks her shoes off at the door, looks up and freezes. There's a woman in her mum's favourite chair. Blonde hair and tailored shoulders. Too small to be Lana. For a watery moment, Ellis knows it's Sally. She's come to threaten or beg Ellis to stay the hell away. The woman turns. It's Jackson.

'Ellis,' she says. She's skinnier and blonder than before but her voice is exactly how Ellis remembers it.

'Sorry, I just . . . you're here.'

'I'm here.'

'It's good to see you.'

'I'm sure you've been just dying to catch up.' She gives her head a little toss. 'Believe me, this isn't what I had planned for my vacation.'

'Where's Charlie?'

'According to your mom, he's at some meeting and can't be reached. Bullshit. I bet you he's at the movies. He's always sneaking off to sit in the dark and eat nachos and pretend he's still a teenager.'

'Kenzie?'

'No one seems to know. My daughter's running wild hundreds of miles from home, and no one's paying any attention.'

'She'll be out on the bike.'

'Your bike, I hear.'

'She's careful.'

'She's also not here and not reading her messages, so I'm just sitting around, wasting time like I've wasted the whole summer.'

'They'd have been here if they'd known you were coming.'

'You think? Anyway, they should've been able to work it out. They're not idiots. Was I going to just sit there, listening to his bullshit excuses while everything goes to hell?' She opens the small clutch bag on her lap and takes out a phone that looks just like Kenzie's. 'What's your wifi password? Your mom can't remember, and I've got fifteen fires I could be putting out if my cell was connected.'

Ellis finds the bit of paper with the password and leaves her to it. Mum's in the kitchen, making a stew. Hiding.

'What's she doing here?'

'Says she's not going to the hotel until she's seen them with her own eyes,' her mum says, jabbing at a simmering pot. Ellis fills the sink, plunges her hands into the hot, bubbling water. Knives float below the surface.

The front door slams. The walls are thick, but Ellis and Mum hear a whole range of snippets. *How could you . . . How dare you . . . What the fuck do you . . . She's my daughter . . . She's not even sixteen . . . You said two weeks max . . .*

Mum picks up a bottle of sherry and nods towards the garden. Ellis follows. The voices are indistinct. Ellis sips. The sun makes her squint. The garden smells like baked fertiliser. Thoughts burble inside: Charlie didn't know Jackson was coming; she'd hunted them down because they hadn't showed up back home when they were expected. Weeks ago, which means he's been lying.

Jackson's life is built around supporting other people's special events and big days. Her calendar is booked years in advance. She must've been beside herself to come all this way on short notice.

The burr of bike wheels turns their heads to the side of the house. The gate goes.

Mum calls out to Kenzie. 'Sweetheart, did you get your messages?'

Kenzie nods. Ellis can't read her expression.

'They're in the living room. Here, give me that.' Mum holds out her hand for the helmet. Kenzie passes it over silently. Ellis sees the outline of the scrawny girl with dry elbows still present beneath Kenzie's new confidence and curves.

Ellis and her mum stay in the garden with the bottle of

sherry, batting away wasps and exchanging quiet words. Mum is fretting over whether she should postpone her week-end away.

'We should have another family lunch while everyone's here. Trev and I can go to the cottage any time.'

'No, Mum. You should have a break.'

'We might not get another chance.'

They're silent for a moment, pretending to ignore the tension emanating from the front room.

'Get-togethers are important, and we've not seen Grant in weeks. Just between us, I think they're having words too.'

'What about?'

'I didn't ask.'

The house, maybe. Grant's hobbies. Or something Lana's done? The kind of thing she wouldn't share with her mum. The more confident Lana is in her position, the more everyone hears about it. The only vulnerabilities Lana keeps secret are her own.

The front door opens and closes. Charlie appears a few minutes later, looking wabbit. 'Sorry about this.'

'Get a glass and come join us,' Mum says. He does what he's told. Ellis makes space for him on the wooden bench.

'Is Kenzie okay? Is she allowed a sherry?'

'She's gone with her mum. To the hotel. She might be back later or she might not.' He pauses to let Mum pour. 'Jackson's booked her a room.'

'In the Balmoral?'

He ducks his head once. 'I'm so embarrassed.'

Mum tells him to hush, it's not his fault. But it is. At least partly. He married her. He had a child with her. He left her and he came all the way here and pretended everything was fine. It's obviously not fine.

'You just kept on changing the dates on your tickets without telling her?' Ellis says.

'I told her.'

'But you stayed even though she didn't want you to.'

'It's been so good to be here.' Charlie looks down at the dry grass between his feet.

Ellis wants him to stay. Wants him to stay so very badly.

'A girl needs her mum,' Mum says softly.

'Sometimes a girl needs her dad more,' Ellis says, wishing that Jackson hadn't come. That she'd had Charlie to herself for a little longer.

'Maybe you're right.' Mum shifts and stands slowly. 'I'll leave you two to it.'

It's only when she notices Charlie's stare that she realises.

'I didn't mean it like that. She knows I love her.' Ellis scuffs her toes in the dirt. The sherry is taking the edge off, but the headache is still there and there's a spongy feeling in her thighs. Jackson scares her. Fighting scares her. 'What are you going to do?'

'I don't know,' Charlie says.

Ellis looks at the colour of his cheeks and worries for him. Charlie's full of good advice and wise words and a sparkling grin, but underneath it all he's concealing the same fears as the rest of them. Worse, there are pegs in there to keep the smile straight.

35

How fitting that the patron saint of dentistry had all her teeth brutally removed. Saint Apollonia, a Christian martyr who died in Egypt in 249 AD, had her pearly whites smashed out by an Alexandrian mob. She then leapt into the fire they had prepared for her rather than renounce her faith. Her feast date is February the ninth. What she's expected to eat, Ellis doesn't know.

Apollonia once had her own church in Rome, before it was destroyed and replaced by a square. An empty spot in the jawbone. The majority of her remains were interred in that church, although a good number were spread elsewhere. Head in one place, arms in another, part of her jaw somewhere else. Smaller relics of her person are scattered throughout Europe, some as meagre as a splinter of bone or a single tooth. In the Middle Ages, there were good profits to be made in trading teeth said to be hers. They were meant to cure toothache. Ellis can imagine being desperate enough to buy one.

It's easier to book in a half-day holiday than it is to try and take off another hour for a doctor's appointment. She sends her request to Richard, and he okays it without speaking to her. The receptionist at the GP wanted her to see the doctor first, but Ellis stood firm. Blood test only. The dentist has said what they're looking for, and she doesn't want to wait the two weeks until the GP's free. The receptionist agrees, eventually, so it's the practice nurse Ellis sees. She takes the blood efficiently, with chatter about the box of chocolates on her desk and how grateful they all are to their patients for gifting them despite everyone being on a diet. Ellis goes home pleased with herself, poking the tender spot in the crook of her elbow. She is convinced they'll find evidence of a wrongdoing in her body.

Her mum welcomes her home enthusiastically.

'What a relief to see a friendly face. It's been nothing but frosty silences and slammed doors all day. And Lana's worried Mia's getting stressed and acting out. I should tell her about those toddler yoga thingies your Becca's going to – Scotty seems to love them.'

Ellis pauses, hand outstretched. Becca's only been going to yoga for the last few weeks.

'When did she say that?'

'Oh, I don't know.'

'Have you been speaking to her?'

Her mum nods reluctantly.

'When?'

'The other day.'

Ellis waits.

Mum fiddles with her ring. 'We had a coffee.'

'Without me.'

'Don't be like that. We're worried about you.'

'No, you're not.'

This isn't true. Ellis knows it isn't true. She wants them to worry, but what right do they have to actually do it? To worry together? To meet up and talk about her?

'Of course we are and we understand. Who wouldn't be having a hard time? We just don't want you to get stuck in it.'

'Don't meet up with Becca and talk about me.'

'Ellis–'

'She's *my* friend.' Ellis stalks out the room.

Becca's always had a soft spot for Ellis's mum. All Ellis's friends do, boyfriends too. It's not enough that she has to share her with Lana; everyone else wants a little of Marion's attention. Now there's Trevor. What if there's not enough of her to go round? She's spending all this time making fucking fudge for strangers, raising money for charity, and Ellis hates it. Hates it the same way she hates Becca right now, especially because she's only trying to help. Hates that she knows Becca was dangling offers of lunches and coffees for weeks and she was dodging them, not wanting to be called out. Becca came to her, and she kept her as close to arm's length as she could manage. Who is she to blame her for going to her mum instead?

Ellis pulls off her jacket and shirt. She sits in her bra and trousers and thinks of the mouthguard that doesn't fit.

It costs more than three hundred quid to have one made that will cleave neatly to her teeth. It doesn't count as essential on the NHS, instead falling into Band Three along with bridges and full-jacket crowns. And they'll have to take new impressions to do it. Another round of that pink goo. Unless that's been scrapped in the last few years. How she hopes it's been scrapped. She's going to have to buy a guard, to endure everything that comes with it, if it's the only thing that might help.

She opens the banking app on her phone. By staying with Mum, she's cut her outgoings, but still she's hardly managed to save anything. Even renting in Edinburgh is ferocious: a one-bedroom will be a third of her salary, and she'll never be able to put anything by.

Ellis needs enough to be able to think about buying, even if it's somewhere tiny. She needs a deposit, a steady salary. If TravelOn fires her, there will be something else eventually, but in the months in-between she'll chip away at those insubstantial savings. She doesn't want a hand-out from Adrian, just what he owes her.

She reads through the information she has saved on her laptop. Adrian has no legal obligation to give her back the money she's paid in and believes he has no moral one. She has barely any standing according to legislation, but what she can do is take him to court to enforce occupancy rights. Chances of her winning are slim, but they exist.

She sits, still in her bra, and types out the most officious email she can manage. She just wants him to be reasonable.

She closes her laptop with a snap, kidding herself she can close the lid on her actions.

★

Ellis is on her way home early. There was an issue with the server, and Richard told them all to scoot. Naila asked if she wanted to get a coffee, and Ellis almost said yes but was beguiled by the hope that she might get an hour to herself in the house.

There is no headache. She's not noticed it all day. Maybe the problem has fixed itself. She pushes away the knowledge that if a tooth is left to rot for long enough, the nerve dies off. She presses the teeth on the left together, waiting for the answering skewer and taking it as proof that the tooth is not doomed.

Her phone lights up as she walks home. Ellis's breath catches but it's only Jackson.

The message is a summons. Jackson has everybody's number, and whenever she wants in the house and there's no one there to open the door, she sends blanket texts. Ellis trudges home to find her cousin-in-law leaning against the garden wall, thumbs flying over her iPhone.

'There you are,' she says. 'Kenzie's late.'

The house smells of singed sugar. Ellis drops her keys in her pocket and gestures to the front room, planning to escape upstairs. Jackson has other ideas.

'While I have you, there's something I wanted to talk to you about.' She marches into the living room in a way that indicates Ellis is expected to follow. 'That fuckwit, Adrian, you're better off without him. But that doesn't mean he should get away with it all, right? Charlie can't get away with his nonsense either. He's not allowed to run across the world like a child when the whole thing was his idea.'

Ellis sits opposite, nodding uncertainly.

'I can't stick around for much longer. Clients are lining up, and not everything can be delegated. I need to get back and so does Kenzie. It's too late for her internship – I've no strings left to pull there – but she's got to get ready for the new term. So tell me, what's he planning? What's he trying to get out of me?'

'He's hardly said anything about any of it. We didn't even know what was happening until he got here. We all thought you wanted space. This is the first I'm hearing of any internship or whatever.'

'Give me a break. I expected them home at the start of the month. Can you imagine?'

'No.'

'You're seriously telling me he's not shared his hare-brained scheme with you?' Jackson clucks her tongue.

Ellis fights off a scowl. The forgiveness she keeps trying to coat Jackson in is tacky and unpleasant. It's one thing to make allowances, another to try and like someone. She thinks of Jackson as a teenager, the perfect overachiever pretending her bruises came from the volleyball court, and the way that experience coloured everything that came after it.

Everyone has a wound at the heart of them, a hurt the body curls around. Jackson's plugged and salved and tended her wound in a way that's hardened her. The knowledge should help Ellis rise above her frustrations. It doesn't. Jackson is a stone-cold bitch.

Someone else arrives home. It's too much to hope that it will be Charlie, or Kenzie. Ellis doesn't expect Lana, but that's who stomps in.

'What's up?' Ellis says.

Lana doesn't indicate that she's heard. It's Jackson she's glaring at. 'You got in, then? Fast enough for you, was it?'

'Beggars can't be choosers,' Jackson says in a voice that reminds everyone she doesn't believe she should ever have to beg.

'Isn't that so? I'm only here so I can say this to your face: no more of this. No calls, no texts, no voicemails. I'm not coming running to let you in, ever. That's the second time your badgering has woken up one of the twins, as if I don't have enough to worry about.'

'It'll be a pleasure to not have to message you again.' Jackson rearranges the heavy chain bracelet on her left wrist so that it lies a fraction flatter.

'I've never been happier to have someone out of this family,' Lana says.

'And what a charming relative you turned out to be.'

Lana's winding up her reply when Charlie calls hello from the hall. The three women stand, lips crimped, as he and Kenzie hurry through.

'Sorry, Mum. We were getting a new bike helmet, like you said,' Kenzie says.

Jackson gives Lana one last glare and turns to her daughter, holding out a hand to inspect the purchase. Charlie raises his eyebrows the tiniest fraction at Ellis; she responds with a small shake of her head.

'See you later,' Lana says to Kenzie. No one else deserves a goodbye.

'Where's the safety certificate?' Jackson says. Kenzie points it out.

★

A handwritten envelope is on the bed. Ellis approaches with caution.

The experiment? He didn't seem like the love-letter kind, but how would she know? He's a blur of gin and laughter and smooth arms and vomit. There's a flicker of pleasure at the thought of being wanted, followed by a whirr of panicked irritation at the thought of having to get rid of him. The itch of wondering how he worked out her address. Her name loops and curves on the front of the envelope. The paper inside is lavender. Ellis flips it open to see the signature.

Sally. Oh God, it's Sally.

Dear Ellis, I know you and Adrian were together for many years and it didn't end in the best possible way and that I have a lot to do with that, but I had to write to you. We didn't mean to fall in love. We tried really hard to fight it but the truth is, you were so unhappy together. He didn't want to hurt you. He still doesn't. He spent a whole weekend working out which furniture you might want, even when you refused to tell him. You have no idea how devastated he was when he read your email about Occupancy Rights. He only ever tried to be fair. Why do you have to throw it back in his face? It's cruel. He's hurting. We all are. But you have to stay away and accept what's happened. Please leave us alone and find your own happiness. Sally.

The words hop around the page. Unhappy. Hurting. Love. All lies. The corner is damp from Ellis's sweaty palm. Anger scorches up her spine. Sally has no right to call her cruel. No right to even think it. Did Adrian read this delicate little shiv? Did he sit beside Sally as she wrote it, suggesting a tweak here and there? Maybe he waited until she was done then checked it over, leaning beside the kitchen sink. There's not a single mistake or bungled spelling. This is a second draft, a third. Carefully copied out on pretty notepaper.

Her fingers twitch to rip. She stops herself. She wants the evidence. Wishes she could show it to Lana, who once would've read it aloud in a scathing impression of Sally's voice.

Ellis turns her head and lifts her arm until her teeth catch the soft skin below her oxter. She bites. The flesh bulges, presses against the tip of her tongue. She feels the muscles shifting under her skin and forces her jaws together. It hurts, and she wants it to. The letter trembles in her hand. No matter how much she wants to bite off a chunk, her body won't let her. It can't. It's like holding your breath. Her teeth refuse to tear. Far easier to slice with a razor or hit a head against a wall. She releases. An imperfect bite is left on the skin, imprinted in white, purple and fast-blooming red. It will bruise.

She knows, because she and her end-of-high-school friends had a biting phase. They took turns marking each other, claiming their friendships. They loved to squirm and shriek and see who could bite the hardest or withstand the pain the longest.

The sensation is familiar, but this bite is not about pride or ownership. It is punishment. Ellis swipes at the saliva drying on her arm. The release is laced with regret. She has to put the letter down to replace her vest top with a T-shirt.

She needs to see Sally in person. Maybe this time she'll tell her what she thinks of her. Ellis is out the house before she's had time to consider how wise it is. The bus comes five minutes after it's supposed to. She sits at the window and shields her phone screen from the other passengers. Not that any of them will care whose Facebook she's looking at.

Ellis takes the usual table by the window. A bored girl shoves a menu at her. Ellis is terse as she asks for the coffee, tries to smile sweetly when it's finally brought to her. It's too hot and has an acrid undertone. She takes the smallest sip, stares. There are Adrian's colleagues. The nice one, the one who couldn't stop talking about the horse she rode when she was twelve, the one who has a plan to retire at fifty-five. No Adrian. No Sally. They knew she was coming. Ridiculous. She didn't even know she was coming. Ellis sits and sits. Doesn't order another coffee because they're three quid and that's outrageous and she can't afford it and she doesn't care that the staff might want the table. Stays until the office lights go off, quietly consumed with rage.

36

Dental records can identify bodies when all other markers fail. The science, which has proven reliable if not infallible, has been in use since 1878.

Would they be able to tell who Charlie was, now that he has generic crowns rather than the formations coded in his DNA? Or is their topography still unique enough for someone to make sense of it? If Ellis pulls her teeth, can she become someone else? Pointless. Even if Ellis changes every single tooth, she will still be the same inside.

Another day, another dentist's appointment. Ellis is resigned, despite her rising frustration. She wakes, removes the mouthguard and suffers for the umpteenth time the memory of a picture she once saw online: a boxer holding a similar guard, each depression in the plastic filled with something that shouldn't have been there. Someone had hit him so hard, every upper tooth was knocked from his head. The roots were bloody although not so much as you'd expect. Ellis will never rid herself of this image. It'll always be there, waiting for her to falter from a mental pathway into this shady back alley.

She arrives at the dentist ready to explain to the nice woman that the mouthguard hasn't been the miraculous cure they hoped for. For the last few nights, Ellis has barely slept. She says her name to the receptionist, who clearly recognises her, and takes a seat. She logs into her work emails, her phone warm from her pocket, and finds one wishing her good luck from Naila. The dental nurse comes to fetch her. It's only at the end of the corridor that Ellis gets a bad feeling.

'I'm meant to be seeing the woman, the new one,' she says.

'Oh, Pamela? She's had to help out at another practice, we're sharing her until Dr Niall's back. It's been quite a month,' she says, leading Ellis into the room. Just as she feared, Dr Conor is waiting for her. His greeting is more subdued than usual but Ellis can already feel the positive spin he's going to put on everything. She should've checked at the front desk. She should've prepared for this.

He asks what he can do for her, Ellis gives him the summary. He nods.

'It's a good sign, that you haven't heard from the docs. No news is good news when it comes to bloods. We'll hurry up and get you in for a mould asap so you can feel the full benefit of a properly fitted mouthguard. Can you check the calendar, Maria? While I just have a little look at what's going on here.' He presses the control that makes the chair tip back.

It's a long time since that awful dentist at the West End accused her of being bulimic. A long time since she was lectured about how acidic vomit is and how bad it is for her teeth, let alone the rest of her. But she feels an echo of the same shame. He thinks he knows what the problem is. He thinks she's bringing it on herself.

Dr Conor is waffling on about clenching and nerves and all the things she's heard before. His voice is patronising and makes her want to clamp her teeth around his fingers. Strip the skin from the bone.

When the dentist of her youth diagnosed her with an eating disorder, she said nothing. Not this time. She's taking off the bib, the goggles, and handing them to the nurse, who starts to reach out then holds her hands up, refusing to take responsibility for them. Dr Conor says something about patience and being kind to yourself. Ellis drops the useless protective gear onto the leather seat, snatches her bag from the floor and straightens up. She will not stumble, she will not fall. She stalks along the corridor, does not Pass Go at the reception desk to receive her bill, and leaves the building.

Ellis is broiling in her skin. The bus is a microwave. It's too hot outside. She's too hot inside. Scotland isn't meant to be this warm. Ellis isn't built for it. She's got to get to the office. She wishes she still smoked. She is a liar. She is distracted. She is spying on a woman she hates twice a week. If she's not careful, she's going to drive away her friends simply by avoiding them. And if she's not careful, she is going to lose her job too.

She checks her phone. A reply from a solicitor. Her finger slips on the screen as she hurries to open it. A hundred and fifty quid for a letter stating her claim on the flat, two hundred and fifty an hour for their time after that, including consultation on home boundary issues.

Ellis pauses before replying. It is a defeat; claiming occupancy rights seems like the kind of thing someone else would do and it's money she doesn't want to spend. But it might force Adrian's hand. Embarrass him.

Yes, she says, in Arial. *Yes I want to claim rights, I'll get back to you on the other part.*

Missive sent. Yes. He deserves it.

＊

The office whirrs with ineffective fans. Ellis takes her seat without looking round, hoping not to draw attention to her arrival.

Adrian has messaged her already, making no sense.

I never thought you could be so spiteful. Couldn't you have given us a day? I was going to call you tonight. I thought you deserved to hear from me, but I should've known you'd be creeping about like a fucking stalker and would find a way to hurt us.

Her chest is shrinking; there's no space for breath. She follows the well-worn furrow that takes her to their Facebook pages.

Sally's profile has an update. Another fucking pastry, flooded with likes and comments. There's a caption: *Eating for two.*

Yes, it's true. There's a little one on the way #blessed #babymumma

Empty. Her heart echoes in the abandoned cathedral of her ribs. A baby. They're having a baby. There's a fizzing in Ellis's gums, a firework in her heart. Sally is having his baby.

Ellis never wanted one. Adrian felt the same. Ellis still doesn't want one. She doesn't want him to have one. How long, how long? How many months? Was it before? It's on Facebook, so Sally is sure. Or brave. If she's sure, it'll be past three months. When did he decide to not tell her? He knew she'd find out this way. Just because he's never on his Facebook page it doesn't mean he's oblivious. He let it happen. He always controlled by stealth. Ellis imagines stepping into his arms, pressing her cheek against his shoulder, smelling his clean smell, sinking her teeth into the skin below his stubble line, yanking at the fibrous tug of the tendons and arteries. She wants to destroy him.

It's all she can do to make it to the staff toilets before the explosion of tears. She cries silently until her throat aches, then returns to her seat with puffy eyes and a twitch in her left cheek. She can't destroy him. Who takes revenge on a baby?

Should she ask the solicitor to send another email saying she's changed her mind? Has she?

Ellis rubs at her face as she opens her backlog of queries. She needs to resolve some. But a baby. *A baby.*

Sally is pregnant, and Ellis has to pretend that misery hasn't looped its arms around her neck. Its stomach presses into her spine, its shins circle her ribcage; stale breath blows in her ears while everyone else types and takes phone calls and finalises spreadsheets around her. Gabrielle will be watching from her little office. Ellis is trapped.

37

Ellis wakes in a sweaty tremble. Her abdomen aches; her heart races with the remnants of dreams. Babies born with teeth, chewing their way out of the womb. Natal incisors ripping into flesh, tearing at the placenta, emptying the woman. Ellis pushes hair out of her face, blinks. He wore a condom, the man from the bar. Her experiment. He wore one. She remembers the juddering friction. Remembers seeing it discarded on his dresser, knotted, heavy and viscous. But it can still happen. They were drunk and clumsy, and he was handsy. The chances are infinitesimal. They still exist. Anything is possible: nothing is probable. She's cramping with no blood.

Later, in the artificial light of the TravelOn office, Ellis knows it is ridiculous. One night, one condom. There is nothing growing in her. No bundle of cells waiting to transform into teeth. Still, there is an easy way to loosen their grip: a test. She can't go to the chemist by work, where someone's always popping in for throat sweets or nicotine gum or hangover remedies. She can't go to the one near home, where the owner knows her mum.

There's a Boots just down from Adrian's office.

It takes a brisk walk to get there on her lunch break, but she does it. She passes the hotel, the bench, the bus stop and hurries into the chemist. The pregnancy tests are legion. She stares at the stacked boxes, unable to tell them apart. There's no time for this. She looks around, grabs one and tucks it under her arm. The lunch fridges run alongside the queue; she takes a vegetarian wrap, drink and packet of crisps as she waits. She feels the box under her arm start to slip. She adjusts, and the bottle of juice seems to grow. Her fingers twitch. She grips tighter; she will not drop it. Another glance round the shop. No Sally, no Adrian. She came here with the inkling she might see them, and faced with the reality that they are just as likely to see her, the muscles between her ribs contract. She's here on purpose. She's set herself up for punishment.

It's finally her turn to be served. She wrangles the pile onto the counter and opens her bag, ready to throw everything in the second it's been scanned. The woman barely looks at her, just asks if she has a loyalty card and tells her the total when she whispers that she doesn't. Ellis pays and escapes at a clip. The street is busy. She bumps into a stranger. She looks up to apologise, and when she does, a jerky movement to her left catches her eye. She's saying sorry to the guy walking round her but she's looking at Sally, who's grasping Adrian's arm like a damsel watching a train wreck. Ellis's heart flames.

She hurries her way to the office and heads straight for the toilets. They're empty. She hangs her bag on the hook on the back of the cubicle door and rips into the cellophane and cardboard as quickly as possible. You're meant to pee first thing in the morning. She can't wait. She thrusts the stick under her, and in trying to make sure the absorbent pad is under the stream, pisses all over her fingers. She dries herself with toilet paper and sits, knickers at her knees. Every footstep in the corridor makes her jump. She stares at the tiny window, willing time to pass.

Lana's teeth fell apart when she was pregnant. Two healthy, twinning, coalescing groups of cells taking all they could – their only purpose, growth. Developing into Oscar and Mia at an astonishing rate, feeding from Lana as they went, only one, strong-boned, iron-willed woman, they took all the resources they could plunder. Lana bloomed, she glowed, she prevailed, and still there was a weak spot for them to attack: her teeth.

One line. There's one line. Of course there is. Ellis is paranoid.

Not feeling right, not thinking straight. She has to pack this away. They didn't give her a plastic bag at the chemist; there's only a small bin for period products in the cubicle. Ellis wraps the test in layers and layers of loo roll. Her head throbs. Her breath is shallow. She's falling apart. She's spent more time in these toilets than she has at her desk, over the last few days.

She flushes and forces herself out of the cubicle, dropping the swaddled plastic into the waste bin and pulling several scratchy green handtowels from the dispenser to layer on top. She washes her hands, eyes avoiding the mirror and the red still staining her cheeks.

*

Ellis sits, damp and hollow, moving her cursor around the screen. Gabrielle is laughing her way down the central aisle. She stops at Ellis's desk and asks her to follow her back to the HR room.

'How are you getting on?' she says, nudging the box of tissues across the table.

'Fine,' Ellis says. A muscle near her eye twitches involuntarily.

'It's just that you seem a little . . . distracted.'

'I'm fine.'

'Are you sure?'

Ellis nods.

'I noticed you've been away from your desk a lot. Do you need to go home? You can tell us if you do . . .' Ellis shakes her head. 'Are you overworked? Feeling stressed? Anything we can do to help?'

Tears threaten to return. She resists, her insides contracting and expanding with thoughts of Adrian and Sally being bound together by the multiplying cells. Making soft, proud expressions at each other.

'I'm sorry,' she says.

'It's just that we've noticed things proving a little . . . challenging for you recently. You've had a lot of appointments for one thing or another. You know we'd be better placed to help if you kept us in the loop.'

Ellis nods as though she believes her. Gabrielle's offer is paper-thin. TravelOn might technically have a mental health policy but it holds no weight. It doesn't matter how many emails they send sprinkled with words like 'holistic' or 'people first', it's the bottom line they're protecting.

'I know I've been off a lot, but the dentist thinks he's finally figured it out.'

'Good, good. And your sister, everything at home okay? You can talk to me about anything – I've heard it all.'

'No. She . . . I'm really sorry . . . The appointments should be about done.'

Ellis bites the inside of her bottom lip to keep her face straight. Gabrielle sighs and tells her to remember that her door is always open. Ellis walks away, imagining Gabrielle rising to stand at the blinds, one slat tweaked to watch her go.

Ellis returns to her emails. Alison is striding across the office floor; she pauses to deposit a coffee by Ellis's keyboard with a quick wink.

She must look dreadful if Alison is bringing her coffee unprompted. She thought that if she tried hard enough, she could keep it all in, but it's seeping out of her. She should've told them the truth in the first place. Updated her status on Facebook, put an ad in the paper, plastered the shame on her forehead. It couldn't have been worse.

∗

Ellis shuts herself in her bedroom. Mum's packing for her long weekend, Kenzie's watching videos about climate change (she can tell by the earnestness of the young voices blaring from the phone speakers), Charlie's talking to people he thinks might give him a job, and Jackson, thankfully, is elsewhere.

Muscle memory thumbs through the recently opened apps and pages on her phone. There's a new post on Sally's Facebook.

Sorry to be back with more on this, but I'm getting scared. She was there at lunchtime today, face all twisted up with hate. Thank God Adrian was with me this time. Why is she doing this? Can I even do anything about it?

Ellis floods with adrenaline. She scrolls down and down, looking for the 'more' Sally referred to. Nothing. Only all the pictures and shares Ellis has seen already. She returns to the post. It has twenty-four comments and is marked Public.

In her distress, Sally has forgotten to click Friends Only.

There are other posts about Ellis. Several, dozens, hundreds, maybe. And she can't see them. Her hand is shaking so much, it takes her several tries to expand the comments. She leaps through them:

. . . so sorry hun . . . restraining order . . . Adrian should get her told . . . probably get over it . . . can't believe this is happening to you . . . this is the kind of bullshit you don't need right now, get her reported . . .

Horror poisons every atom. There's Anna, Adrian's sensible friend who Ellis never replied to, inviting Sally round for dinner and a chat. Adrian's mum has left a picture of a cartoon bear holding a heart. The injustice. Ellis has been so careful, yet she's somehow become a figure of hate.

38

Ellis can't eat. She tells her mum to leave her alone when she taps on the door to say goodbye because she's leaving for her weekend getaway first thing in the morning. She stays awake all night and drinks from the bathroom tap as she gets ready for work. She feels distanced from the world, as if she's moving through molasses. She's late, and she doesn't know how.

She goes right to her desk, switches on the computer, lays down her things, when she notices that the air is wrong, pulled tight with expectation. She looks up.

Lana's in the office. Fucking hell, Lana's in the office. She's walking out of Gabrielle's room, and Naila is right there to meet her. Ellis stands and stumbles towards them.

'Look who's here to see you,' Naila singsongs, with her usual inability to read a room. Alison is on her way over. Ellis searches Lana's face. It is granite with a smile etched on.

'Are you okay?'

'There you are.' The sweetness in her voice is a warning. Ellis's stomach plummets.

'Let's go outside.' Ellis is corralling her to the door.

Lana moves with her, but slowly, while giving each of Ellis's colleagues a good stare. 'Lovely to meet you, Naila. Thanks so much for pointing me in the right direction.' She's speaking in a voice completely unlike her own.

Naila makes all the right noises, but she looks confused now, and her cheery wave flounders. Ellis ushers Lana into the street. Sweat prickles her upper lip. The apologies are lining up, but she keeps them in, just in case she's wrong and Lana's shown up at TravelOn for some other reason.

'What the fuck, Ellis? What the actual fuck?'

'What's–'

'You know, you bloody know. I've spent weeks, actual weeks, trying to deal with this. I know Grant's a good guy, I know it in my bones, but you start hearing things, don't you? And then you have to look into them because what kind of idiot doesn't at least investigate? Then you fucking rip your husband to shreds accusing him of something terrible and you know you shouldn't have, but you couldn't help thinking there's no smoke without fire. And then when you're left with just this wreckage of a marriage, you start thinking, who started the smoke then? Who wanted to break us up?'

They are in the car park.

'God, Lana. I didn't–'

'Of all the people I thought who'd be likely to screw me over, I never imagined my own sister. Did you know what you could've cost us?'

'I'm so sorry, I'm so sorry. It wasn't like that. I love Grant, I love you.'

'You don't want me to have the house that much? Revenge for something?'

'It was a stupid mistake that got out of control. It wasn't on purpose.'

'Everything's on purpose.'

'I didn't want HR to know about Adrian. It wasn't meant to go anywhere.'

'I talked to your friend up there – the whole office knows. They were all talking and you never even warned me. That wasn't a mistake.'

'It was,' Ellis says. 'It is.'

'Don't worry, I had a very interesting meeting with that bitch of an HR lady for you. What? I thought you'd be pleased, seeing as you're not capable of telling the truth yourself.'

Ellis is falling. The gravel beneath her feet disappears. Lana's anger is obliterating the world around her. And, for once, it's justified.

'My own sister. What the fuck is wrong with you?'

'Please, Lana, it was a mistake. I didn't mean to–'

'Same old shit. You're just trotting out the same old shit again. I can't even look at you.' She turns and stalks away. Ellis should chase her. She can't.

She steps to the wall and huddles there for a moment, sun in her eyes and shame in her guts. Lana hates her. She has to go back upstairs. It's hours until lunch. Lana has lobbed her retaliation right where it will cause the most damage. Ellis could leave. She could just walk away. She doesn't have to head back up there. She thinks about walking away and switching off her phone. Except her phone is on her desk, her bag tucked in the footwell. Ellis wraps a tourniquet around her insides and pushes open the door.

Alison and Naila are talking, their heads tilted together. They look up. They pause.

'Gabrielle's asking after you,' Alison says.

Ellis dips her chin to show she's heard and walks straight to HR.

'Well,' Gabrielle says, sculpted eyebrows scrunched together. Ellis stands by the chair, she can't bring herself to sit. 'This is not a situation I've ever had to deal with before. Based on my conversation with your sister and thinking of your general well-being, I think it's best if you go home.'

In confusion, Ellis murmurs something about her emails.

'I'm sure they can wait. I've had a word with Richard, and we'll be having a proper disciplinary meeting soon, but in the meantime, there's obviously been quite a breach of trust. We'll be suspending you until further notice. I understand from your sister that there are some . . . uh, mental health issues that may be at play. We will of course support you in the best way we can. First, let's go and fetch your things.'

That's it. No mention of what Lana's actually said. No way for Ellis to know whether it's the truth or not. Who is she to expect honesty right now? Would it even help her? The condemnation emanating from Gabrielle is enough. She guides Ellis out into the main room, which is quieter than it ever is. Every nerve is singing. They're all going to hate her, if they don't already.

They make it to Ellis's desk. She reaches for the mouse to switch off the computer. Gabrielle stops her, firmly, as if she's going to sabotage their holiday listings. Like she gives a shit about them. Everyone's looking now, even the ones pretending to work. Ellis takes her phone, bag and jacket and flees.

The streets are filled with tourists and parents wrangling their nursery-aged children. Ellis stumbles among them, not sure where to go.

Lana will never forgive her. She's fucked it up so badly there's no coming back. Now she'll never have to deal with the flinty silences and derisive sighs again.

And.

But.

In Primary 6, Lana came to school with a tub of (washable) poster paint and tipped it into the rucksacks of the two girls who were bullying Ellis. She buys expensive, thoughtful presents. She wants to help when disasters fall. Unless you are the cause of your own disaster. Lana wants people to live up to her expectations. Some of those expectations are good and admirable.

Ellis can't cut her out. And she can't live up to expectations.

✳

She walks and walks. She doesn't want to be anywhere. She refreshes Sally's Facebook page then Lana's then Sally's again until her phone runs out of battery. It doesn't matter, no one wants her. Lana hates her. Adrian and Sally are united in disgust.

She's abandoned her friends and pushed Charlie away because she was scared of wanting him. She can expect nothing.

Small mercy that her mum and Trevor have already left for their weekend break. Lana will let them have their holiday. Surely she will. Ellis could get an explanation in first. She won't.

The front door isn't locked. She walks softly but has to pass the living room to get upstairs.

Charlie's by the mantelpiece, Jackson's at the window and Kenzie's standing by the sofa, her hands out by her side. Tension spirals between them, snaring Ellis into eavesdropping.

'I want you to have your bag packed by first thing tomorrow.'

'But, Mum, they're expecting me.'

'Kenzie, I'm out of patience here.'

'I don't want to.'

'We're flying back as soon as possible. Your new friends will understand.'

'You can't make me.'

'No one can *make* you do anything, sweetheart,' Charlie says.

'Can't I?' Jackson raises her eyebrows. 'She's a child and I'm her mother. And at least I'm setting some actual boundaries and making plans to help her with her future instead of dragging her off on false pretences, then spending half the time ignoring her because I'm having some pathetic midlife crisis.'

'That's not what's going on here, Jackson.'

'Really? She could be a week into her internship by now instead of wasting her whole summer. You could've at least arranged a club or class or something that would get her some credits.'

'That's what we all need in our lives, more micromanagement.'

'Wouldn't we all be better off like you. Sneaking off in the middle of the night so you don't have to face me, when it's your bloody insistence on talking things out that's got us in this mess. There's a time when you have to stop talking and start accepting. You're the worst kind of hypocrite.'

'Mum . . .'

'Kenzie, we love you whatever happens,' Charlie says.

'Here we go with the Mr Nice Guy act again. Yes, yes, very good. Better make sure everyone hears what a caring guy you are, while you're busy doing whatever the hell you want with zero respect for anyone else. You know how much money you've cost us? Cost me? How hard it's going to be for me to get those clients back?'

'You didn't have to come.' There's a whine to his voice.

'I think we all know that's not true.'

'If you hadn't been such a–'

'Enough, I'm going back to the hotel. Kenzie, you're welcome to come with me if you've calmed down. Otherwise, I suggest you get packing.'

'I . . .' Kenzie looks from parent to parent, her eyes wet, her mouth open a few hesitant millimetres. There's no right answer.

'Kenzie.' Ellis's voice wavers. She clears her throat. 'Weren't you going to make labels for Mum's tablet? For the craft fair?'

Kenzie snuffles and glances at Ellis, trying to catch up with this lie. She blinks, nods.

'I was. I promised Auntie Marion.'

'For God's sake,' Jackson says.

'Let her do it,' Charlie says.

'Then I'll fetch you in the morning.' Jackson tugs at the bottom of her tailored shirt, pulling herself back into line. 'Hope you enjoyed the show,' she lobs to Ellis on the way past. The slam of the front door shakes the walls and releases Charlie from stasis. He reaches out to Kenzie.

'Sorry, sweetie, I really am.'

'But you still want me to stay here with you.'

'I want you where you'll be happy.'

'Yeah, right.' Her footsteps thud the way to Lana's room.

Ellis rubs a thumb into her palm.

'I've fucked it all up, haven't I?' Charlie says. His eyes are bloodshot. He's never looked this old.

Ellis is exhausted and electrified. 'What did you think was going to happen?'

'I don't know. I just wanted to come home and start over.'

'You can't trick someone else into running away with you.'

Charlie blinks. Ellis wants to comfort him. Instead, she waits.

'She wanted to come.'

'For a holiday.'

'I can't be without her.'

'Then go back with them.'

'The thought of it is killing me.'

'You want her to move here?' Ellis says.

'Maybe she should be with her mum. She's got so many friends. Clubs. Things she does.'

'Don't make her choose.'

'I want to be with her. She's my daughter, but I was half dead all this last year.' He looks so sad, Ellis steps into the space beside him. Her arm lands across his shoulder. He returns the squeeze. It's friendly, reassuring, and she wants the other arm. She wants all her misery crushed away, she wants to smell him and for him to let her tuck her head under his chin. That's not the answer: he can't cleanse her humiliation. She can't make his choice for him. She steps back.

'You'll work it out.'

'The thing is, I got offered a job a couple of days ago. Here. I was waiting for the right moment to say. It could be a whole new life.'

He's looking at her hopefully, like she's meant to give him permission.

It's Kenzie she's worried for. Kenzie has it all coming. She's like Lana, thinking she can corral life with the sheer force of her personality. And, like Lana, she'll be unprepared for the stream of complications and crevices that will open up as the years go by. Her genes will out. Jackson can't eliminate them, no one can. Kenzie needs the chance to be free, to make mistakes and not let down her friends to keep her parents happy. She shouldn't have to choose between her parents at all.

Ellis steps back. 'Don't make her responsible. It's up to you.' His expression is wounded.

Ellis is thinking about Lana. Regret is sucking the moisture from her. She is desiccated. 'I'm sorry, I feel like shit. I got sent home from work sick. I need to lie down.'

Charlie immediately grows solicitous. She waves him off, desperate to be alone and silent.

39

Tooth after tooth loosens from gum and tumbles across her tongue. Each disappears without a spit or swallow, and before she can breathe, another starts to dangle. More. Thirty, forty, fifty. A shark's mouthful. A puca's. They keep coming. There is no end to them. Even when she should be reduced to blunt flesh, a tooth is dangling there, poised to fall. Ellis wakes with a gasp, her mouth dry and blessedly empty.

In the Philippines, a dream about your teeth falling out means that someone you love will die soon. It is a premonition and a damnation. There are two ways to counteract the curse: biting on a piece of wood or never telling anyone about your dream.

At six, Ellis told her dad everything. She told him when Lana broke her piggy bank and when Granny Patrick took off her housecoat and the skin on her chest was all crackled. She told him how good Mum's eggy bread tasted and how yucky her scrambles were. She told him how she prayed for an imaginary friend but couldn't get Eliza Jane to arrive at the end of her bed. She told him about the dream where Lana turned into a robot with blue glowing eyes, and the one where the whole house was empty apart from Ellis. And she told him the one about the teeth.

'They were all gone,' she sobbed.

'It's okay, they haven't gone anywhere,' he said, rubbing small circles on her back.

'There was blood all over me.' Her voice was too loud. She was going to wake up Lana and her mum, and everyone would be cross, and she couldn't help it. She needed him to understand. And he did. Enough. He stayed in the bed with her until she fell asleep again.

There is no one Ellis will tell about this dream.

By the coughing and rustling of papers from downstairs, it's obvious that Charlie is waiting for someone to wake up. Kenzie has surely spent the whole night crying and texting her friends and is avoiding him as much as Ellis wants to.

Ellis drags herself up for a drink to take back to bed. Charlie comes to see who it is and deflates slightly at the sight of her.

'I'm going to see if Jacks will give us a few more days, just to get our heads round everything.'

'Right,' Ellis replies. She yawns. Her eyes are sticky. Charlie looks as poorly slept as she is.

'She'll understand.' He doesn't sound convinced. Ellis says he knows better than she does and leaves him to pace round the kitchen.

She's back under her duvet, drinking a coffee that seems to have no taste when she hears a chapping at Lana's door. Silence. Charlie knocks again, loud enough to be heard by a teen with headphones cupping her soft ears. Still no answer. Instead, the sound of the door opening. No voices. Footsteps, then a bang on Ellis's door. It opens before she has a chance to say anything.

Charlie's expression drags her upright. 'She's gone.'

She asks if he's sure but of course he is. Kenzie's sneaked out while everyone was sleeping. He rings her, one hand tapping at his thigh, staring out the window at the quiet street. Ellis moves to the edge of the bed. Charlie looks panicked.

'She'll be fine,' Ellis says.

'She went to bed crying. Her phone's off.'

He calls again. It goes to voicemail. He calls Jackson. His voice thrums with worry.

Ellis tries to think clearly, but the morning is slipping through her fingers like a handful of spit-slicked teeth.

Jackson arrives while Charlie is checking if Kenzie's favourite coat is still on the rack. It is. It means nothing; it's another scorching day. Jackson barely looks at Ellis. Her fury is reserved for Charlie.

'Where is she? Where the fuck is my daughter?'

'Probably with her new friends.'

'Who are they? What are their numbers?' Jackson says. Charlie holds his palms out to her. 'You don't know? You didn't ask?'

'She's a teenager. She's too old for us to be vetting her pals or finding out who their parents are.'

'Charlie, she's a minor. If she was back home, I'd know exactly where she was and who she was seeing.'

'For fuck's sake, is this really the time for this shit?'

Ellis realises that neither of them has been listening to their daughter at all. It is ridiculous that they have no idea where she might be. As if Kenzie hasn't been talking about nothing but the climate crisis and her new friends and the peaceful protests for days. They've been too busy arguing about whether she should be with her mum or her dad to listen. If they can't put two and two together when it comes to their own daughter, Ellis doesn't see why she should do it for them.

'The bike,' Jackson says. They hurry into the back garden. Ellis uses the opportunity to retreat again. Her room is a cave packed tight with debris. There is no air, no space. She is shipwrecked on the bed, clutching her phone. Their voices needle; she catches a word or two. Of course her bike is gone. Ellis rages at Charlie for choosing Jackson in the first place. He ran away and found someone with too much bite. Someone who would take and take, sure she deserves everything she can get.

No, that's not fair: Jackson is a victim. A perpetrator. They're all victims, all perpetrators. The room is so stuffy, Ellis can barely breathe.

She wants them to shut up. They're meant to love each other, to have loved each other once. They should be kind. They should shut up. Shutting up is Ellis's undoing though.

There is a baby growing who is half Adrian. It will be Kenzie's age one day. Ellis's age. When will the buds of its teeth appear? She checks. The basic core of the tooth forms at six weeks. The hard substance around it won't come until month three or four. They have started. She looks to see if new congratulations have been added to Sally's page. A handful. Nothing else on the post about Ellis.

Ellis checks an update about the protest outside the Parliament. Pictures have been uploaded to the Facebook group. Smiles. Children with globes and rainbows painted on their cheeks. Big, hand-drawn signs. Faces filled with hope or resignation.

They're still fighting downstairs. Ellis refreshes the page. She would like to see Kenzie with face paint. A flower. Birds. Ocean waves. What would Ellis have? Jagged teeth over the lips and down the chin. Tusks curling up alongside her nose. Red eyes painted over her eyelids. No, green. Because it's envy at the root of it. The page flickers and reloads. There is a post at the top, a tiny circular image of a smiling woman and beside it: *GO HOME. DISPERSE, DISPERSE NOW. THIS IS NO LONGER PEACEFUL.* Ellis stares. Refreshes again. Googles the date, Edinburgh, protest in a new tab. There is nothing apart from a story from two days ago with details of the start and end times. Back to the Facebook page. There are replies to the woman's comment. *It's a shitshow . . . fucking far right arseholes . . . the polis are here and all.*

Ellis is downstairs before she has time to think.

'There's a climate change protest in town that's turning ugly and I'm pretty sure that's where Kenzie's gone.'

Jackson's anger is volcanic, but it's the way Charlie avoids her eyes that cuts Ellis deep.

✱

Ellis is pulling on her shoes. Charlie is grabbing his keys. Jackson is already at the door. She's ordered an Uber.

They stand on the pavement.

'Why didn't you say earlier?' Charlie says.

Ellis ignores him.

The driver is young, expansive. Ellis wishes they were in a black cab. She wants the wall of Perspex between them. Jackson's in the front, one hand on the lip of the window, willing the car to go faster.

'The town's rammed. You'd be better off giving it half an hour to see if it calms down,' the driver says.

'What have you heard?'

'Not much, just tried to drop someone off at the station and had to leave them on Hanover and loop back from the West End. Would've been better off at Haymarket but who am I to say?'

The car is thick with his aftershave. The leather beneath her thighs burns. She smells meaty. Her breath is rank. Charlie won't look up from his phone.

The driver's right. After five tense minutes stuck in immovable traffic at York Place they say they'll just walk. The driver doubts they'll be any faster on foot. Jackson snippily promises a tip. The man shrugs, waits for them to get out. They cut back onto Leith Street and head up towards North Bridge and the Royal Mile.

They're walking against the crowd. It's like peak Festival, except there's too much fear and anger mixed in with the excitement. Police are barricading the Bridges on the far side, right by the old *Scotsman* building. No one's looking for ticket money. There's no parade. People are yelling. Charlie and Jackson are arguing with two impassive men in blue, whose faces say, who are these jabbering tourists?

'Our daughter,' they shout.

'We're not allowing anyone past at this time.'

'Maybe go get a coffee,' the younger one says, his collar ever so slightly loose at the neck.

'I will not get a coffee, you–'

'Not now, Jackson,' Charlie says in a handling voice. While Jackson is not handled, she does refrain from saying anything else she shouldn't.

Charlie leads them a little way back down the Bridges. Ellis says they should go round. Charlie says, of course, and Jackson is furious no one suggested there was another way to try. They split up. Charlie and Jackson will backtrack to Waverley and get onto the Royal Mile by cutting through the station and up Blair Street. Ellis is going to head east and check Calton Road. She'll go all the way to Abbeyhill, if she has to. They're running now. Ellis is the most unfit of the three, and every step thuds through her head. The air doesn't want to stay in her lungs.

Sweat streaks her face and her hair is matted at her neck. She must look like a madwoman. The worst part of her, the smallest most despicable bit that twists in her, worries that Sally and Adrian will walk past and see her.

Only Kenzie matters. Kenzie has to be okay. Edinburgh's too noisy – everything's louder than it should be. It's like Hearts v. Hibs on steroids. She's in a film. The people running past her shouting and crying are extras. A man has blood around his mouth. She has to stop, a hand against the hot brick, the stench of pigeon shit pushing down into her throat. She stumbles on, dazzled by the light as she steps out from under the tunnel.

For a moment, she falters, then pushes on through an unyielding crowd. Just as she's thinking there's no chance in hell, Ellis spots her.

Kenzie is crying at the side of the road, looking one way then the other, unsure where she is or which way to go. There is glitter all over her cheeks. She looks so vulnerable. Ellis shoves her way past the milling bodies, standing on feet and shouldering backs in her determination to reach her cousin. Kenzie feels hot and clammy, her arm so slender, the bones so small. She pulls against Ellis's grasp then relaxes into it with relief.

'Thank Christ,' Ellis says.

'I lost everyone.'

'It's okay, it's okay. You're fine. Your folks, we have to tell them.' Ellis is already dialling; she holds out the phone. Kenzie shakes her head. 'They already know you came,' Ellis says, but Kenzie still refuses to take the phone. Charlie is breathless, and when he hears Kenzie is fine, relief garbles his response.

Ellis tells him to make his way to the Playhouse. As they hurry to meet them, Kenzie tries to explain. She'd never thought there could be so many people or that it could be so scary. Edinburgh is so small compared to home, but it'd suddenly felt huge, when she was in the middle of it all. A woman had helped drag her from the worst of the crowd, and then she couldn't work out where she was or what to do.

'I was so scared,' she says.

'We've got you,' Ellis says. They hurry past the Omni Centre and wait, silently, until they see Jackson moving like a steam train. Her certainty is a relief. Kenzie allows herself to be hugged by both parents, and they stand swaddled, oblivious of the steady stream of people pushing past, trying to get to Leith Walk. The mood of the passers-by is not jovial, and finally the family acknowledges the bodies buffeting their own.

'Hotel,' Jackson says.

'There's more space at Auntie M's,' Charlie says.

'The hotel's closer.'

Charlie nods, pulls Kenzie close again and gives Ellis a cursory goodbye. Kenzie says thanks, and the family turn away, leaving Ellis to walk home. She found Kenzie, but they're all leaving her anyway.

*

The phone is still clutched in her hand when she wakes. It is night, and she's on the sofa, where she'd passed out in a sudden desertion of adrenaline. The temperature's dropped, but Ellis is sodden with rancid sweat. Kenzie is safe. Ellis should be happy. Everyone should be happy. She feels twisted. There are goose-bumps running from her lower back right up her spine. She rubs her face. The headache is worse. Heatstroke? She's never had it before. The tooth, surely. But, no, she's fine. They promised her she was fine. Whatever it is, it's her. It's in her.

Charlie and Kenzie didn't come back. They're with Jackson, like they're supposed to be. She swallows half a slice of bread that clags up her throat and follows it with two paracetamol and two ibuprofen. She gulps a little water to wash everything down. A cold shower might help, but she can't face it. The old thermometer Mum used to stick on their foreheads isn't in the bathroom cabinet.

Ellis can't sleep. Her brain is simmering, her thoughts bubbling over. Her head aches, her stomach turns, her heart shrivels at the memory of Charlie's glare. Jackson's anger. So like Lana's. Like Adrian's and Sally's. They all know she's rotten.

She stares at the ceiling, barely changed since she was first shunted into this room, and rages at the years she's let pass. She probes the roof of her mouth, searching for sore spots. She feels the edges of her teeth and they're the same as they were the day before. They are there, demanding protection, giving her nothing but trouble. Why are they called eye teeth if they can't fucking see anything?

She finally falls asleep, and only when the sun spikes round the edge of the blind does she blink awake. She's missed a call from her mum. There's a voicemail.

It's me, sweetie. Sorry for calling so early but do you know what's going on with your sister and Grant? She sounds in a right state. We're on our way back there now. Let me know. Love you. x

Ellis doesn't call back. She is guilt. She is rage. This is all Adrian's fault. Everyone will hate her now. She deserves to be hated. Ellis will not live like this.

40

She leaves the shoe rack for her mum's sake. Everything else left over from her life with Adrian is dragged out to the back garden. Ellis works quickly, humping box after box downstairs and stripping the front room of its firelighters and kindling, worried she won't have as long as she needs.

She stands and surveys. There is a scattering of paper and photos. A ridiculous cushion. A flimsy throw, clothes she never wants to wear again, the rocking chair, the chest of drawers she had to pull apart and still barely managed to get outside. She grabs the small axe her dad used for splitting logs. It feels good in her hands. Ellis swings its balanced heft; the blade thunks firmly into the wood. She pulls it out and sends it crashing down again, again. The rocking chair shatters into pieces. She should've done this ages ago. Now the set of drawers. Her dad's axe bites into the chest's hollow centre. Ellis steps forward, relishing the collapse.

She knows how to build a fire. Learned before she was even allowed to strike the match. You need space for the air to get in, there are layers, there's a system. The pictures of her and Adrian smiling, holidaying, making polite conversation with his family, will flare. The home decorating magazines she'd never thrown out and he decided she wanted are scrunched into loose balls of paper. Wooden spoons are tepee-ed, a pair of bamboo tongs balanced on one edge. Firelighters crumble in her palms, and she sprinkles the greasy white lumps throughout. There's liquid in Dad's old shed too, the tin almost rusted through. She douses the hunks of smashed furniture liberally.

The blaze blooms, shrivels, then grows again as the photos catch. Ellis sweats. It's too hot. The flames kick and leap as she feeds and feeds it, letting the anger climb higher and higher in her chest.

The smoke is acrid, thick with the chemicals in the plastic cushion filling. The cover melts in moments. This is no bonfire: it is a pyre. It burns rapaciously. It's time for the larger pieces of wood. More. More.

Wait. She turns and rushes to her mother's room. She pauses for a second, the smell of primrose moisturiser eliciting a wavering, childlike apprehension. Ellis overrides it and lunges for the drawer. The little pot of teeth is where it always sits. It rattles when she snatches it. She takes the stairs two at a time, feet confident on the worn centre of each step.

The fire is big now. Big enough. Hot enough. She twists the lid and lets the teeth fall in before dropping the pot behind them. She sees the painted fluffy chick, devoured by flames. She listens for a popping sound, doesn't really expect one. All that matters is that they are consumed and she is set free.

Ellis is tangentially aware of the neighbours at their windows. She doesn't care, she wants it all gone. Fuck it. Her eyes and nose are streaming, the back of her throat seized mid-cough. She pulls her T-shirt up over her mouth and tips a block of memo pads into the heart of the fire. Dust sparks in the air. The sound below the thumping in her ears is a siren call. They're coming for her. She throws on a drawer liner, a tea towel, a last handful of rocking-chair fragments.

She'd wanted love so desperately that she'd given up on her other wants. She'd been full of them. Everything on this pile, she'd wanted once. She lets the useless furniture burn and cries for all the other things she'd cared for. The box of crayons that melted in the midday sun, the sticker sheet her favourite teacher gave her that Lana emptied before she'd had the chance, the newspaper her dad had been reading the day he died, which she'd taken to her room and kept as it yellowed and thinned. Her mother chucked it out when she redid Ellis's bedroom for Granny

Patrick. The things didn't matter, yet it still hurt to lose them.

The fire's too big. It's too big. The heat draws sweat to her skin; a breeze pushes the flames towards the bench. They're eating the dry grass, advancing on the shed. Only in these moments does Ellis appreciate the danger. She drops the axe and hurries to the outdoor tap. Water splashes onto the dry grass. A small pool spreads, slowly, slowly.

The siren crests, stops, and is replaced by the sound of doors opening and feet hitting the road.

She leaves the fire, runs to the street to greet them. 'It's gone a bit far,' she says to a man whose neck emerges, white and vulnerable, from a thick, protective blue collar.

'I'd say.' He looks at the house; her eyes follow his. The column of smoke behind it is a thick, dark brand. 'Stay here,' he says, moving past her and towards it before she replies. His team are unhooking the hose in preparation; one holds out a hand to stop her when she tries to head back into the garden with them. Her anger still fizzes and crackles, but shame is creeping through it now.

The firefighters get to work, treating the mess she's made with gravity. They gesture her out, into the street, and no one looks at her as they work. She pictures the boundary wall. If the fire could've eaten that too, she'd have one less decision to make. But it takes the crew no time at all to extinguish the whole thing.

A police car arrives. She is being told, sternly, that bonfires need a permit and that household junk cannot be burned willy-nilly at home when Trevor pulls up in a muddy rental car. He parks in the neighbour's driveway and hurries over.

'Is this your home, sir?' the policeman asks, his partner leaning against the car, making notes. Trevor shakes his head and explains, but the lecture is now directed at them both anyway. Materials unsuitable. Look out for your neighbours. Be responsible. Ellis is done being responsible, but the flames that crackled through her have been doused. She nods, knowing she should feel fear but unable to get hold of any.

Finally, the firefighters efficiently pack the hose back onto the engine and leave. With one last unsympathetic look, the police follow. Trevor says nothing. He just stands nearby, waiting. The energy that propelled Ellis has gone. She says they'd better look, and they traipse around the back. A thuggish layer of smoke remains, the same consistency as Ellis's headache. She is ashy and insubstantial.

'If you were having a barbecue, you could've waited,' he says.

'I didn't plan it,' Ellis says. 'It just kind of . . .'

Trevor surveys the blackened mess at the centre of the lawn. 'Is that a chest of drawers?'

Ellis nods, and the world wobbles.

'Are you okay? Ellis, are you okay?' His voice is so sharp, so serious.

Ellis looks away, heads for the shed. The spade is where it always is.

'Yes. I'd better . . . before Mum gets home.'

'Shutting the stable door a little late there, aren't we? She's at your sister's. Grant's gone off somewhere. I said I'd bring everything back and pick her up later, but . . .'

'Is she all right?'

'Who? Lana? Everyone's fine, Ellis, but what about you?'

'I just didn't want the things. Adrian's things.'

The waterlogged garden is the scene of a massacre. The flames inched so close to the bench, it could've gone up. And if the bench, then also the shed. And if the shed, then perhaps the gate, and if the gate certainly the house, and then there'd be nothing left to fight over.

The grass at the heart of the blaze is gone. Grey water pools on the dry soil. The flowers around the edges are greased with smoke. The handle of the axe, which Ellis had put down a metre from the flames, is scorched but still solid. Ellis reaches down and cradles it.

41

Ellis is reduced to a jaw. A jaw and the knowledge that something is wrong. This isn't her. She knows it's not all in her head. No. It *is* in her head, just not in her mind. It is a part of her. Swelling, spreading, controlling her lip, her cheek. Tendrilling towards her brain, groping its way upwards, inwards. It will eat the bones around her sinuses away until she is hollow, then travel into her brain and poison it. It's poisoning it already.

It must be real: it isn't real. She was fine until she found out that Sally had been working away at the roots of her relationship all along. But it's not Sally that's the problem. It's not Adrian either.

She turns to Trevor.

'You're going to say it's stress, it's me, it's nothing, just like the rest of them, aren't you?'

'Ellis?'

'It's not. There's something in there. It got in when they filled it. Or they didn't get it out. They sealed it in. I don't know, but it's there and it's growing.'

'What are you talking about?'

'My tooth. Does my face look the same to you?'

Trevor steps forward, puts his hand on her upper arm and looks carefully, calmly.

'There is a bit of a discrepancy between the left and right, you know. Is there something wrong?'

'You tell me, you're the fucking dentist.'

'Right. Okay, then, I will.' He steps back, takes his phone from his pocket. He's talking to someone. Ellis stands on shifting ground, smoke in the back of her throat, her thoughts spiralling upwards.

Trevor hangs up and gently pushes her towards his car. 'We're going to the surgery,' he says.

Ellis isn't resisting. It's what she wants – someone to take her seriously. She feels like she's floating high above the city, deep below the streets. Her blood is running hot, too hot to contain.

Trevor's speaking to her. 'How long has it been bothering you?'

'Months.'

'Pain? Discomfort? What kind?'

'All the time. It's just there. All the time.'

He parks. The pavement is busy. Ellis looks at Trevor and thinks she could walk away, if she wanted to.

He leads her in and nods to the woman on reception. She waves them through with a smile, so much nicer than the woman at Ellis's practice. Or she's smiling for the dentist. They always smile for the dentists. At least someone smiles for them. It's bright, so bright. Her eyes hurt. Her face hurts. Her cheekbone is the sun.

'You're seeing Orla. She's squeezing you in. Come on.' He ushers her down the corridor. Ellis follows. The dentist waiting is young and sharp and has frown lines that look older than the rest of her. Trevor speaks to the woman as Ellis sits. Amongst the jargon, she hears 'infected' and Ellis expands with hope.

'I got a blood test a couple of weeks ago. They said they'd let me know if it was important and didn't have anything when I called them,' she says, marvelling at the strength of her voice.

Trevor makes a noise in the back of his throat, then asks for her GP's details, typing them into his phone as he backs towards the door. He leaves her with the stranger, who nods for her assistant to place dark goggles over Ellis's eyes. Thank God.

The inspection is assiduous, and she barely feels it. There is an X-ray. Biting, more blood. The woman returns and glares at her screen before grasping her pick and asking Ellis to open her mouth.

Ellis does as she is told.

The woman is typing. Ellis is shivering. Trevor is back. Time is not behaving as it should. She's in the staff room. There's a pot of yoghurt and a pill in front of her.

'I got your bloods. They filed them accidentally. You're right: it's an infection. A periapical abscess,' he says, 'high up on the root. Hard to spot. I'd get it drained this second, but it's going to take some effort to reach and you're too feverish. So I'm advising emergency antibiotics for now, and we'll keep an eye on your temperature.'

'It's real,' she says.

'Sure is. Day after tomorrow, we're booking you in for a root canal. Orla will take care of you.'

Triumph fires through her.

*

Trevor takes Ellis home and installs her on the sofa. He acts as if he has every right to treat the house as his own and Ellis as his to care for. She is grateful. She is weak with vindication. She'd known there was something fermenting where it shouldn't, and she was right. She'd put her trust in the wrong people, the wrong places.

Trevor fetches a glass of water and the duvet from her mum's bed. He's phoning her mum now, telling her everything's fine. Even if he ruins it all and breaks her mum's heart by leaving her for someone younger, Ellis will love him for this.

'How's Mum?'

'She's grand. She sends you her love and says she'll be home as soon as possible. And not to worry, Lana will be fine. Grant's back.'

'It wasn't meant to happen.'

Trevor nods and says never mind, obviously not sure what she's on about. She shuts up, and he goes to hunt through the medicine cabinet.

She's falling asleep in a haze of childhood sick days spent in front of the TV, the sound of her parents going about their business in the background. There are few feelings as precious.

Ellis wakes to her mum saying goodbye to Trevor. She wants to call out a thank-you, but her throat is too dry. Her mum comes through and places a hand on her cheek. Her fingers are so soft, softer than Ellis has ever known them.

'Come on then, my silly girl. Wouldn't you be comfier in your own bed?'

'Sorry about the garden.'

'Sounds like it's the least of our worries. Bed.'

Ellis rises, heads to the toilet. She pees drowsily then cotton-steps to her room. The house is still sour with the smell of things that shouldn't be burned. Shame lingers in the smoke. Ellis rejects it. She is responsible: she is not ashamed.

✳

It's dark and the house is quiet. She's slept for hours. Ellis rolls over, feeling she's been woken by a sound. The knock on her door is tentative. She can't think who it is. She says hello.

Kenzie steps into the room.

Ellis wipes her face, sits up a little.

'You okay?' Kenzie stands awkwardly by the window, in the space that had been filled with crates.

Ellis nods.

'I'm sorry about your bike. We went back to look for it again but it's gone.'

'It doesn't matter.'

Kenzie picks at the window sill with one perfectly filed thumbnail. 'Dad is so angry.'

'He'll get over it – he was just scared for you. They both were.'

Kenzie nods, and the tears, the uncertainty Ellis saw on the street, have vanished. 'I can take care of myself,' she says.

Ellis doesn't doubt it. And she doesn't want Kenzie to have to. 'I know. But no one's invincible.'

'Thanks for finding me.'

'It's not your fault it turned out like it did. Anyway, you're talking to someone who just torched half her belongings. You think I'd be mad at you over a bike?'

'Only because everyone else is.' Kenzie smiles. Ellis wants to say: stay, don't go back to America, grow up where I can see you. It wouldn't be fair, so she smiles instead. 'You're a good kid, Kenzie. Now go to bed – don't get me in trouble for keeping you up.'

Kenzie leaves behind a trace of mango and passion fruit to mingle with the scorched grass and wood that Ellis now realises is oozing from her own skin. She listens, wondering if Charlie's in the house. If he is, he isn't coming to see her.

Ellis picks up her phone. It's one in the morning. She writes an apology and sends it. Stares upwards as her phone's artificial glow dulls then disappears. She's starting to drift off when it flashes bright again. She opens the lock screen and there is Becca. *Love ya too, lady. You'll always be my best bud, no getting rid of this bitch xxxx*

42

It's muggy, and the house booms with emptiness. Ellis is not at work. TravelOn have been informed that she's been properly ill. She doesn't know if they'll believe her, considering the mess she made, but feels insulated from the consequences. They can't fire her. She roams the house in bare feet, grateful for the absence of headache.

Charlie's taking Jackson and Kenzie to the airport. He'll follow in a few weeks, after he's tied down a few of his contacts (according to him) and played out a bit more of his crisis (Jackson). Kenzie wants to finish high school. After that? No one's saying. No one knows. Kenzie will work it out when the time comes, and Charlie will have to decide what he wants too. Ellis is glad she blew that up by sleeping with a stranger. It could never work with Charlie; her feelings for him are embedded in their childhood. It's time to make new ones.

The house has been so busy and felt so oppressive all summer, Ellis has forgotten it can be like this. The fabric of home is so tightly woven, she's been blind to the strands. Padding from the hall to the front room, she catches the edges of what it might be like for her mum, rattling around in such a lot of space. Stacking up bottles of wine from sort-of-friends, repapering Ellis's bedroom for Grandma Patrick and then again when she stayed only a handful of times before her death, filling quiet rooms with the smells of a relentless baking schedule.

Ellis moves to the photos on the wall. She's barely looked at them in years. Her favourite is the picture of her mum and dad the summer before he died. They look so young. They were so young. Younger than Ellis is now. Mum was a god to her daughters, then. And that's how they judged her. Every mistake deliberate. Every bad situation a punishment. She was just a young woman with two children doing her best. It's impossible to guess the right answer. There is no right answer for everyone.

She moves to the kitchen. Her mum's back, Lana in tow.

'You said she'd be out.'

'I know, but I don't want to have to say this twice.' Mum pauses. Ellis is by the window, her feet naked and vulnerable. Lana is perfumed and heeled, her arms folded across her ribs. Their mum stands between them.

'Say what?'

'I'm not selling.'

The air is thick. Lana frowns, disbelieving. 'Why now?'

'I wasn't ever planning to sell. I just wanted to know how much it's worth for my own peace of mind. And I wanted you to know too.'

'Funny way of showing it,' Lana says.

'I would've told you right from the start if you hadn't acted like I owed you it.' Her voice is harsher and firmer than it ever is, especially with Lana. Mum normally soothed rather than shouted. Who could give birth to such a ball of conviction and expect to stay in charge? But something is shifting. Instead of the shouting match she's primed for, Ellis hears a sniff. And then another. Lana is crying. Ellis feels sick.

'But Trevor?' Lana says.

'For God's sake, Lana. You think I'd sell my house for some bloke I hardly know? For anyone? You think I'm the naïve one?' Her gaze turns to Ellis. 'And you, skulking around like a teenager, never saying what you think out loud and huffing and puffing instead. I know you've not been yourself this last wee while, but don't think it's gone unnoticed, or that Trevor couldn't tell how you two felt about him.'

'I'm sorry. He's a good guy.'

'I know.'

'How could we trust this total stranger you picked up at a dentist's surgery?' Lana says.

'You didn't have to, you only had to trust me. And anyway, you've got your own family and husband to worry about.'

'I almost didn't, thanks to her.'

This is what guilt feels like. Real guilt. Thick, hot guilt that smothers. Ellis did this. It's not one of the imagined slights Lana has used against her for years. Ellis chose this. She'd looked in Gabrielle's eye and chose it.

'I said something I didn't mean to . . . I didn't think . . .' She stops, swallows. 'I fucked up. I lied about Grant because I was ashamed. I'm so sorry, Lana. If I'd ever really thought I might cause you guys actual problems . . .'

'I'm sure you didn't mean to–'

'No, Mum, I didn't mean to. But it's not the point, is it?'

Lana stares at her for a long time – so long Ellis is desperate to look away. Her sister's gaze goes too deep, plumbs depths she is not welcome in. Finally, she dips her chin in a tiny nod.

'If I'd known you had a reason for being such a raging bitch, I'd have got you to the dentist weeks ago.'

'I wasn't being a bitch.'

'You bloody were. Lying, sneaking about saying things you just can't say.'

'I know. I thought they might fire me if I didn't give them a reason and I was so angry. And jealous.'

'Jealous?'

'Of you. Grant. Everything. Don't make me say it.'

Lana glares so hard that she fails to blink away her tears. 'He almost left, Ellis. He almost left me. Because I thought there might be something to it. He said me not trusting him is the worst thing I've ever done, that it was too much after everything else. I've never seen him like that.'

'What do you mean, after everything else?'

'Things have been a bit rough. We've been arguing. I didn't think it was a big deal. He says he's exhausted.'

'Lana, have you ever thought about why it is that you're so angry all the time?' Ellis holds her breath, can barely believe she's said it.

'I don't know. He asked the same thing. He wondered if it was him, or the kids. God, how could it be? It's me, not them. And it's not like I mean to be. Maybe I should do something about it.' Lana's voice is small, her shoulders rounded. Their eyes meet, for just a second, and it's Lana who looks away.

'That might be good,' Ellis says. 'But Grant knows this was my fault, right? I could go speak to him?'

'He knows. It'll be better if you just leave it. Look, Ellis, I'm sorry. I didn't mean to get you fired.'

'You didn't. But I need a change anyway.'

'Good, they were an awful-looking bunch.'

'Some of them aren't so bad.'

'If you say so.' Lana walks to the back window and surveys the patchy grass. 'You know, it's meant to be symbolic – a love letter or two. Not a bloody inferno.'

Ellis laughs. The relief is so intense it crests into something else. A kind of pride. She's powerful. She almost caused a tragedy. She's been telling everyone it got out of hand, even though she's not sure it did. Lana's peace offering can't diminish it.

'I'm done with symbolism. It was a fire because it needed to be.'

'Fair enough. Maybe just destroy your own garden the next time though?'

'We'll sort it out,' their mum says.

Lana says she needs to get home because Grant's watching the twins and she owes him a lot, right now.

Lana's known what she wanted from the moment she was born. She decided what she desired and she achieved it. She knew what was hers and that she could have it, the same way she's taken everything she's wanted. But Ellis doesn't have to give all the time just to accommodate it.

'Mum, I know you're saying you're not planning to sell just now, but if you do decide to at some point, you need to look into the stuff with the wall first.'

'What was that about again?'

'It's over the boundary line.'

'And that's something I need to get fixed?' She's rifling through the cupboard.

'Not now. Just remember to mention it to whoever's dealing with it if you change your mind.'

'Will do.' She pulls out a small bottle of vanilla extract. 'I'm in the mood for madeleines. Fancy doing the mixing?'

Ellis is still too hot, and her mouth still aches and her heart is still swollen with hurt, but she wants to help her mum make cake. She says yes.

The house is just a house. Teeth are just teeth. People survive without either. They recover from break-ups. They struggle on when they've been ripped away from everything they care for. People are dumb animals and they are miraculous too.

✱

Ellis is waiting for Naila. She doesn't remember saving her number, but it was there in her contacts when she looked for it. It's lunchtime, and the heat is already mellowing towards autumn. Ellis has chosen a bench on the edge of Leith Links.

Naila arrives slightly out of breath. Ellis apologises for asking her to meet so far from the office and hands over a sub filled with hummus and vegetables. Naila thanks her effusively.

'No worries if you've got something already. I just didn't want you to miss your lunch. Thanks for coming.'

'Don't be silly. I'm so glad to see you. Alison sends her love. She says to check your emails if you can – she sent you an article about how good goji berries are for fighting infections.'

'I'm not sure I can. I'm kind of suspended and, to be honest, I don't think I'll be coming back.'

'No?' Naila is sad, not surprised.

'It's my own fault.'

Ellis wants to say she got screwed up when her dad died. That her sister is a bitch and her ex quietly sadistic. And that her teeth are fucked and that the dread that courses through her every time she thinks about having to submit to another treatment is overwhelming.

Except everything is only half true and none of it justifies lying about Lana. Or fobbing Naila off over and over again when she's been trying so hard to be kind. Explanations aren't excuses. Everyone has to climb out of their own pit or get comfortable grubbing about in the dirt. Ellis can't stay where she's been, wrapping grimy hands round the ankles of friends and acquaintances who're trying to pull themselves up.

Naila is ready to comfort without question. Ellis owes her something.

'Adrian and me, we broke up. A while ago.'

'You did? Oh, Ellis, I'm so sorry.' Naila's face crumples.

'And Lana . . . I said it was her and it wasn't. Grant didn't cheat on her. It was Adrian cheating on me.'

A stream of thoughts scud across Naila's open face. It darkens, lightens, darkens again.

'I didn't want to admit it. I felt like such an idiot,' Ellis says.

'It's okay. That's okay. You're not an idiot.' Naila is patting her arm. Ellis melts towards her and then abruptly draws back. This kindness is unfounded, undeserved.

'It's really not okay.'

'But I understand.' Naila's voice is steady. She waits until Ellis meets her eyes and nods, once. 'I understand. It's your business anyway. You didn't have to tell us anything at all. Richard's pretty angry at Gabrielle about the whole thing. Jean heard him having a go, but we thought it was about making you work when you were sick.'

'Not so much. The tooth part is true, but Gabrielle didn't know how bad it was. None of us did. Still, she should've been keeping her mouth shut.'

'True. How's your sister? She seemed pretty . . . uptight.'

'She's been better, but she'll be fine.'

Naila nods, pleased for someone she barely knows. How does she wear such hopefulness close to her skin? Ellis used to pity her for it; now she's envious. They don't have much time left, Naila needs to get back to her desk, so they start in on goodbyes. Ellis asks her to say hello to Jean and Alison, realises she wants to know if Naila has spoken to Greig and decides to ask her next time. Naila hurries off, blending into one of the groups of young schoolkids who slouch and dance on their way to pick up sandwiches.

★

When Ellis gets back, she finds a reply to her email. She opens it silently.

Adrian's tone matches the legalese of her own message. He accepts her terms. He will pay her a lump sum of four and a half thousand pounds in three instalments. In return, she will not pursue occupancy rights and will officially give up any claim on his flat or its contents.

Only the postscript reveals his anger.

I thought you were better than this.

The words are poison that is supposed to eat through her elation. It won't. The money is a moral victory. The shame she feels for spying on Sally, for thinking her worthy of suffering, wakens and turns. Ellis pushes out her lips. She has committed no great crime. Her shame is small, manageable. Does she have to care whether Adrian is disappointed in her? Not any more. He gave up the right. His opinion is void.

It's not enough money for a deposit, but it's a foundation.

Ellis is grateful for the time she might spend in this house, with her mother and its memories. Moving on will be bittersweet but necessary. She'll be happy for her sister to have it one day, seeing as it means something so vital to her – but not for nothing, not without compensation. Lana can sell her own home if she wants this one.

43

Ellis no longer remembers every tooth lost. She's been hewn down to the highlights: the very first; the flying front two; the one that embedded itself in toffee before she knew to fear it.

Trevor's colleague, Orla, thought the left molar might need to go too. Warned her, prepared her, but managed to save it after several root canals. Ellis hated every second. She sliced nail-shaped crescents into her stomach like always, but survived every appointment until the day Orla sat back with a smile and said, 'All done.'

She's registered at Trevor's practice now. Dr Niall decided to take early retirement, Dr Conor bought in as a partner and the nice woman who was so sure Ellis's whole issue was stress has gone elsewhere.

Ellis thanks Orla profusely, she always does. Orla nods professionally. She isn't the sort to report back to Trevor, Ellis can tell, and she's glad.

He's waiting for her after the final treatment to take her for a coffee – lukewarm spearmint tea, in her case – and ask her opinion on the paintings of snow-capped mountains they've just hung in the surgery corridor. She says they're nice. He's easy to talk to, and her mum is so happy she's switched to his place.

'Thanks again,' she says. 'It's such a relief. I just wish I didn't have such shitty teeth to start with.'

'It's not the teeth,' he says, licking milk foam from his lips. 'They're fine in and of themselves. It's your saliva that's the problem. Too acidic and, worse, a breeding ground for bacteria. Just one of those things, runs in families. You just have the kind of chemistry that's inhospitable to teeth.' He lifts his cup again, drinks with satisfaction.

Ellis runs the tip of her tongue over the smooth edges and rough tops of her molars. All this time, blaming the teeth. Blaming herself and her diet and her laziness and her inability to follow the instructions all her friends must have, because they only needed a filling every few years. And it turned out that tending her teeth was never enough to keep them intact. The humiliation she's felt in dozens of dentist chairs over the years begins to thaw. The teeth aren't weak; they're under assault.

Adrian, Sally. The betrayal was a fracture. Ellis bit down on her normal relationship and the truth of it cracked her. In her vulnerability, she'd had the hole filled and something undesirable slipped in. And in the warm, dark wetness of Ellis, it multiplied. It grew. Rot isn't inexorable. Sometimes there is something that can be salvaged. The pulp can be scraped out and packed with filler to halt further degradation and give the tooth the best chance of survival.

✳

Later, Ellis is making dinner for her mum, Bolognese with a big glug of red wine. A good one, to replace the depleted stash by the microwave. She tops up her glass and her mum's too.

'Becca's coming round tomorrow afternoon, if you want to say hello.'

'And you're sure you don't mind me being here?'

'That's why I'm asking.'

'We were just worried about you, you know.'

The pursing of Ellis's lips says, *funny way of showing it.*

'We weren't talking about you behind your back.'

'Yes, you were. But I get it.'

'Oh, Elly, don't cry.'

Her mum shuffles closer for a hug. The warmth is so welcome.

'Lana still hates me.'

'No, she doesn't. Lana has her own problems to deal with. They're not yours to fix.' Mum has been the bringer of brusque cheerfulness and practical solutions for so many years that Ellis barely grasps the validation she's hearing.

'I suppose so.'

'Lana will get over it. You know, Ellis, that she always needed more than you. Ever since you were tiny. You were so self-contained and she was just exhausting. We tried to make more time for you. I know I let you down after your dad died, but you turned out okay. He would be proud of you.'

Ellis starts to scoff – *what does he have to be proud of?* – and stops herself, allows the pain to spread across her breastbone instead.

'I still miss him.'

'He's your dad. You'll miss him forever.'

It's true. She does, she will. And it doesn't mean she can't change other things. The Patricks have survived all sorts of breaks, yet their bones only grow stronger, more solid each time. Their teeth might need constant fortifying, but maintenance demands so little and gives so much. Ellis was born with one sort of mouth. It's up to her how she chooses to use it.

Acknowledgements

A huge thank you to all of the people who put up with me refusing to talk about writing, apologies to the patient and ever supportive Jenni Hamilton and Martha MacDiarmid-Tait in particular. My friends and family are stellar. Shout out to Karen Thirkell, Gillian Caddy and Owen, Evan and Neil Hamilton, as well as my uncles, cousins and the Crambs for all their support and inspiration. And to Martha, Mandy Price and Candice Purwin, for being wonderful. To my agent, Sara Langham, for 'getting it' and giving excellent feedback and to my publisher, Polygon, and editors James Crawford and Alison Rae in particular.

Part of this book was written at Shakespeare and Company, an experience I am beyond grateful for. Big thanks also to the whole team at Scottish Book Trust – Caitrin Armstrong, Lynsey Rogers, Kayleigh Bohan most of all. Sorry you've never been able to get rid of me.

There's also a ton of great writers to thank, including R. A. Martens, Kirsti Wishart, Caroline von Schmalensee, Helen Jackson, Lucy Ribchester (whose description of this book will always stick with me), Graeme Macrae Burnet, Catherine Simpson and many, many more. A special mention to Jenni Fagan, for her insightful advice and support.

And a massive thank you to Fin Cramb, your pursuit of a better story (and indulgence of nonsense) is everything.